THIRST

THIRST

JILL WILLIAMSON

Thirst
Copyright © 2019 by Jill Williamson. All rights reserved.

This book or parts thereof may not be reproduced in any form, stored in a retrieval system, or transmitted in any form by any means—electronic, mechanical, photocopy, recording, or otherwise—without prior written permission of the publisher, except as provided by United States of America copyright law.

This is a work of fiction. Names, characters, places, and incidents are products of the author's imagination or are used fictitiously. Any similarity to actual people, organizations, and/or events is purely coincidental.

The author is represented by MacGregor Literary Inc. of Hillsboro, OR.

Cover Designer: Emilie Hendryx
Editor: Brad Williamson
Proofreading: Kaitlyn Williamson

Library of Congress Cataloging-in-Publication Data
An application to register this book for cataloging has been filed with the Library of Congress.

International Standard Book Number: 978-0-9985230-6-4

Printed in the United States of America

To my Explorers, for reading the stories I write.

Other books by Jill Williamson

The Safe Lands series
Captives
Outcasts
Rebels

The Kinsman Chronicles
King's Folly
King's Blood
King's War

The Blood of Kings trilogy
By Darkness Hid
To Darkness Fled
From Darkness Won

The Mission League series
The New Recruit
Chokepoint
Project Gemini
Ambushed
Broken Trust
The Profile Match

RoboTales
Tinker
Mardok and the Seven Exiles

Stand-Alone Titles
Replication: The Jason Experiment

Nonfiction
Go Teen Writers: Write Your Novel
Go Teen Writers: Edit Your Novel
Storyworld First: Creating a Unique Fantasy World for Your Novel
Punctuation 101: A Fiction Writer's Guide to Getting it Right

PROLOGUE

Six days into our wilderness survival adventure in the La Plata Mountains of Colorado, Comet Pulon passed by the earth. We had no way of knowing that it had come much closer than expected, that it had forever changed our planet, and that it had left a killer among us. Oblivious, the twelve of us camped in a clearing, cheered as the bright yellow fireball soared overhead, roasted marshmallows, and toasted with canteens of water we had purified ourselves.

And as we celebrated in awe of nature's majesty, the rest of the world began to die.

1

"First!" I jogged up the split log steps of Deadwood Lodge and yanked on the antler door handle. It didn't budge.

"This ain't a race, boy." Andy Reinhold clumped up the stairs behind me. "What? Is it locked? Shouldn't be." Our guide and the owner of Wilderness Way Adventures was a retired US Army Ranger who had become the quintessential mountain man. His hair and beard were so bushy that his eyes, nose, and cheeks were pretty much all you could see of his face.

I cupped my hand against the glass window on the slab door and peered inside. "The lobby is dark." I shrugged off my pack and let it fall to the planked porch. My shoulders loved the weightless freedom. The twelve-day extreme survival training camp had been awesome, but I was ready to go home.

Reinhold stepped past me and tugged on the handle. "No biggie. I got a key stashed over here."

While Reinhold approached the aspen tree on the side of the building, I turned back to the yard. The dirt parking lot held four vehicles: Reinhold's rusty Ford pickup, Mark's Impala, Antônia's Prius, and Riggs's fancy new Range Rover Evoque. No sign of my dad. Bummer. Our group had left our campsite at dawn. I checked my watch. It was 9:40 a.m. We were a bit late, if anything, so Dad should be here by now.

If we left soon we'd be home in time for dinner. Mom, knowing we'd be eating vegan meals all this time, had promised to grill steaks tonight. I honestly hadn't minded the camping food, but I missed me some meat.

Across the grassy clearing, Riggs trudged out of the forest with Jaylee, followed closely by Kimama, Reinhold's eleven-year-old daughter. Jaylee's reddish-brown pigtails swung as she walked. She laughed at something Riggs said. The sound carried all the way to where I stood and gnawed at my stomach. Stupid Riggs, anyway. When Wayne had gotten sick, Riggs had jumped in at the last-minute to be our "male leader," but the dude was only two years older than most of us.

Squeaking hinges diverted my attention from Riggs and Jaylee. Reinhold stepped inside the lodge. I followed. In the lobby, a strong, fishy odor hung on the air.

I wrinkled my nose. "Smells like Chipeta's been eating salmon."

Reinhold inhaled deeply. "Don't know what that smell is, but it ain't salmon." He flipped the light switch. Nothing happened. "Power's out." He walked to the front desk and snatched up a sheet of paper. He squinted, tilted the paper toward the light from the open front door. His eyes flicked back and forth as he read, eyebrows scrunched. He grunted and his hands fell to his side, the paper crumpling in one fist.

"What's it say?" I asked.

"Chipeta's home sick."

"Must be bad to keep Chipeta home." Reinhold's wife, a Ute native, could have led any wilderness adventure on her own. She was one tough lady.

"I'll give her a call." Reinhold walked behind the desk and picked up the cordless phone, put it to his ear, then slammed it back in the charger. "Cursed technology. Got a corded phone in my office." He strode down the hallway, his boots clumping on the hardwood floor.

I went back out to the porch, expecting to see Jaylee and Riggs, but Kimama sat alone on the bottom step. I sank down beside her and stretched out my legs. My hiking boots were dusty from the Colorado mountain trails. "How you doing, Kimama?"

"I just like to give them a moment, you know?" Kimama looked at me and smirked. "It *has* been twelve days."

Only a kid like Kimama would think of something like that and not be weirded out. "No worries. Your mom's not in there. She left a note that said she's home sick."

Kimama frowned. "Mama doesn't get sick."

I shrugged and looked back out over the grassy yard. Zach, Josh, and Cristobal were crossing the lawn, followed closely by Antônia, our female sponsor. A hundred yards behind them, Mark and Erin had just stepped out of the forest. They looked bad. They'd gotten sick a couple days ago—or one of them had gotten sick and given it to the other. For the past few nights we'd been awakened in the middle of the night by the sound of dry heaves.

Maybe they'd caught something from Reinhold's wife before we left.

Still no sign of Logan. Big surprise. I hoped Riggs hadn't murdered him and left him for dead.

A horn beeped in the parking lot, making me jump. I stood up, looking for our silver Honda minivan, but there were only the same four vehicles in the lot.

"They're in his car," Kimama said.

My stomach slid into my boots as my gaze shifted to the Range Rover. Sure enough, I could see Riggs and Jaylee's silhouettes in the front seats. Jaylee in the driver's seat. I slumped back to the step, propped my elbows on my knees, and ran my hands through my greasy hair. I needed a shower.

"You like her, don't you, Eli?"

I tensed and glanced at Kimama. She looked just like her mom. Tanned skin, round face, dark brown eyes, and black hair twisted into two braids that ran down to her waist. She was giving me that look. The one my sister always gives me when she knows I'm lying. I hadn't even said anything!

"She doesn't deserve you," Kimama said. "Mother says, 'those who have one foot in the canoe and one foot on the shore are going to fall into the river.' Jaylee is nuts to chase after Riggs."

Now it was my turn to question her. "You don't like Riggs?"

She thought about it. "Mother also says, 'It is better to have less thunder in the mouth and more lightning in the hand.' That's his problem, I think."

I chuckled, recalling my parents' discussion about this very topic in regards to Riggs. Mom didn't trust him. Said he was all talk and no brains. Dad didn't trust him, either, but he'd argued that Riggs had volunteered to chaperone, and that had said a lot. Dad said we should be thankful for his generosity. I'd stayed quiet, torn, because I knew Riggs had only volunteered because Jaylee had begged him, but if I'd told my parents that, they might not have let me come.

But seriously. Talk about a no-win situation. I'd spent the last twelve days asking myself what Jaylee saw in Rigley Orcutt, which was dumb because the guy was twenty, a college student, rich, and drove that spaceship of a car. He had a trim goatee and a massive tattoo of wings on his shoulder blades that ran down the backs of both arms to his elbows. Plus every girl in my youth group—including my sister—said he was hot.

It was nice to know at least one girl didn't think Riggs was all that great, even if she was only eleven.

I glanced back to the parking lot, past the Evoque to the road. Where was my dad? My cell phone was dead in my pack, and I couldn't charge it with the electricity out.

Footsteps on the porch behind us preceded Reinhold's deep voice. "No answer at home. She must be sleeping it off, whatever it is. Your dad ain't here yet?"

I shook my head.

Reinhold stepped between us down the five porch steps and turned to offer a hand to his daughter. "Let's get your pack in the truck so we can take off as soon as their ride shows. I want to get home and see your mama." Reinhold hoisted Kimama to her feet, and the two set off for the parking lot. He glanced over his shoulder. "Eli, go use my office phone to call your ride."

I dragged my weary body back inside Deadwood Lodge. It really did reek like rotten fish. The light from the door and front windows lit the hallway enough so that I didn't run into the walls as I inched my way into the building, but I couldn't see squat in Reinhold's office. I fumbled around until my eyes adjusted enough to spot the outline of a desk. I managed to find the phone, and when I lifted the receiver, the dial tone rang in my ear. Weird that the phone got power when nothing else did.

I couldn't remember Dad's cell number, so I dialed home. It rang and rang—the answering machine didn't even pick up. I also tried Lizzie's cell since it was only one number off from my own. The call went straight to voicemail.

I left a message for my sister then stumbled back out to the porch. My gaze scanned the parking lot for the minivan. Still no sign.

Where was my dad?

Something hit the top of my head, fell to my boots, and rattled across the porch. A pinecone. I looked up and took another to the forehead. My best friend Zach peeked out from behind a massive ponderosa, cackled, and pelted me with a few more.

I scooped up the pinecones and returned fire. "You're just mad 'cause I beat you back, slowpoke."

Zach blew a raspberry. "First is the worst, man."

I ran out of ammo. "Oh yeah? What were you, sixth? If first is the worst, what's sixth?"

"Kimama said seeing six crows brings gold and wealth, so I figure that's a win." Zach approached the porch, slung off his pack, and dropped it on the ground. He fell onto the grass beside it, groaning. "No Silver Bullet?"

The Silver Bullet was Zach's nickname for my parents' minivan. "Nope." I yawned. "Man, I want a shower. I feel like I've been deep-fried."

"Mmm. Deep fried. I want some KFC. And some Cold Stone. I'm starving."

"You've clearly wasted away under Reinhold's

cooking," I said. "I'm surprised you're still alive." Reinhold had provided meals of rice, beans, pasta, potatoes, whole-grain breads, nuts, granola, and oats, along with an assortment of fresh fruits and vegetables. It hadn't been a good fit for Zach, king of the junk food junkies.

"I need sugar, McShane. White. Granulated. Just a five pound bag and a spoon will do me fine."

"You're suffering from withdrawal. You should get into a support group before you go on a binge and hurt yourself."

My youth group was not comprised of professional hikers. This was *my* obsession. *I* had wanted to come here. *I* had talked my youth pastor into it. *I* had organized fundraisers and begged people to come along. But then Pastor Wayne had gotten sick, and Riggs had stepped in at the last minute to take his place as chaperone.

And ruined my plans to hike for twelve days with Jaylee Jennings.

Most of the others were lying in the grassy lawn, spread eagle, packs strewn about. From the sound of things, Mark was off in the trees being sick again. Poor guy.

Movement in the distance caught my eye, and I was relieved to see Logan finally dragging his way across the clearing. His face was flushed and his blond afro looked like clown hair, but he'd made it. I was proud of him.

We hung around outside the lodge, waiting for my dad to show. Jaylee and Riggs finally emerged from the Evoque and sat in the grass with the others. Those with vehicles packed up their gear. Reinhold dragged me back to his office so I could try calling home again. Still no answer.

Antônia and Erin left first, the Prius barely making a sound as it rolled away. Antônia hoped to make it back to Phoenix before the Urgent Care closed. Jaylee had ridden up with them, but I guess she'd be coming home with us now.

Dad would never let her ride back alone with Riggs. I couldn't help it. This made me smile.

Mark and my dad had convoyed on the way up, but I couldn't blame Mark when he, Josh, and Cristobal piled into the Impala and took off. Sick or not, after twelve days in the wilderness, everyone was ready to go home. That left me, Zach, Logan, and Jaylee.

Oh, and Riggs, of course, our so-called male chaperone.

Reinhold got impatient and started a portable generator so I could plug in my iPhone and try my dad's cell. But when I finally got power, I had no service.

"You had service before. All y'all did!" Reinhold stalked off, muttering to himself about the ills of technology.

Jaylee, Zach, and Logan went inside to try Reinhold's old-school phone. Now that my iPhone had some power, I wrote down my parents' cell numbers on a sheet of paper from my journal, just in case I needed them again. When I was done, I joined everyone in Reinhold's office.

"The power must be out in Phoenix too," Logan said. "None of us are getting through."

Jaylee clicked her tongue. "Land lines should still work."

"Only if they're corded phones like this one," Logan said. "Does your apartment have a corded phone?"

Jaylee rolled her eyes and left the office.

I took the receiver from Logan and tried my parents' cell phones now that I had the numbers. Both went to voicemail without ringing. I pressed my thumb against the reset button. "This is starting to freak me out."

"If our country was invaded, they'd attack the big cities first and cut the power," Logan said. "That would hamstring most our population."

"You know what?" Zach said. "It's probably aliens."

"It could be," Logan said.

"Dude, I was joking."

"Still, it's not an impossibility," Logan said, "though an invading country is more likely."

I wasn't in the mood for Logan's conspiracies, so I headed back outside. Zach and Logan's footsteps clumped behind me in the hallway, Logan still working his point.

"I'm just saying, we've made ourselves vulnerable to infiltration from the inside. There are plenty of sleeper cells living in America, and when they're ready to attack, they'll take us by surprise. Boom. Done."

"Okay, I got you," Zach said. "But how about you keep that quiet, okay? Reinhold won't like it if you get Kimama all scared."

"Good point," Logan said.

I grinned, amused by Zach's cleverness and the knowledge that not much in this world could scare a kid like Kimama.

I stepped back onto the porch and squinted in the sunlight. Jaylee was standing beside Riggs, who was doing pushups with both hands on the rail. Show off.

"I can't get through," I said. "I just get voicemail on cell numbers, endless ringing on land lines."

Jaylee looked right at me, fixed her big, brown eyes on mine. "How are you going to get home?"

The question tangled the thoughts in my brain.

"Us?" Logan said. "What about you? Why didn't you leave with Antônia and Erin?"

"Because I didn't want to catch whatever Erin has," Jaylee said, turning her attention to our male sponsor. "And Riggs said I could ride with him."

My gut churned, and I again searched the driveway for signs of my dad.

"What about the rest of us?" Logan asked.

"Hey, it's no problem." Riggs shoved off the railing. "I

got belts for five."

"Shotgun!" Jaylee said.

No, no, this was *not* happening. The only reason my dad had taken a day off work to drive us up here was so that we would *not* be in the car with Rigley Orcutt. I couldn't very well say *that*, so instead I tried, "But what if my dad gets here and we're gone?"

Riggs shrugged. "We'll probably pass him, but go ahead and leave a note on the door just in case."

"Seriously? A note?" I couldn't believe Riggs was being so nonchalant about this. "The man drives seven hours to pick us up and we're not here?"

"What if something happened to him?" Jaylee said, tugging on one of her pigtails. "What if the van broke down or something and he's stranded?"

"Eli's dad's a mechanic," Logan said. "He could handle it."

"But he might not have the parts or tools or whatever," Jaylee said.

"Yeah," Riggs said. "What if he's miles from anywhere? Has to walk to a gas station and call a tow? By the time he gets the van fixed, we could be to Flagstaff. And if we don't pass him on the way, you'll have reception by Flagstaff and can call him and tell him what's up."

"I think it's a great plan," Jaylee said, beaming.

Sure she did.

"Makes sense," Reinhold said. "Might as well get on the road while it's still early. Likely will save time in the long run."

Great. Now even Reinhold was siding with Riggs. I looked to Zach. At six-foot-one, he was taller than anyone here, Riggs included. I needed him on my side. "What do you think, man?"

Zach met my gaze, and his eye twitched, a sign he was

thinking hard about this. "Your dad's never late. Something must be up. It's pretty desolate for miles. If we don't see him, one of our phones is bound to have some bars by Flagstaff."

Traitor. I was completely outnumbered. "Fine. Let's go home."

Jaylee whooped and ran toward the Range Rover. I went back for my pack. I wrote my dad a note, and Reinhold stapled it to the door so it wouldn't blow away.

"Hey," he said when we'd finished. "I know this is the last thing you wanted at the end of this trip."

He was talking about Riggs. There'd been a couple nights up in the mountains where Riggs had gotten on my nerves. I might have vented to Reinhold about it a time or three.

I sighed. "It's fine. I'll be fine."

"I know you will. But if things get hard, remember what I told you. The guy is just a substitute teacher. There's more to being a leader than telling people what to do."

"I know." People actually needed to listen. The sad thing was, no one ever listened to me because I wasn't a cool, tattooed college student or a six-foot-one athlete. "I guess I'm just worried about my dad," I added.

"Your dad's a smart man. I'm sure he's fine."

I hoped so.

I said goodbye to Reinhold and Kimama, who reminded me to follow the wolf, whatever that meant. Then we loaded up Riggs's Evoque. The thing was like an iPhone on wheels. It was candy apple red with a tinted sunroof that covered the whole hood of the car. It had a touchscreen computer console with GPS and internet—internet that couldn't find a signal either. A pewter skull hung by a string from his rearview mirror. Seemed kind of ominous.

Jaylee sat shotgun—she *had* called it, after all.

"Jaylee," I said, standing beside the car, "you're really going to make Zach fold himself into the back?"

She looked out the open window and turned a pouty smile on Zach. "Do you mind? Would you rather have the front?"

Say "Yes!" I thought. But Zach just shrugged. "Don't matter to me."

Jaylee beamed, "Thank you!" then pulled the seatbelt across her lap.

Zach caught my glare. "What?" he asked, then a smile stretched across his face. "Oh, I get it." And he switched to baby talk. "Did I wooen aww your pwans to sit wiff Jaywee?"

I shoved him away from the vehicle. "Shut up."

Honestly, though, I wasn't sure what bothered me more, that Jaylee wanted to sit by Riggs or that she'd force someone as big as Zach to squish into the back seat for a seven hour drive.

Regardless of my internal conflict, Zach, Logan, and I crammed into the second row. I lost rock-scissors-paper with Logan and had to sit in the middle. Forget Zach. There wasn't much leg room for any of us back there, but I guessed it beat walking.

And so we headed for Arizona. Riggs put on some music, loud enough that I couldn't hear what he and Jaylee were saying to one another. The Colorado roads were barren but for road kill. We saw two dead skunks, several squirrels, and three deer. Strangely, we never saw one moving vehicle, even when passing through some small towns, though there were several abandoned cars on the roadside.

It wasn't *that* early in the day. Where was everyone?

Logan must have been thinking the same thing, because he said, "What is this, Christmas day?" then guffawed at his own joke.

Logan's laugh . . . I'm not even kidding . . . it's loud.

I didn't find the situation funny. I kept thinking about how the cell phones weren't working and the power was out and my dad hadn't showed to pick us up and how, at that moment, Riggs had steered the Evoque into the opposite lane to avoid driving over a dead coyote.

We passed into Arizona and continued to see an unusual amount of road kill. I don't think we passed a mile without seeing a dead bird, snake, or javelina—these hairy, wild pigs.

The first place Riggs stopped for gas was closed. The second place was boarded up. Someone had nailed one-by-sixes over the windows and doors. I would've guessed the place had been out of business for years except we'd stopped there on the way up.

True to form, Logan was the first to panic. "We're not going to make it home without gas. What are we going to do? Phoenix is another 400 miles!"

In the rearview mirror, Riggs's cold blue eyes flashed our way. "Don't start freaking out, kid. There are more than two gas stations on this highway, I promise you."

Logan had driven Riggs nuts the past twelve days. Logan can do that to a person. Still, Logan's concerns made me feel a bit better, knowing I wasn't the most paranoid person in the car, until Riggs said, "Dude, is that your dad's van?"

My gaze shot out the front as Riggs steered into the oncoming lane and slowed to a stop, nose-to-nose with the Silver Bullet. I shoved Zach toward the door, my pulse skyrocketing.

"Get out of the car, man. Move!"

"I'm going!" Zach climbed out, and I followed, leaving the door open.

The Honda was parked on the gravelly shoulder of

the road, northbound. The doors were locked. No sign of my dad. I circled the van, checked all four tires. What was going on?

Logan yelled out Zach's open door. "Check under the hood, Eli."

I lifted my hands. "The doors are locked!" I could pop it if I got on the ground under the engine, but I'd need a long screwdriver. Riggs didn't have any tools.

"Do you have a spare key?" Riggs asked out the driver's side window.

"No. And I'm not going to break a window, either, Logan, so don't suggest it."

"If you did, I could hotwire it," Logan said.

"You could not." Zach slammed the door on Logan's rebuttal and walked to where I stood between the two vehicles. "What do you want to do, Eli?"

My skin crawled, heat rolling from my stomach to my chest. I read the concern in Zach's eyes but shrugged it off with a deep breath.

"I don't know." I checked my cell phone. "Still no signal." I squinted out over the endless sagebrush. "Let's wait a few minutes. He could, uh, could be out taking a leak."

"Good point."

But the minutes ticked by, and my dad didn't show.

"What are we doing, people?" Riggs asked from the car.

"May as well keep moving," Zach said. "I mean, we didn't pass him walking."

I nodded. "Yeah, okay. He probably headed back the other way, to a gas station or something."

Back at the Evoque, I ripped a sheet of paper out of my journal and wrote my dad another note. I secured it under the driver's side windshield wiper and hoped he'd see it. Then I climbed back into the Evoque, but it felt wrong, like I was leaving my dad for dead, like I would regret this choice for the rest of my life.

"What's the plan?" Riggs asked once we were inside. He'd shut off the music, and everything seemed extra quiet.

"Keep going," I said, as if it were no big deal, though I felt sick saying it. "He must have walked south since we didn't see him on the road."

"South it is." Riggs stepped on the gas and steered back into the right lane.

Helpless, I watched the van as we rolled away, craned my neck until it hurt.

"I can so hotwire a car, Eli. Anyone can. It's not that difficult."

"Logan," Zach said. "You're not helping."

"But you guys are acting like you don't believe me, and I—"

"Fine," I said, fire shooting through me. "You could have hotwired it. But what good would that do us or my dad? He's probably just up the road. We can't steal his ride."

"Oh. That's a good point," Logan said. "But once we find Mr. McShane, he might need my help to get it started. What kind of engine does that Honda have? A four-cylinder?"

I pushed down my desire to throttle Logan, my eyes scanning the road for any sign of my dad. "Six-cylinder."

"I think the wires on a six cylinder are on the side, near the center of the engine. I'd have to take a look to be sure."

I gritted my teeth and glanced at Zach. His lips were curved into a small grin.

I elbowed him and whispered, "Laugh it up,

chuckles."

Riggs slammed on the brakes.

Jaylee screamed.

I jerked my gaze out the front windshield. About ten yards away, a body lay on the side of the road, a red gas can beside it.

The sight just about stopped my heart.

2

Riggs swore.

Jaylee rocked in her seat, repeating, "Oh my gosh, oh my gosh" a hundred miles a minute.

I just stared at the body, unable to breathe, unable to move. A chill broke out over my arms, but the rest of me felt hot, like I'd just run a marathon.

"I'll go look," Zach said, climbing out.

The sound of the opening door yanked me from my daze, and I scurried after him. We strode toward the body until the smell of dead fish slowed our steps. It was a man. I took in his red windbreaker and leather loafers.

"That's not my dad." Relief flooded through me,

followed by a subtle horror of being pleased that someone else was lying on the side of the road.

From that point on, like a scene from some horror film, everything rolled into slow motion. I could hear my shaky breath, a Velcro strap on the man's windbreaker flapping in the wind, and my hiking boots scraping to a stop over the old concrete. Foreboding built in my mind as I inched closer. I didn't want to look. My legs were trembling, but Zach appeared so calm and cool that I tried to keep my face passive so he wouldn't know how freaked out I was.

The smell was worse up close. The man looked to be in his fifties. He was bald, his scalp shiny under the bright sun. His eyes were open and so bloodshot they looked to be bleeding. His face and neck and head and hands were pink and blistered.

"That from the sun?" I asked, jiggling one leg.

"Naw, it's some kind of zitty rash." Zach used the toe of his hiking boot to tip back the dead guy's chin, peering inside his mouth. Zach was a lifeguard at the pool. We'd all taken basic first aid with Reinhold this past week, but I was glad Zach was here.

"You going to do CPR?" I asked.

"No use. He's been dead a while. Besides, I don't want to touch him. Whatever killed him could be contagious."

My stomach dropped at the idea that my dad might have talked to this guy—touched this guy. I slid back a step. "He stinks like Deadwood Lodge."

Zach looked at me then, our eyes exchanging a question neither of us could form.

"Mark had a rash on his arms," I finally said. Reinhold had thought it was poison oak.

Zach gave the slightest shake of his head. "Don't go there, man. Not yet."

Too late. My insides were starting to writhe with the

implications.

Zach leaned down, head sideways. "I don't see the lump of a wallet in his front pockets. Don't want to turn him over to check the back. I hate to just leave him, but I think it's the smartest thing to do."

"Then let's go," I said.

Zach straightened and walked past me. "Don't mention the rash to the others."

I started to follow, then paused and kicked the gas can. It was empty. But if the Honda was out of gas, maybe my dad could use it. "You think the gas can could be contaminated?"

Zach turned back. "Some viruses can survive on door handles for a week. I wouldn't risk it."

So I left the gas can with the body and followed Zach back to the Range Rover. We got in, and Riggs drove on. Jaylee hid her face as we passed the body, but Logan rolled down his window and looked out.

Once we had picked up speed, Logan rolled up his window and leaned forward, resting the top of his head on the back of Jaylee's seat. He looked at me and Zach. "That guy was dead?" he asked.

"Yeah," I said, though it was more of a breath than an actual word.

"Hit by a car, you think?"

"No," Zach said. "He probably had a heart attack or a stroke while he was walking."

"That's so sad!" Jaylee said. "We should have put him in the car. Taken him to the next gas station and called the police."

"We are not putting a dead body in my car," Riggs said.

"But coyotes and birds will eat him!" Jaylee said. "You guys! We have to go back."

"We're not going back," Riggs said.

"I didn't see that he had a wallet," Zach said, "or I would have taken it to give to the authorities."

We rode in silence. I thought about how Zach had used his boot to tip back the guy's head, how he hadn't wanted to touch the body long enough to look for a wallet. I kept picturing that man's pimpled skin and how it reminded me of Mark's rash and imagining my dad talking with that guy and catching some horrible disease.

A rush of panic pulsed through my veins. I felt trapped, squished between Zach and Logan in the back seat. I wanted out of this car. I needed to walk. My breath was shallow, which I knew was making things worse. I forced myself to calm down, to breathe deeply.

"Here," Riggs said, reaching up to the dash for his cell phone and handing it to Jaylee. "Put on some tunes."

While Jaylee played DJ, I focused on the road, my gaze darting from one side to the other, vigilant for any sign of my dad. Twenty minutes later, we came to another car, this one stopped in our lane. Riggs drove around it, and as we passed by we could see that it was empty.

"Bet that was the dead guy's ride," Riggs said.

"That was the first time I've ever seen a dead body," Logan said.

"I couldn't look," Jaylee said. "I knew I'd have nightmares later. Last year, I saw my grandma's body at her funeral. It was an open casket. I had nightmares for two months after."

"Yeah, I've been to open caskets," Riggs said. "Never saw someone dead where he fell, though."

Jaylee twisted and looked between the bucket seats. "How about you guys?"

I tried to change the subject before she pressed Zach. "How 'bout we play twenty—"

Jaylee cut me off. "Zach?"

Okay, it ticked me off when people forgot Zach's mom. I mean, she'd died six years ago, but it's not like Jaylee had just moved to Phoenix last year or something. She'd been in seventh grade with us when Zach's mom had gone through chemo and everything.

But Zach handled it like a pro. "Not like that guy," he said. "You got any 21 Pilots on there?" And just like that, Jaylee was distracted.

Not me, though. As we settled in for the long drive, I couldn't stop stewing over that dead guy and my dad. When I forced myself to think of something else, I'd obsess about Jaylee and how wrong she was for me. She was gorgeous, so there was that, and when she talked to me, I felt like there was some kind of magic force circling the two of us. But this trip had made it clear just how completely different we were.

Like any of that mattered. She'd never even looked at me longer than three seconds. She'd had a huge thing for Zach last year that had about killed me. He'd finally had to tell her she wasn't his type. I still wondered if that was true or if he'd lied for my sake.

I really needed to get a life.

The problem was, there was history here. It had started when we were in the same table group in Mrs. Muir's fifth grade class and Jaylee had laughed at my jokes. But now that we were about to be seniors, I really needed to snap out of it.

I heard her voice, teasing Riggs, and the sound made my gut churn with something so toxic I put my face in my hands so I could casually press my thumbs over my ears to block out her voice.

A nudge to my side. "Hey," Zach said. "I'm sure he's fine."

I exchanged a nod for his concern and let a deep breath roll through me. It felt good but didn't change the weight pressing against my chest. I closed my eyes like I might actually sleep, then realized, with a jolt, that I could miss spotting my dad. So I went back to watching the road. It was too hot, though, even with the air conditioning. I stripped off my hoodie and threw it in back. Zach was reading a book on his cell phone. Logan had pulled out his Nintendo Switch. Jaylee repeatedly tried to text Erin but the messages weren't going through. I kept watching for my dad, trying to keep my thoughts on that task and nothing else.

Jaylee put her hand on Riggs's shoulder and started toying with the brown and black puka shell necklace he always wore. I hated that thing. The guy could do lots of cool stuff, but he was no surfer. We lived in Phoenix, for Pete's sake.

"Check it out," Riggs said. "Another abandoned car." He sailed past a black Nissan king cab parked half on the road, half on the shoulder.

This one had a body in the front seat. A woman, her eyes open, staring.

Heat shot through me. Stunned, I glanced at Zach. His eyes were wide. Neither of us spoke, but Zach looked at me a long time, like he was trying to think of some way to rationalize what we'd seen.

Two dead bodies. Could they be related? Maybe they'd been in the same vehicle, eaten something bad. Had gotten food poisoning.

After that, I tried hard to keep my eyes on the road, but it was difficult not to see that woman's face in my memory. My hands began to shake, and I stuffed them between my knees, trying to hold it together. Somehow, it seemed Zach and I had been the only ones who'd seen that the driver have been dead.

"How much gas do we have?" Logan asked.

"Plenty," Riggs said.

"We'll have to fill up, though," Logan said. "One tank won't get us to Phoenix."

Riggs's eyes glanced back in the rearview mirror. "We're fine."

Yet his tone didn't sound so fine. I straightened, tried to get a look at the gas gauge, but I couldn't see past Riggs.

Seeming to have the same idea as I had, Jaylee leaned toward the driver's seat. "The low fuel light is on, Riggs."

"Yep. We're definitely going to need some gas," Logan said.

"How about you people let me drive the car?" Riggs said.

"If we run out of gas, we'll have to hitchhike." Logan's voice cracked.

"We're not hitchhiking," Riggs said.

"Hitchhiking is dangerous," Logan said. "That man could have died from heatstroke."

"Dude!" Riggs glanced over his shoulder. "Do you have an off switch?"

"Hey," I said, not liking Riggs's tone.

"Everyone calm down," Zach said. "It's going to be okay."

Logan started rocking in his seat and mumbling. With his bushy blond afro, his bony limbs, braces, and the terrified expression on his face, he looked twelve, not sixteen. "Please help us, God. Don't let us die. Please help us. Please, oh, please, oh, please."

It was weird to see him so freaked out. I mean, Logan freaks out a lot, but we hadn't run out of gas yet, plus my dad was the one who was missing. How about a prayer for him?

"Did you see that?" Jaylee whipped around to look over her shoulder and out the back window.

"What?" I'd been so busy watching Logan, I had neglected my job of watching for my dad. Hopeful, I looked back but didn't see any people.

"That sign back there said, 'Gas ahead'."

"Where?" Logan twisted onto me, trying to see out the back window, his bony elbow spearing my side.

I shoved back. "Dude, get off!"

"There's another one!" Jaylee pointed forward.

We all stretched to look out the front, our heads turning as we read the spray-painted words on plywood.

"Gas—Open. One mile," I read aloud.

Logan whooped and started clapping, like we'd all worked together to solve some big dilemma. Jaylee grinned and said something to Riggs that I couldn't hear. I felt relieved to see the sign but wondered why such a sign was necessary. What was going on that would close gas stations?

Sure enough, we found a Texaco station with another plywood sign announcing gas available. Riggs pulled into the lot. The place was really run down, but so was most everything in the Navajo Nation. Riggs parked at a pump and shut off the vehicle.

"See now?" he said. "Everything's cool. I'll get the gas. Eli, you go in and ask about your dad."

"Look!" Logan said. "Here comes someone."

All heads turned and focused on a man who had exited the Country Grocery and was headed our way. He wore dingy gray coveralls, the knees baggy and blackened, and a green baseball cap that read "SKOAL: a pinch better." He had long black hair and round cheeks that made his age difficult to guess.

He walked up to the driver's side window, which Riggs rolled down. An oval-shaped patch on his coveralls declared his name: Pete.

The man whistled. "That's one fancy vehicle. What you

call this thing?"

"It's a Range Rover Evoque." Riggs patted the dashboard like the vehicle was a *good boy*. "Gets 18 miles a gallon. Best mileage in a Range Rover to date."

"That right? How can I help you kids?"

"Fill her up," Riggs said.

"You have cash?"

"Uh, yeah. I think so."

"Price is five dollars a gallon."

"Whoa!" Riggs said. "That's kind of steep, don't you think?"

"It was ten yesterday. You're the first car to come by since then, so I figure I'd make you a deal." Pete stepped back from the car and pointed across the gravel lot. "Pull over to that pump there." Then he started walking toward it.

"I don't get it," Logan said. "What does he mean?"

"Probably that I should follow him to the pump that's working," Riggs said, starting the car.

Riggs drove the Evoque to the pump and climbed out. The rest of us got out too. My legs had felt like pretzels in that backseat, so it felt good to stretch them out. The pump looked like an antique. It was skinny, had a glass container on the top, and a long handle attached to the base.

Jaylee tucked a loose strand of hair over her ear and asked Pete. "Is your store open?"

"Sure is. Just don't use the bathroom. You need to go, you can use the outhouse." Pete nodded to a port-a-potty on the side of the building.

Jaylee wrinkled her nose and headed toward the brown and beige plastic structure.

Zach walked up to Pete. "Sir? Do you have a number for the highway patrol? We found a dead man on the side of the road about fifty miles back."

Pete rubbed his chin and sighed. "The number's on the

counter in the store, but I don't think anyone will answer."

Zach frowned at Pete. "Why not?"

"Probably no one there."

I cut in. "Have you seen a man come through here, mid-forties, white, about my height, dark hair, probably wearing an orange Phoenix Suns cap? We found his Honda Odyssey a ways back, so he might have been walking."

Pete started to crank the handle on the pump back and forth like it was some massive slot machine. "Haven't seen nobody come by on foot since about two days ago."

My stomach turned to lead. I stepped up to Zach and lowered my voice. "If he didn't go north, he had to come by here."

"I want to know why this guy thinks the cops won't answer their phone," Zach said. "They should be able to help us track down your dad too."

"We were sure glad to see your signs," Riggs said to Pete. "Tank was almost empty, and no place else was open. What are you doing?"

Pete was still cranking the handle, but now the glass jar on top was filling up with gas. "What you think I'm doing? I'm pumping your gas. This is a globe gravity flow pump. It was used when my grandfather built this station in 1936. We used to keep it on display inside, but with the power out and people needing gas, I figured I'd better hook it up and put it to work."

"The electricity is out all over?" I asked.

"I don't know about all over, but it's been out here for the past three days."

"Three days!" Zach said. "That's a long time to be without power."

"Looks like pee," Logan said, staring at the gas in the see-through tank.

I snorted. "Nice, Logan."

"Well it does." Logan slurped at his braces. "I've never seen gas before. I didn't know what color it was."

"You know why the power is out?" I asked Pete.

He slid the pump nozzle into the Evoque's gas tank and flipped a switch. The gas in the globe started to drain. "All I can figure is that everyone got too sick to work the grid."

The word *sick* stole my breath. "Something going around?" I asked, thinking of the dead man, the dead woman. Thinking of Mark and Erin . . . Chipeta . . . Lizzie and my dad.

"How come none of you've heard of the sick?" Pete asked. "It all but took over the world the past two weeks."

Logan's eyes widened.

"We've been camping," Riggs said.

My stomach twisted. Zach raised his eyebrows at me. Yeah, Pete was giving me the heebie jeebies too.

"What happened?" I asked.

The globe had emptied. Pete flipped the switch and went back to cranking the handle. "I had a blood sugar test over in Kayenta. Had to fast from food and drink the day before. That's when it hit around here. It all happened real fast. By the time I got to the doctor's office, the place was a madhouse. Doctor told me not to drink any water that wasn't bottled. That's why I'm still standing."

"Something in the water?" I asked, looking to Zach.

"Something bad," Pete said.

"You guys!"

I looked up. Jaylee was standing outside the store, waving us over and pointing to a sign on the door. She didn't have to ask me twice. I took off at a sprint.

Zach and I reached the store together and took in the sign, which had been printed on a sheet of regular typing paper.

HEALTH ALERT

A new bacterium has been found in fresh water sources in various parts of the country. People who visit these affected areas and do not take preventive measures are likely to suffer infection and spread the disease to other areas. This notice is to remind you of the need to practice personal and environmental hygiene at all times.

Do not consume or bathe in any ground, lake, or river water until further notice. Drink only bottled or canned beverages.

If you think you have been infected, visit your nearest medical clinic or health facility immediately.

LET'S WORK TOGETHER TO PREVENT DISEASE

Department of Health and Human Services
Center for Disease Control and Prevention

3

My stomach fluttered. This was not good.

"Sounds like cholera," Zach said.

I folded my arms in an attempt to hold it together. "Yeah, wasn't there a cholera outbreak in China before we came up here? I saw it on the news."

"I don't watch the news," Jaylee said. "It's too depressing."

"No, you're right," Zach said. "Something to do with that tidal wave and the flooding."

It had seemed so far away—most disasters did. "This couldn't be the same thing," I said. "Not in Arizona."

"Cholera can spread quickly if people aren't careful."

Logan eyes fixed on mine. "It can be lethal within hours if a person is not treated."

"Thank you, Logan," Zach said. "But, guys. Think about it. This is what our government does. If there is one case of cholera in the US, they have to post warning signs everywhere, otherwise some tightwad will sue for millions when their dog dies and they weren't properly warned."

That was true. The U.S. government did tend to go above and beyond where these things were concerned, which was a good thing, really. Better safe than sorry. "Still . . . I think we should heed the sign—and Pete—and stick to bottled water till we get home."

"Done," Zach said.

Jaylee's eyes shone wild with fear. "Do you think this is what's wrong with Mark and Erin?"

"How?" Zach said. "They were in the middle of the San Juan National Forest."

"Though that body we passed on the road . . . He could have been infected." Logan looked from me to Zach. "I hope neither of you touched him."

"We didn't touch him," Zach said.

"Good," Logan said. "I would hate to have to quarantine you two."

I ignored the rush of anger inside me at Logan's words.

"You guys are freaking me out," Jaylee said. "I'm going to get my wallet so I can buy something." She took off running for the Range Rover, her ponytails bouncing behind her.

Zach nudged me. "Stare hard, McShane."

I shoved him. He pushed me back, then tucked me into a headlock. Nuts. I could never get out of Zach's headlocks. Despite his baby boy face, the guy was built. He had a full ride to the University of Arizona for swimming and would be training at the Hillenbrand Aquatic Center this fall for a shot at qualifying for the next Olympic games. He was that good.

I, on the other hand, liked to hike and hunt and fix cars. These activities did not require a muscular physique. Still, I knuckle-punched his leg as hard as I could. "Let go!"

He laughed. "Oh ho ho! The string bean fights back!"

"Come on!" I twisted my head, but Zach's hold was like medieval stocks.

"Admit you love her!" he sang in my ear.

"Dude. Cut. It. Out." It was one thing to tease me about Jaylee when we were at my house or Zach's or Logan's. But not here. Not where she could hear and I could die of humiliation when she laughed in my face.

My desperate tone did the trick. Zach let go, shoved me toward the Evoque, then ran for the store.

"You're a jerk," I said, smoothing my shaggy hair out of my eyes as I followed him inside. Oh yes. I'd sure told him.

Zach used Pete's phone to call the highway patrol, but no one answered. I tried home again. No luck.

While Logan was on the other end of the store, I said to Zach, "You think that man and that woman both had what this health alert is warning about?"

"They must have," Zach said.

"I don't like it," I said.

"Me either, man."

We all bought extremely overpriced snacks, and Riggs threw a fit when Pete said the gas cost eighty dollars. But soon enough we were back on the road, all scarfing our snacks like we hadn't eaten for a week.

"Hey, Riggs," I said. "Why don't you try the radio? See if you can find out anything."

"Radio won't work out here," he said. "And even if it did, they never put local health scares on the radio."

"Sure they do," Logan said. "Remember that measles

outbreak in the schools a few years back? That was all over the news."

Riggs growled, his patience with Logan so thin it was about to break. "Whatever, okay? Try it if you want, but I think it's a waste of time."

When no one moved, I had to speak up again. "Jaylee? Would you mind?"

"Oh, okay, sure." She put the paper sack with her snacks down on the floor, then pushed a few buttons on the console until the sound of static spilled out of the speakers. She fumbled with the knobs and eventually found a station playing music in Spanish. A few more clicks brought in the faint sound of classic rock.

"You're going to have to pick one and leave it," Logan said. "People will only talk when there is a break between songs."

But Jaylee kept flipping through. "I didn't like any of those channels." She finally settled on a Fallout Boy song, then dug back into her bag of treats from Pete's store.

"Reese's mini, anyone?" she asked.

"Uh, yes," Zach said, reaching between the seats. "Where'd you get those?"

"They were on an end rack," she said, pouring the bite-sized morsels into all our outstretched hands.

"I totally missed them!" Zach dumped his handful into his mouth, then made a sound similar to gargling. "Oh. So good. I love you, Jaylee Jennings. You are my candy hero."

She giggled and winked at Zach. "Well, I love you, too, hot stuff."

She settled back into her seat, and I glared at Zach.

He leaned close and whispered, "See? That wasn't so hard. If I can do it, so can you. Go on, McShane. Tell her. Confess your luh-hu-huv."

I elbowed him, then ate my Reese's.

"That Pete guy was creepy," Jaylee said. "And I think that Health Alert sign was a fake."

"Why would anyone put up a fake sign?" I asked.

"To scare people," she said.

"No," Logan said. "Something is going on. The power, the phones, the Health Alert sign, Eli's dad, the dead guy, the fact that there is no one else out on the roads . . ."

"We're not getting all paranoid over Prickly Pete, okay?" Riggs said.

"Hey, Eli," Logan said. "Wasn't your dad and Lizzie sick before we left?"

Heat flashed over my body. Logan had no tact whatsoever.

"*Logan*," Zach said.

"And Pastor Wayne too. Think him and your dad and Lizzie all got cholera? Think it somehow got to Phoenix?"

"Shut up, Logan," Zach said.

"What?" Logan asked. "What'd I say?"

Zach leaned forward to glare past me at Logan. "Just stop, okay?"

But Logan wasn't wrong to wonder. Lizzie *had* been sick all last week, and Dad had gotten sick a few days before the drive up. He'd planned to camp with us but figured he was coming down with whatever Lizzie and Pastor Wayne had. When I thought about the cholera outbreak in China, however, it just didn't make sense that the two were connected. The outbreak had only shown up a week or so before we'd left, and cholera couldn't spread that fast. Could it? Besides, the US had excellent water purification systems in place to keep diseases like cholera away.

"Check out this guy," Riggs said, slowing the Range Rover.

A maroon Honda Accord was coming toward us, currently straddling the center line of the two lane highway.

Riggs rolled onto the shoulder to get out of the way, and we all watched the vehicle roll by. It couldn't have been going more than ten miles an hour.

"There are people inside," Jaylee said.

"What is he doing?" Logan asked.

I turned in my seat to watch as the car continued on a slight diagonal across the road. It finally rolled in front of us and off our side of the road, into the sagebrush, stopping about five yards from the highway.

"This is nuts," Riggs said, his seatbelt flying back as he unbuckled himself and climbed out of the vehicle.

"I'm coming too," Jaylee said.

"I don't think that's a good idea," I said, but as usual, no one was listening to me.

Logan got out, so Zach followed.

"Just to make sure no one touches anyone," he said.

I started to get out, but before my hiking boots touched the pavement, I heard Jaylee scream. Then Logan, Riggs, and Zach were all shouting at once. I looked over to the Honda in time to see Zach dragging Logan back from the opened driver's side door, a limp arm hanging out of the opening.

Jaylee was hugging Riggs, the two of them already heading back this way.

"They're dead," she said as Riggs opened the passenger side door. "All four of them."

But for Jaylee's quiet sobbing, we rode in silence all the way to Flagstaff. It was truly a record for Logan. We were all of us seriously scared now. The radio went from one song to the next and never did give us any information. Images of my dad and Lizzie and Pastor Wayne covered in zitty rashes haunted my thoughts. Were such rashes a symptom of cholera? I didn't have a clue. I wished I could Google it and know for sure.

Riggs slowed as we entered the outskirts of Flagstaff. I'd expected to see a lot more cars in the road here, but there were no more than what we'd seen before. We still saw plenty of dead animals—cats and dogs instead of game. The storefronts along the road had been vandalized. Broken windows, mostly. Looted, I imagined. But there were no immediate signs of life, no cars driving on the roads, no people on bicycles, no pedestrians. A band of pressure wrapped around my middle. What did this mean? Was everyone sick?

Distant bells caught my attention. In Flagstaff, Route 66 ran parallel to the train tracks. Right now, the crossing signals were clanging and flashing, but there was no sign of a train. "If the signals are on, does that mean there's electricity here?" I asked.

"I think it's pretty obvious," Logan said.

I dug out my cell phone and checked it. "I've got a bar!" I quickly dialed home. It rang and rang. The answering machine still didn't pick up. Zach and Logan tried to make calls too. I tried my dad's cell next. It went straight to voicemail, so I left a message, told him where we were.

"I got a text from Antônia!" Jaylee said.

I leaned forward. "Where are they?"

"She didn't say. Just that nothing is open. She sent it this morning."

"I didn't think to ask Pete about Antônia or Mark and the guys," Zach said.

The pressure in my chest seemed to increase as I thought about my friends. "Antônia wouldn't need gas for the Prius," I said. "They're probably still on the road. But we didn't see Mark's Impala, so they must have filled up at Pete's."

"I don't know why Antônia didn't respond to the rest of my texts," Jaylee said.

"Probably because there's no power in Phoenix," Logan said. "That's likely why our calls have all gone to voicemail. No power equals no working cell towers for our cell phones to connect to."

"Thank you, Einstein," Riggs mumbled.

That made sense, though. I tried to distract myself from despair by watching for my dad, but the split highway made it so much harder to look for him. What if we drove by and I missed him? I really didn't think Dad could've walked this far already. He must have gotten a ride with someone. Maybe Mark. Or he might have hiked north to the campground.

Then why hadn't we seen him on the road?

We passed a sign that marked the road to the hospital. What if my dad did have cholera or whatever this illness was? He could have ended up at the hospital. Maybe that's where everyone was. At the hospitals or home in bed, sleeping it off.

"I'm hungry for real food," Jaylee said.

Zach leaned his head between the seats. "Ooh! Downtown Diner!"

"Where?" Riggs asked.

"It's that's place with all the license plates on the counter," Logan said as if that made the location obvious to everyone. "They have the best milkshakes."

The mere thought of a Downtown Diner milkshake made my mouth water. "Why would Downtown Diner be open?" I said. "Nothing is open."

"Doesn't hurt to look." Riggs glanced over his shoulder. "Where is it?"

"By the toy shop," Logan said.

"You're going to have to do better than that," Riggs said.

"Turn by the Painted Desert place," I said.

Riggs eyed me in the rearview mirror. "Painted *what?*"

"It's by the . . ." I wracked my brain. "It's a one way street going right."

"At the Amtrak station," Zach said.

"Yeah! But before the Amtrak," I clarified. "The one-way street before it."

"There!" Zach pointed at the Painted Desert store on the next corner. "Turn on San Francisco Street."

Riggs turned right, and just like that, we were on a mission. We had a task, small as it was. We had purpose, and it united us. Gave us something to think about other than the obvious.

"Left up here on Aspen," Zach said.

"But that's a one-way!" Logan said.

"Who cares?" Riggs said. "We're the only ones on the road." He steered the Range Rover up the one-way street.

And just like that, our cooperative environment ended.

"But, Riggs," Logan said. "That's illegal."

"That's very true, Logan," Riggs said, "very true. But I'm going to risk it. This once. Because if there was a cop, I'd be so happy to see him, I'd pay for ten tickets. Though even if he did choose to run my plates, he wouldn't be able to because there's no electricity."

"We've already established that there's electricity in Flagstaff because of the train crossings," Logan said. "Plus a cop car would have its own power from the car battery, and an officer of the law doesn't need to run your plates to give you a tick—"

Riggs laughed maniacally. "You just keep going, don't you? Five years later, you're still talking, and I'm in the nuthouse."

I couldn't help myself. I had to butt in. "Give him a break, Riggs." Only Zach and I got to razz Logan. That's what friends were for.

Riggs slammed on the brakes and turned to look over his shoulder. "You got a problem with me too, high school twig?"

Yes, I absolutely did, but before I could tell him that yelling at Logan was no way to be our adult chaperone, Zach leaned in front of me, saving me from certain death. "Dude, Downtown Diner! It's right there. On the left."

Riggs turned the wheel, and parked perpendicular to the sidewalk, the front of the car facing the restaurant. We all stared. The windows of the Downtown Diner had been shattered. Piles of debris littered the sidewalk out front. Someone had tagged the walls with the words "It's the end of the world and we know it."

"What do you think happened?" Jaylee asked.

Before even Logan could speculate, two guys ran out of the diner, wielding baseball bats. We all screamed. Riggs put the car in reverse and hit the gas. We rolled back, but when Riggs stopped to put the car in drive, it slowed us enough that one of the thugs managed to swing his bat against the back windshield, cracking the glass like desert clay.

4

"Go! Go!" I yelled, while Riggs called the thugs a string of swear words that would have caused my mother to wash out his mouth.

Riggs cranked the wheel left on Leroux Street, accelerated, and then slammed on the brakes so hard that Logan smacked against the back of Jaylee's seat. A few more curses from Riggs pulled my gaze out the front windshield.

Jaylee screamed.

A body lay in the middle of the street. Behind it, the rest of the road was gridlocked with empty vehicles. The smell of fish was overwhelming.

Jaylee gasped. "Oh my gosh, look!"

Dozens of people were clustered along the base of the wall, sitting on the sidewalk as if they'd been waiting in line for days. Men, women, and children. None were moving. Many sat huddled in groups, some with their arms around each other. A few dozen lay on the ground, some right on the pavement, others under blankets or tucked inside sleeping bags.

Rashes covered their skin.

The people stretched along the sidewalk and right up to a glass door that had one of the Health Alert signs taped to the inside. A sign on the building said Flagstaff Urgent Care.

"Dude, they're zombies!" Logan whispered.

"They're not zombies," I whispered back, trying to keep Riggs from hearing Logan's latest. I couldn't bring myself to tell Logan that if they weren't all dead, they would be soon. I could barely even think about what that might mean.

Jaylee swatted at Riggs's arm. "I want to leave," she said, her breath coming in short, gasping breaths. "I want to leave right now! Riggs! Get us out of—"

CRACK!

Jaylee screamed again as the back window of the Evoque took another blow. The guys with the baseball bats were back.

"Get out of the car!" one of them said.

"I don't think so." Riggs cranked the wheel hard to the right and floored it. The Range Rover's wheels spun long enough for a bat to hit Zach's window. The wood bounced off of the glass. Once. Twice. I tucked my head between my knees, shocked the glass actually held.

Just as we shot forward, the bat struck the window again. This time it shattered, spraying us with glass. Riggs didn't turn tight enough, though, and the Ranger Rover plowed through one of the white wooden pillars of the Hotel Weatherford. Wood shards splintered over the windshield and sun roof as we sailed back onto Aspen—still going the wrong way. Jaylee was bawling Logan hugging me. I grabbed the headrests of the front seats to keep from falling onto Zach.

Riggs turned down Beaver Street, which was, thankfully, vacant, and everything became peaceful again.

I released my breath. "You okay?" I asked, looking at Zach, who had glass in his hair.

"Doesn't look like I'm cut. Check it out," he said, picking up an ice blue wedge of glass off his leg. "It looks like rock candy."

"It's tempered glass," I said, helping him brush the fragments onto the floor. "The only people who get cut by it are the installers who handle the unfinished product."

"Were those people all dead?" Jaylee asked, her voice high-pitched and soft.

"Sure looked like," Zach said.

Jaylee sniffled and wiped tears off her cheeks. "What does that mean? Why wouldn't that Urgent Care have let them inside?"

"Can everybody, please, just be quiet for a few minutes?" Riggs asked. "Just until we get out of here?"

We obeyed. I don't know if we needed the silence or were shocked by Riggs's use of the word *please*, but no one uttered another word.

Once we were back on Route 66, Riggs drove like someone from a *Fast and Furious* movie, taking a ninety-degree corner at seventy and breaking our silence with another round of screams from us all. I'm pretty sure the Evoque went up on two wheels for a second there.

The car approached another clanging railroad crossing, but Riggs didn't even slow down. I winced as the wheels clunk-clunked over the tracks, thankful not to see a train on this visit to Flagstaff.

By the time we hit I-17, Riggs was going ninety-five. Wind and heat whipped in through Zach's broken window, tickling the hairs on my arm. I just sat there, sandwiched between Zach and Logan, gripping my knees as if that might help me if we crashed.

Jaylee started flipping through radio channels. A lot more were coming in now, which made me feel better for some reason. She clicked past a few country channels, one playing classic rock, some eighties and nineties music, three classical channels, and a sports show in which the host was interviewing someone from the Arizona Sun Devils. She stopped there the longest.

"I thought it was news," she said finally, hitting the scan button again.

A familiar, high-pitched tone blared from the speakers. Jaylee turned, wide-eyed, to Riggs. "Is that what I think it is?"

We fell silent as the tones played again.

"It's the Emergency Alert System," Logan said.

Sure enough, a man's voice was talking, saying familiar words. ". . . broadcasters of Coconino County in voluntary cooperation with federal, state, and local authorities, have developed this system to keep you informed in the event of an emergency. The CDC has been alerted of a HydroFlu outbreak in your area. A new bacterium has been found in fresh water sources in various parts of the country. People who visit these affected areas and do not take preventive measures are likely to suffer infection and spread the disease to other areas. It is imperative that everyone practice personal and environmental hygiene at all times. Do not consume or bathe in any city, well, ground, lake, or river water until further notice. Drink only bottled or canned beverages. If you think you have been infected, visit your nearest medical clinic or health facility immediately."

The tones began to sound again, and the message repeated.

Riggs switched off the radio.

"What's HyrdoFlu?" Jaylee asked.

"Water sickness?" I guessed.

"This is what the Health Alert sign at the gas station was warning about," Logan said. "That's why we aren't supposed to drink anything but bottled water."

"And suddenly I'm very thirsty," Zach said, his hair blowing in the wind.

"If Flagstaff was that bad, think of Phoenix," Logan said. "What do you guys think happened to our parents?"

I felt sick just thinking about Lizzie and my mom. "Let's not speculate," I said, hoping to keep Logan from doing just that.

"Let's not even discuss it," Riggs said. "We've got two hours until we're home, and I don't want to spend the next two hours listening to you all freak out over nothing."

"Nothing!" Jaylee cried. "Riggs, you saw all those dead people."

"Dead people in Flagstaff do not equal dead people in Phoenix. So everyone relax."

"But what about Erin and Mark?" Jaylee said. "They were sick!"

"Sick, not dead," Riggs said. "Let's just get back to Phoenix. We'll know more then."

"There are over four million people in the Phoenix-Mesa metropolitan area," Logan said. "I doubt there's enough bottled water to serve that many people for long."

"Shut it, Logan," Riggs said.

"In fact, if this is an outbreak, we'd be wise to avoid metropolitan areas at all costs."

Riggs glared at Logan in his rearview mirror. "Anyone got some duct tape?"

"I have some in my pack," Logan said.

I almost laughed. "Logan, please. I'm begging you, man. Let's wait and talk about it later." I shot him my most serious "work with me, please?" look, and he finally clammed up.

"We *should* make a plan, though," Jaylee said, her voice laced with tears. "Something we can do to stay safe. I mean, Logan is right. If there were two guys with baseball bats in Flagstaff, there will be two hundred guys with baseball bats in Phoenix."

"We're going to Phoenix, and that's final," Riggs said.

"We have to know what happened to our families," I added.

"Listen," Riggs said. "No one is giving in to paranoia. Everything will be fine. I'll take you all home, you'll see that I'm right, then I can go home and shower and sleep for a week."

Jaylee's jaw dropped. "But you can't just leave us!"

"I can and I will. Home is the best place for us all."

"If we even have a home left," Logan said. "Phoenix could be gone. Without power, something could have happened to Palo Verde. Just like what happened in Japan."

I shut my eyes. Leave it to Logan to bring up a nuclear meltdown.

"Logan, shut your mouth, or I'll do it for you," Riggs yelled.

"No! I want to hear this." Jaylee turned in her seat so she could see Logan through the crack between the seat and the door. Tears glazed her eyes. "You think there might be radiation in Phoenix?"

"It's a conceivable theory," Logan said. "Back-up generators only run for so long. If no one is alive to work them they—"

"You know what?"

Riggs pulled onto the shoulder of I-17, slowing the car so fast the tires slid two yards in the gravel. Logan and Zach both jerked against the seatbacks. I stopped myself by grabbing the center console. Dust drifted in through Zach's window.

Riggs twisted in his seat and glared back at Logan. "I think you need to hoof it."

"Walk?" Logan said. "No way!"

"If I hear one more paranoid, know-it-all conspiracy statement out of any of you, you're hitching. You hear me?"

"You can't do that," Zach said. "You're our adult leader."

"Watch me."

No one said anything else. We all just sat there, waiting for Riggs to chill. He finally pulled back out onto the road, but the ride to Phoenix was agony. No one said a word, which gave me nothing to do but imagine the worst about my dad and Mom and Lizzie and Phoenix and this HydroFlu business. Fear never lifted. It merely shifting from the feel of a smothering blanket to some kind of critter, gnawing at my bones.

We passed eighteen abandoned vehicles. I know because I counted. Had they run out of gas? Or had their drivers died?

"Look!" Zach said, pointing at a car on the opposite side of the freeway, moving, heading north toward Flagstaff. It was a silver Chevy Cavalier, nothing I recognized.

We all watched it in silence. Once it was out of view, no one spoke. I wondered if the driver had seen us, if he or she knew what was going on, if he or she was sick.

A few miles later we passed a man sitting on the roof of a Subaru Outback, holding a sign that read, "Need Gas."

"Riggs!" Jaylee yelled. "We should stop and tell him about Pete."

Pete, who was a 250-mile hike away.

"I'm not stopping for no one," Riggs said. "I'm in charge, so can it, all of you."

That was the last thing anyone said until we reached the city and Logan's arm flew past my face, finger pointed out Zach's open window. "There's a fire!"

There was more than one. A gray haze clouded the Phoenix sky. Hundreds of black plumes of smoke drifted up as if one in five buildings in the city were some kind of factory. Riggs kept the Evoque steady at sixty five, pausing only to weave around stopped cars. Every-so-often we sped past a moving vehicle, and I felt the need to duck my head. I don't know why.

"Phoenix is burning," Logan said. "It's like the whole world is asleep and no one is left to put out the fires."

Which meant what? That it would burn until nothing was left? I didn't voice my question aloud for fear of what Logan's reply would be. Nothing pleasant, I was sure.

Someone's cell phone sang. Jaylee jumped. "I got a text!" She scrambled for her phone. "It's Antônia! She says, 'Many gas stations closed. Country Grocery Texaco open.'"

"Been there, done that," Riggs said.

"What else she say?" I asked.

"'Nothing open in Flagstaff.' Then about twenty minutes ago she wrote 'Something wrong in Phoenix. Urgent Care closed. Be careful.' Then next she wrote, "No one was home at my mom's or Erin's, so we're driving over to my grandma's house in Peoria.'"

"Wait," Logan said. "Was that Antônia's Prius we passed on the freeway?"

"It wasn't a Prius," I said. "And she wouldn't have been that far north if she was going to Peoria."

I dug out my phone and checked my messages. Nothing.

"Anything from Lizzie?" Zach asked.

"Nah," I said. "She doesn't really text much, anyway." Though she did more than my parents. Neither of them had adapted all that well to smart phone technology. "You hear from anyone?"

Zach shook his head.

"Jaylee, tell Antônia about the water," I said. "Then see if you can get through to Mark or Cristobal."

"I've already texted everyone I know," she said. "What carrier do you guys have?"

This sparked a pragmatic discussion about phone carriers that lasted a good ten minutes without any of us thinking about the horror of what was happening outside the vehicle.

As we neared my place, Jaylee changed the subject. "You're going to Eli's house first, right?" she asked Riggs. "Then Zach and Logan's?" Her tone suggested that this was the only acceptable plan.

"Eli's place, your place, then Zach and Logan's."

"But I want to stay with you!"

"No way." Riggs shot her a look. "I'm taking you to your house. To your mom."

Jaylee folded her arms and slouched down in her seat. "Fine."

I had a sister, so I knew that "fine" actually meant "not fine" in girl speak. That Jaylee was upset with Riggs made me a little bit lighter inside for the briefest moment.

Riggs took the Camelback Road exit. The surface streets looked like a riot had passed through town. Buildings were on fire: a couple raging, most only smoking. Cars clogging the streets forced Riggs to keep it under thirty. The stores we passed looked to have been completely pillaged. Had this all happened during a power outage?

Every now and then I saw a group of people walking

down a side street, or one or two inside a store. They all seemed to be carrying something. I saw a few with rifles. Whenever one of us saw human life, Riggs stepped on the gas. It was weird. I felt like I should be relieved to see others alive, but it terrified me.

There were signs too. Lots of them. Some on store marquis, but most had been hastily thrown together like the one at Pete's gas station.

Don't drink the water!
Quarantined.
Don't boil! Don't filter!
Bottled water only!
Stay out! Infected inside!

The closer we got to my house, the sweatier my palms became.

"This is unreal," Zach said.

"Which street is yours?" Riggs asked me.

"I'm on 14th," I said. "But it doesn't go through, so you have to take 13th to get there."

"Right. I knew it was something like that."

My street was deserted. My neighbors had a sign on their yard that said, "Keep out! Watchdog not infected!" I found that strange, considering the Mendozas didn't own a dog.

Riggs pulled the Evoque in the driveway in front of my house. The carport was empty. That the truck wasn't here killed the hope inside me.

Everyone piled out into the scorching heat. My place smelled like burning asphalt, which I preferred to the fishy smell of the HydroFlu.

Riggs helped me get my stuff from the back. "Call if you need—"

A gunshot rang out. I practically jumped out of my skin. Jaylee yelped. Logan fell to his stomach on the sidewalk and rolled under the car. Riggs, Zach, and I just stared in the direction the sound had come from. Southeast. By the shopping centers.

"Probably just a firework," Riggs said.

"No, it wasn't," I said. "I've fired enough guns in my life to know the difference."

Gunshots had two sound components. The blast itself and the boom of the bullet breaking the sound barrier. Just then, I'd heard both.

Riggs trained his cool blue eyes on mine. "Best lock your doors, then. And, like I said before, call if you need anything."

"Sure." But if I needed anything, I was calling Zach, not this egomaniac.

"We'll wait until you get inside," Riggs said.

Gee thanks.

"I'm walking him in," Zach said. "Don't leave me."

"Whatever. Let's go, people! The rest of you, back in the car." Riggs climbed into the driver's seat and shut the door.

Jaylee hugged me. She somehow managed to smell like peaches despite not having showered for twelve days. It was a quick hug, but one I'd remember for a long time. She pulled back, and her brown eyes met mine. Makeup free eyes. I liked them better this way.

"I hope your dad's okay," she said. "And Lizzie and your mom too."

"Thanks," I said. "Um, if things are bad, let's all go to Logan's house, okay?"

I glanced at Logan, who was back on his feet. He nodded eagerly.

"Okay," Jaylee said.

Logan and Zach lived next door to each other, but Logan's house was bigger. And since his parents were never home, that's where we usually hung out. Jaylee's apartment was only three blocks from there, so it should be easy for her to make the trip if she had to. She blessed me with one last wave, then jumped into the vehicle.

"Let's go in, yeah?" Zach asked.

"Yeah."

I didn't have my keys with me but found the spare on the top ledge of the living room windowsill. Once I got the door opened, we went in. I called for my mom. I called for Lizzie. When neither answered, Zach and I did a quick pass through the house. It was empty.

Where was everybody?

"Well this sucks," Zach said, checking his phone. "Why wouldn't Lizzie text?"

I didn't know.

"You want to come to my place?" Zach asked.

"Not yet," I said. "I'd like to wait a few hours. Give Dad time to get back. I'll call you."

"You got a corded phone?"

I nodded. "It's probably in storage though." There were still a dozen boxes we never unpacked after the move here two years ago. This house was smaller than our old place and just didn't have room for everything.

A car horn honked out in my driveway.

I looked to Zach. "Why doesn't he just give the gunman a lift to my house?"

"He's an idiot," Zach said.

No argument there. I walked Zach out.

Before he got into the car, he lifted his fist toward me. "Later, McShane."

We tapped knuckles. "See you soon."

Logan waved out the window. "Bye, Eli."

I nodded back. "Bye."

The Evoque backed into the street, then peeled away, the motor quickly shifting through four gears as it receded down 14th. I watched until it was out of sight. I felt weird, standing here while Zach and Logan went to their houses. I should have gone with them to see if their families were okay, but all I could think of was my own.

From the outside, my house looked like it always had. No strange warning signs posted in our yard. It was 5:30, and twilight was settling in. I stood there, listening to the sounds around me, but there were none. No sprinklers or airplanes. No hum of cars on the distant freeway. No TVs or people talking inside nearby houses. No dogs. Not even the crickets that were normally singing at this hour.

A silence so loud it was alarming.

Until someone yelled out, calling to a friend, maybe. It was a male voice. Adult. Sounded a few blocks away.

A different male voice answered, angry.

Another gunshot. Closer this time.

I slipped inside and locked the door.

It was darker than it had been when Zach and I were in here a few minutes ago. I tried the light switches. Nothing. I walked to the kitchen, found the junk drawer, and pulled out Dad's big flashlight. I flicked it on and headed down the hallway to the bedrooms. I whistled for Sammy, but my golden retriever didn't come running.

Lizzie's room was pristine as always—bed made, floor spotless. In Mom and Dad's room, their bed had been stripped down to the mattress, which was weird.

I pushed my rising panic down deep as I checked the rest of the house, looking for clues. Found Mom and Dad's bedsheets in the drier. Mom never left such tasks unfinished.

She must have taken off in a hurry.

I tried to stay calm, but my insides were twisting, and all the liquid was crawling north to my mouth and eyes. I ran into Mom and Dad's bathroom and stood over the toilet. I breathed deeply, stifling the nausea. The smell of bleach hit me, along with the faint scent of something fishy.

No. Not here.

I shined the flashlight on the sink and noticed that someone had rubber-banded a Ziploc bag over the faucet. I opened the shower door. Same deal. A Ziploc over the showerhead.

HydroFlu.

I checked out the other bathroom and the kitchen sink. Every faucet in the house had been wrapped in plastic. I imagined Mom and Lizzie home alone, watching the news for details on the outbreak.

This was *not* happening.

A little more snooping, and I found a note on the refrigerator whiteboard. I shined the flashlight there as I read.

> Seth & Eli,
>
> They're saying on TV that the water is dangerous. Be careful. Don't shower. Don't drink any water that isn't bottled. There's some in the pantry and storage shed. I turned off the water to the house. We can't get through to you on the cell phones. I pray this warning is not too late. We weren't feeling well and went to St. Joe's. Come look for us there. Hope to see you soon.
>
> Hugs,
> Mom

St. Joe's. The hospital.

All I could think about was the group of people sitting outside the Urgent Care in Flagstaff. My eyes stung. I dug my cell phone out of my pocket. Still no service. I dropped it on the counter. My nausea returned full force, so I slid down the side of the island and sat on the kitchen floor, fighting it back with deep breaths. Desperate prayers ran through my mind. I begged God to keep Mom and Dad and Lizzie safe. And me. And Zach and Logan and Jaylee and their families. My thoughts spiraled out of control as I imagined everyone dead and me the last guy on the planet.

"Stop it," I told myself. I needed to keep my head. I might not be out in the wilderness, but my survival training should apply here too. If I was going to make it through whatever this was, I needed to get my act together and fast.

Think, McShane.

Okay, Reinhold taught us an acronym while we were up in the mountains. His S-U-R-V-I-V-A-L checklist should work here too. S: Size up the situation.

My health was fine. I didn't seem to have ingested any contaminated water. I could sure use a bath, though.

I was in Phoenix. I shouldn't stay here long. If people were shooting guns in my neighborhood and there were no cops, things would get ugly fast.

As far as supplies went, Mom said there was water in the pantry. I got to my feet and verified this. Sure enough, a flat of forty-eight water bottles sat on the pantry floor. I dragged it into the kitchen and went out the patio door to the storage shed in the backyard, stepped around a couple dead squirrels—animals must have been drinking the water too. That explained all the road kill we'd seen on the drive.

In the shed I found two more flats of bottled water— and after a lot of digging, the old corded phone. I carried it all inside. By the look of some of the food in the fridge, the power had been out a while. But I had plenty of packaged and canned food. My stomach ached. I hadn't eaten anything all day but the junk food we'd gotten at Pete's gas station.

Later. I could eat once I was safe.

I grabbed some cardboard boxes from the shed and filled them with nonperishables. I added a can opener. A few sets of silverware. A couple plates and bowls. How many?

I stopped. What was the matter with me? I was acting like a machine. I needed to find out if Mom and Lizzie were okay. And my friends and their families too. I shook my head and got back to Reinhold's list.

U: Undue haste makes waste. If Mom and Lizzie were okay, we'd probably wait here for Dad. In that case, all this packing was a waste of time. I needed to think before I acted. Always. I'd think my way through Reinhold's checklist, then see if I could track down my family. But I should keep pulling useful things from the shed while the sun was up. I didn't want to have to leave the house after dark.

R: Remember where you are. I was home. In Phoenix. But it wasn't the Phoenix I knew and loved. There were too many variables I had no control over. And Dad was stranded somewhere, likely upstate. The most important thing about survival was locating a clean water source. This bottled water would last a few months if I was careful, but I needed to find more.

I suddenly understood what the gunshots were all about.

Which led me to V: Vanquish fear and panic. I went to my parent's walk-in closet and got the rifles out of the gun safe. My dad had a Remington 30.06. Mine was a .243. Dad and I hadn't gone hunting since last fall. The guns were both unloaded, so I grabbed the crate of shells and hauled everything back to the kitchen. You'd think having a gun nearby would make me feel safer. It didn't. I continued my checklist as I loaded each gun.

I: Improvise. I could do that. Though I sure didn't want to shoot at anyone.

V: Value staying alive. I certainly did. I was not about to go down without a fight.

A: Act like the natives. Arizonans were useless to me at the moment because I was not going to go around like some kind of warlord, shooting people for water. However, if I looked back further, Native Americans had been living on this land for thousands of years, and electricity hadn't existed for most of it. Where might they have dug up clean water? Not in the city—or the desert. I needed to get back to the country. North. To the wilderness. Where Dad was.

I wondered what Reinhold and Kimama were doing right now. Chipeta's note had said that she'd been sick. I hoped she hadn't been drinking contaminated water.

Vanquish fear and panic, McShane, I reminded myself. I looped my rifle over my shoulder and pulled my thoughts back on track.

L: Learn basic skills. I had plenty of basic skills. I even knew how to treat contaminated water. But the signs had warned against that, so until I had more information, I'd stick with the bottles.

Checklist done, I went back to collecting supplies, thinking over how I might find my family. I'd have to drive to St. Joseph's. Once I found Mom and Lizzie, we could head north and look for Dad.

The lights suddenly flicked on. Music blared from down the hall. Lizzie's room! I ran there and shut off her radio. I also turned off all the lights but the living room lamp, which was really dim. Maybe I was being paranoid, but it would be fully dark soon, and I didn't want anyone seeing lights on here. Then again, if the power had originally gone out at night or in the early morning, there might be lights on everywhere right now.

If the power was back on, maybe that meant things were getting under control, that everything was going to be okay.

Regardless, I closed all the blinds, including those that covered the patio door. The only light I turned on was the little one above the kitchen stove. It gave me just enough light to see my supplies in the kitchen. I needed clothing. My favorite outdoors stuff was still in my pack, filthy. Would washing my clothes make me sick?

Aw, man! This was nuts. What could have happened to the water, anyway? Cholera? In the U.S.? It just didn't make any sense.

It occurred to me that I had power now. I ran to the living room and clicked on the TV. The sight of 265 channels made everything seem normal. A lot of stations were running news. The same kind of news.

HydroFlu.

Some were only broadcasting the Emergency Alert System with the same information the radio station had shared. I found a channel just starting up a news report and turned up the volume. A man and woman sat at a news desk, a HydroFlu graphic on the screen behind them.

The male reporter said, "Thanks for joining us for News 12 at 5:30, I'm Alan Andrews."

"And I'm Carol Metzer," the woman said. "HydroFlu spread like wildfire around the world over the past week, and the United States was no exception. Health officials are working hard to try and stamp out the deadly disease. News 12's Charles Rodriguez has more."

The scene shifted to footage from China. A man voiced

over video of mobs of sick people. "Over the past month we've been closely following the outbreak of cholera in China. But HydroFlu—the pandemic that has ravaged the world—is in no way connected to this cholera outbreak. Just three days ago on July 22, the first reported cases of HydroFlu in the US came out of Kendall, Florida, a suburb of Miami. Since then, the pandemic has reached all fifty states. Over six million cases in the US have been reported. And at least sixty countries have acknowledged similar catastrophic numbers of infected, including Great Britain, Russia, Japan, and China. Health officials are baffled as to how groundwater became infected worldwide."

Three days ago? That would've been the twenty-fifth, but today was the twenty-ninth. This news was old. The realization made me shiver. I sat down in the recliner and flipped to another channel.

A newswoman sitting at a desk. "Only one week after the first reported case, the growing HydroFlu outbreak in Florida has now claimed at least two million lives. CBS medical correspondent, Dr. John Saul, has more from Miami."

Dr. Saul was outdoors, weaving his way through dozens of people who were sitting on the ground in a parking lot, like the people outside the Flagstaff Urgent Care. In the distance behind him, olive green army trucks had lined up bumper to bumper, forming some kind of blockade.

Dr. Saul spoke into a microphone with a CBS logo on it. "Health officials confirm more than ten million people are sick with a new strain of bacteria that researchers have never seen before. The hospitals here are overflowing. I walked around the sides of this building, down around the back, in the parking lots, and courtyard. The sick are laid out all over in stretchers, cots, makeshift beds. In the hospital itself, patients are lying on the floor in the hallways and waiting rooms. Medical staff is completely overwhelmed. Many patients have IVs, some are just drinking fluids."

The footage flicked to the face of a frazzled nurse. "People are being delivered to the hospital in the backs of pickup trucks, on motorbikes. Most can't walk. We're doing our best to try and help everyone, but it's been very difficult. We can't help people fast enough."

I flipped channels again.

A male reporter in a studio. "A state of emergency has been declared in the US. One UNICEF representative said, 'We cannot find an uncontaminated water source. No one can.' The World Health Organization has released no official statement other than to warn people to stay away from all groundwater sources until an alternative can be found. It's also important to note that boiling water does not help.

"The National Guard and the Red Cross are distributing bottled water to the public. Call the number at the bottom of the screen or go to www.hydroflu.com to find a clean water distribution area near you.

"The main concern at this time is stopping the spread of the disease. We asked the CDC what can be done to keep people safe."

The scene went to a man standing in front of some office building, a dozen microphones around his face. He spoke in a firm voice. "People need to be informed so they can protect themselves. Watch the news. Stay alert. If you are symptomatic and feel you have been exposed to the bacterium, go to a medical center right away. Take care to avoid any water that isn't bottled. Boiling water or using purification pellets or a Lifestraw does not kill the bacterium."

I changed channels. Two men were sitting on chairs, facing each other.

One said, "This is not the flu. It's an aggressive

bacterium that was deposited into our water in the wake of Comet Pulon. HydroFlu is a misnomer."

The other man said, "Does it really matter what we call it?"

"Yes!" the first man said, his face flushing. "It matters a great deal. People are confused. They're medicating themselves as if they have the flu, and that won't help. This disease is different. It's not passed from person to person like the flu. It's waterborne. That means you can only become infected if you ingest infected water. At all costs, abstain from drinking or bathing or even touching water until you receive further instructions. In the meantime, drink soda, juice, bottled water—anything canned or bottled is safe. The government, the CDC, and the World Health Organization are working around the clock to find a treatment."

I switched back to News 12. Alan Andrews was now sitting with some guy in a navy suit.

"The question everyone is asking . . ." Alan said, "is this the end of the world? What do you say, Congressman?"

"No question about it, Alan. With over three billion reported dead worldwide, even if those still living recover, the change in population is so drastic, planet Earth will never be the same."

Three billion reported dead.

The band around my chest was back, squeezing hard. This couldn't be real. I didn't want to hear about the world ending, but flipping to BBC was no better. "More street fighting in London as bottled water shortages continue."

On CSNBC, a reporter stood in front of a protesting crowd. "People are dying literally hour by hour. Panic is widespread. The real concern is where to get safe drinking water. Here in Jaffrey, New Hampshire, hundreds are gathered outside this Red Cross distribution center, demanding water for themselves and their families. But there is no water here."

A clunk outside the house sent me leaping from the recliner. The screen door rattled. I clicked off the TV and grabbed my rifle. Something banged, and the door hinges squeaked.

I'd locked the door, hadn't I? I was sure I had.

I couldn't see the entry way from where I stood, so I held up the gun and gave my warning from the living room.

"Stop!" I yelled, heart racing inside my ribcage. "There's nothing for you in this house. Leave and you won't get hurt."

The door shut and footsteps crossed the foyer.

Trembling, adrenaline pulsing through me, I stepped closer and trained my rifle on the shadow moving in the foyer. My thumb hovered over the safety.

"Come on, now," I said, faking a deeper voice than I really had. "Don't make me shoot."

6

"Eli?" a soft voice said. A girl.

"Lizzie?"

I threaded the gun strap over my arm and fumbled for the flashlight on my belt. In one motion, I clicked it on and pointed toward the shadow. The bright light shone over Lizzie's squinted expression. She turned her head to the side and raised her hand between us.

"Lizzie!" In a breath, I embraced her. Hot relief flashed over my skin as I squeezed my sister and she squeezed back.

Longest hug of my life.

I pulled away first and looked down into Lizzie's eyes, which were only a glimmer in the deflected beam from the flashlight."

I could barely force out my next words. "Mom and Dad?"

Liquid pooled in her eyes. "Dad's not with you?"

"He never showed. We found the van . . . just inside the Arizona border. It was empty. No sign."

"You just left him?"

Defensiveness rose inside me, hot and urgent. "We left the van because he wasn't there. What were we supposed to do?"

"Look for him!"

"We did! I didn't know what else—"

A gunshot rang out. Out on the street, a woman screamed. Lizzie clapped her hand over her mouth. I lunged past her, shut and locked the front door, this time adding the bolt and chain. I held the flashlight's beam against my leg to dim the light and peeked through the window that ran alongside the door. I didn't see anyone. Dad's truck sat in the driveway now. No sign of my mother.

I dropped the curtain and turned back to Lizzie. "Where's Mom?"

She shook her head. Tears dropped down her cheeks, and my sister started to cry.

Oh no.

I held my breath, tried to keep it together. "Hey." I put my arm around her shoulders and led her into the living room, propped my rifle against the side of the sofa and sat down, pulling Lizzie with me. I clicked off the flashlight, and we sat together in dark, which was somehow more comforting.

"Tell me," I said.

She sniffled and released a shaky breath. "You know we were sick, Dad and me. Well, Mom had us on a non-stop diet of Gatorade, orange juice, and chicken broth."

Mom's prescription for any cold. "The liquid cure."

"Right. And Mom got sick too, after you'd left. The news reports started then too, about the Hydro-Flu killing lots of people. It was all so confusing. 'Don't drink the water' was all anyone would say. No one knew what was wrong. Just 'Don't drink the water.'

"The three of us tried going to the store to stock up on bottled anything, but it was insane, and there was nothing left to buy. Dad said we should stay home and ration the water we already had—wait this thing out. Mom got really bad the day before Dad needed to go get you. He was worried, I could tell. He tried to stay here, said you could get a ride back with Riggs. Mom didn't want you riding with Riggs, though—you know how she is about him. Did Riggs bring you home?"

"Yeah," I said.

"Well, Mom and Dad fought about it. Like, really fought. I never heard them lose it like they did. Dad kept saying you were smarter than Riggs and that you'd keep everyone safe, but Mom was worried you might not know about the water. Dad finally gave in and left."

It felt nice that Dad had so much confidence in me, but all I could think about was what Lizzie hadn't said. "And Mom?"

She choked back a sob in the darkness, and when she finally spoke, her voice came high-pitched and soft. "I tried to take care of her, but I was so tired from being sick, I didn't know what else to do. We weren't even sure she hadn't just caught what Dad and I had. Then the power went out, so I couldn't go online or watch TV to know what to do. All I had were Dad's survival books, but nothing I tried seemed to help. When the rash broke out on Mom's face and arms, she insisted I drive her to the hospital.

"Eli, it was the most horrifying thing I've ever seen.

People were everywhere, shoulder to shoulder, and desperate. A nurse put me and Mom in chairs in some random hallway. Gave us IVs with fluids." She paused, took another ragged breath, and when she spoke, her voice was a hoarse whisper. "I got better. No one else did."

No one else.

Lizzie lost it then, and when she hugged me, I lost it too.

I don't know how long we sat there, but at some point I sniffed and noticed how tight the skin on my cheeks felt from the tears that had dried there. It didn't seem right that I could feel anything when my mom could not. The band around my chest cinched tighter, and the darkness began to press against me. It had taken my mom and it wanted the rest of us. Why were we still alive? Why was this happening?

I repeated the questions out loud, hoping my sister had some kind of insight that I did not.

But all she said was, "I don't know."

Lizzie had a strong faith. It was more real and intense than anyone I knew, even my parents. "Why did God let this happen, Liz?"

"I don't know."

And that was that. If Lizzie didn't know, who would? My mind leapt from one thought to another, needing to make sense of something. "What about that end of the world thing?" I asked. "Could this be it?"

"The rapture?" she asked. "I guess, but . . . I'm pretty sure God would have taken us too."

Her, maybe. I wasn't so sure about myself. God and I . . . I don't know. What Lizzie had, it wasn't like that for me.

"You think Daddy is alive?" she asked.

He had to be. "How sick was he when he left?"

"Not bad like Mom was. I think he and I were okay because we hadn't been drinking water. Just all that

Gatorade and OJ. I think we were just regular sick."

With all that was in me, I hoped so. "Then he's probably okay," I said, now more sure of it than ever. "He just ran out of gas. A lot of people did. There were cars stranded all over the roads. Most the gas stations were closed because of the power being out. I bet when Dad realized he couldn't get gas, he headed toward Colorado, thinking we'd cross paths."

"You think he'll turn around and walk back to Phoenix?" Lizzie asked.

"Eventually, but I think he'd walk to Wilderness Way Adventures first, to try and talk to Reinhold, to find out what happened with me. For all Dad knows, we got sick up there in the forest and died. Since he was closer to the camp, he'd want to confirm what happened to me before going back to Mom."

At least that's what I'd do.

"That sounds like him," Lizzie said. "I'm so glad you're here. That you're okay."

My arm was still around her, and I squeezed her close. "Same to you."

Lizzie reached past me and pulled a tissue from the box on the end table. She used it to dab her eyes and nose. "Why do you think people are shooting guns?" she asked.

"They're panicking. Those who aren't sick are looking for bottled water. It'll be worse now than it was when you and Mom went to the store. Though there aren't nearly as many people as before, those who are still alive are desperate. They'll do anything to get what they need."

"What about us? What are we going to do?"

I flicked on the flashlight and stood up. "We're getting out of here."

"And going where?" Her voice cracked like she was trying not to cry again.

"North," I said. "Back to Colorado. To see if we can find Dad. Plus . . . It's just a feeling, but we'd been drinking the water up there for two weeks. We purified it with our tablets, but the news said that wouldn't help. So I'm thinking that maybe the water up there is okay."

"We can't know that," Lizzie said.

"No, but even so, we have a much better chance of surviving someplace rural and forested."

"Because there's not as many people?"

"Exactly," I said. "And because we can't stay here." I walked to the kitchen and lifted the corded phone out of the pile on the floor.

Lizzie followed. "Eli! All this stuff . . . You're so smart."

I shrugged. "I did just spend two weeks at a survival camp."

"Yeah, but you're always smart. I'm so glad you're my brother, but not just because you're smart about this stuff. You're an amazing person."

I flushed at my sister's praise. She was like that, always saying nice things about people. It usually embarrassed me, but not today. I unplugged the receiver for the cordless and plugged in the old phone. I held the handset to my ear. The familiar buzz of the dial tone drew a sigh from my lips.

"It works?"

"Yeah. I'm going to call Zach."

Lizzie came closer, eyes wide and hopeful. "He's okay?"

"He was when they dropped me off a couple hours ago." I turned away slightly. Her expression brought too much responsibility to my shoulders. Plus she looked a lot like Mom. Our mom was Mexican, our Dad white. Both of us favored our mom with dark skin, hair, and eyes, but Lizzie was Mom's mini me.

I didn't know Zach's home number and had to look it up in Mom's address book. I always thought it was weird how she still used a landline, but now I was thankful. The phone rang seven times before I pressed the hang-up button.

"No answer," I said.

Moisture glossed Lizzie's eyes. "Maybe he doesn't have an old school phone."

"Or he's at Logan's." I flipped the pages in the address book until I found Al and Deb Graham written in Mom's loopy handwriting. The whole side of this page was covered in doodles of blue ink. I could tell by the amount of doodles on this page that mom had spent many hours talking to Logan's mom. The sentimental thought tightened my throat and tried to take hold of my emotions, to drag me under. I fought it back. I had to get Lizzie someplace safe. Then I could think about Mom.

I dialed the number and chanced a glance at Lizzie through the first ring. She was still watching with those desperate don't-let-me-down eyes.

"Graham residence."

"Logan!" A thrill shot through me at the sound of a familiar voice. "It's Eli. You okay? Is Zach with you?"

"Zach and Jaylee are both here. I need to ask you something, Eli. This is very important. Have you consumed or bathed in any water since we left you?"

I actually smiled. "No, Logan. I'm still fine. How about your parents?"

"I can only assume that my parents have perished," he said, as if he were giving a science report.

"Oh, Logan," I said. "How do you know?"

"They left a note that they'd gone to Banner University Hospital. We just returned from there. No one is alive."

Lizzie had said the same thing about St. Joe's, but the idea of Logan and Zach and Jaylee looking for their families in a place like Banner made me a little woozy. "I'm so sorry, man."

"Your mom and sister?"

"Lizzie's here," I said. "My mom didn't make it." And just like that, tears flooded my eyes. Everything blurred. I blinked wildly, needing to keep my emotions under control. Logan was saying something, but I'd missed it. "Uh . . ." I took a breath. "Can I talk to Zach?"

"One moment, please."

His formality made me grin through my tears, and I was suddenly so thankful for Logan's quirky ways. I rolled my eyes at Lizzie. "Logan."

She laughed. It was a great sound, but she let it go on too far, let it be funnier than it was, like she wanted to keep laughing. Like she needed to.

I totally understood.

"Eli!" Zach's voice rang in my ear. "Lizzie's okay?"

"Uh, yeah, actually. She's here now. My mom is gone, though. Not missing. I mean she's . . ." I sighed. The few words I'd managed had used up all my breath.

"No way." Silence stretched over the line, then, "Why is this happening?"

The frustration in Zach's voice took me off guard. He was usually so calm and collected. I supposed this kind of catastrophic event could shake even the strongest individuals.

I forced myself to keep talking, though it was practically a whisper. "No sign of Sammy. Or Dad."

"Your dad is probably still up north somewhere, trying to get gas or whatever."

"Yeah, I was thinking he probably hiked to the camp to talk to Reinhold."

"He totally would. He'd want to check on us all."

"What about you? Logan said you guys went down to Banner?"

Zach didn't answer for a moment. I heard footsteps, a door close.

Lizzie inched closer, watching me. "Is his family okay?" she asked.

"I don't know," I whispered.

A shuddering breath on the other end, then Zach was back, a watery weakness in his voice. "Uh . . . I saw them, E. I d-didn't know what to do. I was only home, like, two minutes. I just saw them there. All together. All four of them. I saw them, and then I ran back to Logan's like a coward. They're dead, Eli. My family is dead."

7

It was too much. Tears blurred my eyes again. Dripped down my face.

A breath from Zach. "I should go back, right? I should go back and, and . . . Um . . . I should bury them? Yeah?"

A rush of heat came over me at the idea of Zach's parents and sisters dead. I rubbed my eyes with the heel of my palm. How could this be happening? It was too much! It was all too much.

Lizzie nudged my arm, but I waved her off.

"Jaylee walked over here," Zach said, his voice strained but in control again. "She said her apartment was empty. Said it was Paul's week to have the kids, but no one was home at Paul's place. No sign of her mom or Melissa and Willie. She's kind of a wreck after the hospital. Logan's parents left a note about going to Banner. That's why we went over there. It was bad. Worse than the dead guy on the road, the Nissan, the Honda Accord, Flagstaff Urgent Care, and my family combined."

"Lizzie took our mom to St. Joseph's," I said. "So I can only imagine."

"Ah. Okay . . . probably more of the same." Silence stretched over the line.

Lizzie tapped my arm. "Zach's family?"

I shook my head. Lizzie covered her face with her hands and wandered into the living room. I could hear her crying again.

"What do we do, Eli?" Zach finally said. "I don't know what to do, man. Logan is driving Jaylee nuts. She keeps screaming at him. He's prepping to go underground for the next decade, but Jaylee wants us to go look for Riggs. We drove by his place, but he wasn't there. She's worried about him. Thinks he never made it home, but I don't know how that could be. He's only two minutes from here. I didn't tell either of them that I saw my family. I just said they weren't home. I just . . . I couldn't . . . Can you guys come over here?"

"You bet. But only to grab you all. Lizzie and I are going to drive north."

"Back to Colorado?"

"That's what I was thinking. We've heard more gunfire around here. People are probably fighting over supplies. We need to get out of the city."

"Yeah, okay. You think Reinhold is still alive?"

"He's gotta be," I said. "He's, like, invincible."

"That's what I was thinking too."

Just then, the power went out. "Oh," I said. "We lost

power again."

"Us too," Zach said.

I felt for my cell phone and flipped on the flashlight, used it to look for the real one. "Lizzie and I are gathering supplies now," I said. "We've got some bottled water and canned goods. A few sleeping bags. Two rifles and some ammo. See what you guys can pull together over there."

"Logan's already on it."

I found the flashlight on the floor by my supplies and turned it on. Put my cell phone away. "Right, okay. We'll bring my dad's truck. You got the keys to your mom's van?"

"I can get them."

"Okay, that will give us plenty of room to haul stuff."

"Great. Pack up and get over here before Jaylee kills Logan."

"Will do."

• • •

Easier said than done though, leaving everything behind, possibly forever. It wasn't so much the house; we hadn't lived there very long. It was the stuff. Our stuff. The stuff of memories.

Dad's recliner with the subtle indentation of his shoulders and head. Sammy's dog dish that I'd filled a thousand times before. The key hook in the kitchen that said HOME in different colored fat wooden letters with a brass hook on each one. The handmade clock Grandpa Ed had made for my parents' wedding. The little bathroom stool we stood on as kids. So many family pictures. The sign hanging above the couch that Mom painted the year Lizzie was born. It said: "As for me and my house, we will serve the Lord."

A lot of good that had done any of us.

The bitter thought stopped me, and my mind sort of

froze. I wanted to yell at God. I was so angry. On the edge of despair, really. But I also didn't want to talk to him, like maybe if I ignored him, if I put my thoughts on hold, I wouldn't have to deal with this crisis of faith that was staring me in the face.

I glanced at Lizzie, who was standing in the living room hall, moving her flashlight from one picture to the next. She'd changed into clean clothes and was now wearing black leggings and one of her old soccer T-shirts. It was green with the number fourteen on back. She was normally pretty tough, but she'd been weeping steadily ever since we started packing. I understood. There was nothing to distract from our bleak reality, nothing for our minds to do but think.

Mom was dead. Dad too, likely.

Dead.

Forever.

Stop it.

I gritted my teeth. I could grieve later. Right now I needed to be the strong one, at least until we got to Zach. Once we got on the road, Zach would take over. He'd be a great leader. Everyone listened to him. He was a rock. Once we got to him, Lizzie could turn her big worried eyes his way, and I could have a moment to breathe.

"Hey," I said to my sister, pushing down the panic that was threatening to swallow me whole. "Bring everything you want into the kitchen, okay?"

She nodded and trudged down the hall.

It would have been easier to pack up with the power on. I'm sure we'd forget stuff we just couldn't see in the dark. Stuff our flashlight missed. Still, we kept adding to my pile in the middle of the kitchen floor. Flashlights, batteries, candles, matches, lighter fluid, all the water and food we could find, warm clothes, Mom and Dad's hiking boots—Lizzie put on hers. I was still wearing mine—the guns, the ammo, Dad's toolbox, gloves, tents, camping chairs, canteens, Mom's bible, and Dad's spare set of keys for the van. I found a few more tools out in the shed, including a vinyl hose we could use to siphon gas. I wondered if we should go by dad's auto shop and see what we might take with, but the hose was the most important thing.

Lizzie also packed a duffle bag of stuff. An envelope of pictures she'd taken out of the frames, the "important documents" file from Mom's room, Lizzie's flute, her bible and journal, her PrismaColor markers, her stuffed bunny—I didn't ask—her copy of *Pride and Prejudice*, and a little blue ceramic cross.

I didn't understand why she put half that stuff in there. I would have left everything, except Mom's bible. I understood why she wanted that. To be fair, it was only one small bag, and I figured, for a girl packing up her life's possessions, Lizzie was doing pretty good.

I also shoved Mom's address book into Lizzie's duffle. I figured once we were someplace safe, maybe we could call some relatives and see if we could get through to anyone. I did call the Wilderness Way office, but I wasn't surprised to get no answer. I didn't have a home number for Reinhold. I tried to look it up on my phone, but I didn't get anywhere.

It was 9:30 by the time we'd finished, and while it was dark, I didn't feel comfortable going out right now. I thought it best that we wait until the wee hours of the morning before driving across town. I mean, even crazy looters had to sleep, right? I called Zach and told him the plan. He'd managed to chill Jaylee with some romance novel of Logan's mom's. I wrote a note for my dad and hung it on the fridge. Then I set my alarm for 3:30 and put the phone on vibrate so it wouldn't make too much noise.

Lizzie cried herself to sleep. I dozed a bit, but I couldn't manage to shut off my brain. When I finally did sleep, I had a vivid dream. I was hitchhiking on U.S. Route 160. I came across a body lying face-down in the road. I rolled the person over, and it was my dad, face covered in a blotchy rash, eyes open and bloodshot.

I sat up, breathing hard, the band around my chest tighter than ever. I also had a splitting headache.

I told myself it had been a dream, that Dad was likely fine, up north somewhere, probably with Reinhold.

I went looking for some Advil, and it occurred to me that I was likely dehydrated. I hadn't taken a drink of water since that morning. I rummaged around, found the Advil, and pulled a single bottle of water from one of the flats on the kitchen floor.

I twisted the cap free, popped the Advil into my mouth, and took a sip.

The water ran over my parched tongue and throat. I closed my eyes, soothed by the cool moisture. I hadn't realized how thirsty I'd been. Tears dehydrated a person, and I'd shed plenty.

Lizzie had cried for nearly two hours.

Shame engulfed me. I felt like I was stealing something, drinking water in the night while my sister slept. But that was nonsense. We both needed water to survive. We'd just have to ration it. A bottle a day would do to start. Three flats of forty-eight bottles each was one hundred and forty-four, divided between Lizzie and me was enough for seventy-two days. If we had to share it with Zach, Logan, and Jaylee, it would only last us a month.

Didn't seem like enough. At some point we might need to stretch one bottle for two days. For now, we'd do a bottle a day.

I found a Sharpie and wrote Eli on the cap. This would be mine for the next day. I labeled one for Lizzie. She would need to drink some when she woke up.

I felt better having a plan for the water.

I tried to go back to sleep, but I couldn't shut off my thoughts. I got up four times to add stuff to the pile: My fishing rod, my Teeva sandals, my Suns cap, Dad's survival books . . .

The alarm never did go off because I shut it off myself at 3:15 and started hauling stuff to the truck. Dad drove a red Toyota Tacoma access cab, and by 3:40, I'd packed that thing to the brim. I woke Lizzie and waited as she said goodbye to every room of the house. I stood by the door, trying not to think that I'd never come back to this place. I had no desire to drag this out, but I didn't want to rush Lizzie. I didn't want her to have any more regrets than she already had.

Finally she walked toward me, face tear-streaked. She took my hands in hers and squeezed.

"I want to pray," she said.

My stomach twisted. Of course she did. Praying was one of Lizzie's things.

"Okay," I said.

She closed her eyes, so I did too. "Heavenly Father," she said, "you are God Almighty, all sufficient, all we need. We're afraid. We don't understand. But we trust that you're in control."

I wasn't sure I did.

"We believe that our friends and family who have died are with you."

They had to be. They just had to.

"And we pray, precious Father, for your guidance for those of us still here. Help us know what to do. Help us be strong and courageous and do what we must to survive without falling into despair. We know you're with us. You won't leave us or forsake us."

Actually, it kind of felt like he'd done that already.

"Thank you for having a plan, God. Thank you that Eli

and Zach and Logan and Jaylee and Riggs and Antônia and Erin are all okay. Please be with Mark and Cristobal and Josh. Please help us to grieve the loss of our families. And please help Erin and Mark. Heal their bodies. Show us the way and keep us safe. In Jesus name, amen."

"Feel better?" I asked.

She nodded and squeezed my hand. Then she let go and walked past me out the door. I shut and locked the door behind us. I mean, if all this blew over, maybe we could come back someday and see if the place was still standing.

We climbed into the truck. I hung my rifle on the gun rack, then I gave Lizzie the bottle of water I'd labeled for her last night.

"This is yours for the day. Drink some now. I don't want you getting dehydrated."

"I'm not really thirsty right now."

"Just a sip then," I said. "If you get sick, you'll need a lot more water, so take care of yourself."

She quirked an eyebrow. "Yes, *Papa Eli*."

She could mock me all she wanted, but I didn't start the truck until she took a drink. The electricity was still out—the streetlamps dark—but the moon was bright enough that I could see where I was going. That made it possible for me to leave the headlights off as I backed out of the driveway and took E Rancho Drive to 16th. I went south on 16th. I could have taken the freeway down an exit, but for some reason I felt the surface streets would be safer.

"I know it's just stuff, Eli," Lizzie said. "I know I shouldn't care about it." She looked out her passenger's window and sighed. "Remember that one fork with the crooked tong? Whenever I took a bite of food and realized I'd gotten that fork, it made me smile."

"Yeah, I remember the fork." Girls were weird.

Now she was weeping again. I left her to it, focused on

driving. For Lizzie, her suffering was immediate and intense. She'd run headlong into it like a soldier on the front lines. I, on the other hand—I'd pushed mine off. It gnawed at me, scratching at the back of my mind like I'd forgotten what I'd been about to say. For me, it had to be this way. I wouldn't be able to function, otherwise. I wouldn't be able to get us to Colorado.

At the CVS Pharmacy, we turned onto Camelback, which stretched across most of Phoenix. We passed many of our familiar haunts: Denny's, Chipotle, Starbucks. Bunches of signs warning people, "Don't Boil. Don't purify. Bottled only." Too many windows were broken. A lot of stores had been looted or defaced with ominous graffiti.

The six-lane street that was normally packed with traffic was deserted. Occasionally I had to weave around a car that sat in the middle of the road. I no longer looked to see if they were occupied or not. We passed over SR 51, which was also deserted.

Past Best Buy, past the Biltmore golf course, through five blocks of residential area, then back to commercial districts. In the daytime, I'd be able to see Camelback Mountain looming in the distance, growing ever nearer as I approached Zach's neighborhood, but now the sky was simply a black void where I knew the mountain slept.

"I'm worried about Zach," Lizzie said. "He loved his Dad and sisters so much. I know he'd never say it, but he's a really squishy guy."

"Squishy?"

"He has a big heart."

Yeah, he did. Zach had been my best friend since first grade. He'd always been there for me. He'd always been strong and steady. I hated how shaken he'd sounded on the phone. I didn't tell Lizzie that he'd found his family in the house. That was his business.

"When we get there, could you try talking to Logan?" I asked. "Zach said he was getting on Jaylee's nerves. Maybe you could talk to her too."

"Why me?"

"Because you have a way with words that people respond to," I said. "I could probably get Logan in line. For a couple hours, anyway. But I think he'd take it better coming from you. From me . . . I don't know how to explain it, but—"

"He loves you," Lizzie said, "so criticism from you hurts."

I frowned. "I'm not sure that's quite it. But kind of."

"I'll talk to him," Lizzie said.

"Thank you."

I turned right on 40th and passed over the canal. It was weird how I was noticing everything I usually ignored because I was listening to music or the radio or whatever. This drive was different. My last one, maybe. Jaylee's apartment complex loomed on my right. The Camelback Apartment Homes consisted of a field of massive five story buildings. I couldn't see Jaylee's balcony from the road.

I turned onto East Coulter and followed the curvy road through the residential area. The shadowed prickly pear and jumping cholla trees made the vegetation seem like moving creatures in my peripheral vision. I jolted at least five times for that same reason.

I finally pulled onto Logan's wide, flagstone driveway that was edged in rigrag. His massive house sat on a desert scape lot. Four-car garage. Pool out back.

I stopped the truck. Lizzie jumped out and slammed the door.

"Way to be discreet," I said. I could see Zach's place through the Acacia trees that edged Logan's property line. My gut clenched at what Zach had told me about his family.

Later, I told myself. *Right now, get Lizzie inside.*

I didn't like leaving the truck in the driveway with our supplies exposed, but it was only four a.m. and I hadn't seen a single vehicle on the ride over.

I shut off the truck and got out. I stood there and listened. So quiet. Too quiet for Phoenix at any hour. I made my way to the front door, which was hanging open. Lizzie was already inside. She stood with Zach in the entry way, hugging him like she had me. He was hugging her back, and she was crying again.

"Hey," I said.

Zach, his expression grave, looked at me over Lizzie's head. "Hey," he said, remarkably calm compared to how he'd sounded on the phone.

Lizzie's hugs had that effect on people.

Before I could go in, the garage door started rolling up, manually. The dull roll of wheels jerking over metal was so loud it made me check the street. I don't know what for. Logan exited the garage, waving his arms as if directing traffic. "Bring her inside, Eli. We can't risk anyone getting at our supplies."

I smirked at Logan's level of intensity but was secretly relieved. I jumped back into the truck and steered it into the empty space between Zach's mom's Toyota Sienna and Logan's dad's Porsche. Logan pulled shut the garage door behind me.

In the house, boxes lined both sides of the hallway, making a narrow path to walk down.

"We did what you suggested," Logan said. "We gathered all the supplies we could and put them in boxes in here. Easy loading location to the garage."

"It looks great," I said, my spirits lifting at the sight of two, five-gallon Sparklets bottles filled with water. That right there was another forty water bottles.

"There are only five of us," Logan said. "Taking two vehicles will waste gas, won't it?"

"I'm not worried about fuel," I said. "I brought a hose we can use to siphon from any car we see." And there were plenty of cars out there.

"That's a relief," Logan said. "Not having to worry about fuel will help Jaylee calm down."

"Lizzie?" I jerked my chin toward Logan.

She grabbed his arm. "Logan, sweetie, can I talk to you in private?"

His eyebrows shot up. "Sure," he said.

"How about we go into the kitchen?"

"Yeah, okay."

As he led her out, I mouthed the words, "Thank you."

She winked.

"What was that all about?" Zach asked.

"I asked Lizzie to talk to Logan about going easy on Jaylee."

"Good idea. Coming from Lizzie, he'll feel like he's being a hero."

"That's what I was hoping for."

Zach and I passed the time loading the supplies in the hallway into the back of my dad's truck. That took all of five minutes, and we soon found ourselves standing around, trying not to eavesdrop on the conversation happening in the kitchen.

"I'd like to do something about my family," Zach said.

I glanced at my friend. The six-foot-one, Olympic caliber swimmer looked pale. Weak. "Let's go now."

We left Logan's and walked across the desert scape lawn toward Zach's place next door. Despite my anger and confusion at God, I prayed for strength and courage every step of the way for what we were about to face.

Some things are so shocking, they scar for life, like the time my dad hit a dog that had run out into the road. Dad had stopped to check on it. He told me to wait in the car, but I didn't listen. I was ten at the time, and when I saw that dog . . . Well, I still think about that poor animal. And I know I'll remember Zach's family for the rest of my life.

Still. It was the right thing to do. I know that much. And I think it gave Zach some closure that I might never have with my mom.

Zach's dad, stepmom, and two little sisters had died, huddled together on the king size bed in his parent's room. The fishy, sick smell overwhelmed me from the moment we stepped inside. It had taken us a while to decide what do to. We didn't have time to dig a grave. That would have taken a couple days. I suggested the pool out back. It had been drained. But Zach didn't want us touching their bodies, even after I told him what I'd heard on the news about HydroFlu. That it was a waterborne disease. In the end, we left the family where they were, but pulled a big sheet over them, then covered it with flowers from the front garden. Every flower we could find, actually.

Zach's face was streaked in tears. Seeing him like that . . . his family . . . it brought the sting of tears to my own eyes. He asked me to say something, and I suddenly wished we'd brought Lizzie along. She was far better at such things and would have known exactly what to say.

"Uh . . . I'm glad that Zach's family was together in the end," I said.

Zach nodded, his thick eyebrows creased deep.

The fishy, sick smell was really getting to me. "Uh . . ." I shook one leg, anxious to be done. "They're not here anymore. They're in heaven now." Because the alternatives were too awful to think about.

"Thank you, God," Zach said.

Had I said something good? I hoped so. "I, uh . . ." I thought back to my grandma's funeral, tried to remember what the pastor had said. "Uh, thank you that we got to know them. That we were all here on earth together at the same time. That we got to experience life together. For a little while, anyway."

"Can we sing something, Eli?"

Musicians, anyway. "Whatever you want, man."

Zach started in on the old hymn "Joyful, Joyful" and I sang along, thinking it a strange choice. I didn't know the words as well as he did, but he thankfully stopped with the first verse. The silence stretched out, and I supposed maybe

I should say something to end this.

"Uh . . ." Pastors always said something about ashes and dust at funerals, didn't they? I couldn't remember what. "You take care of them now, God. We're going to take care of Zach. Amen."

My words had felt stupid and clumsy, but Zach wiped his eyes with the back of his hand and said, "Thanks, E. Let's get out of here."

Gladly. We started back. I felt grimy and wanted a shower more than ever. I also wanted to find a dark closet and hide for a few hours, to try to deal with the madness piling up in my head.

No time for that, though. Had to keep moving.

At Logan's, Zach and I passed through the garage and saw that more stuff had been loaded in the minivan. It was almost five. Time to take off. Another forty minutes and the sun would be up.

We stepped out of the garage and into the hallway. The smell of coffee hung on the air.

Who was making coffee?

"Hey! Almost forgot to load my guitar." Zach stepped past me to the laundry room and picked up the hard case covered in stickers of his favorite bands.

I continued into the kitchen. No one was there, but sure enough, a saucepan sat on the stove, steaming with recently made coffee. Beside it on the counter were three empty water bottles.

Fire shot up my spine. I stalked into the living room, ready to ream someone for their stupidity. Lizzie, Logan, and Jaylee were sitting on the couch, talking about Bobby Flay cooking shows.

"Who made coffee?" I asked.

"Eli!" Jaylee jumped up and tackled me in a hug. She smelled all flowery and clean, and I wondered how she'd managed it. She released me all too soon, and wiped the side of her finger under one eye. "I'm so glad you and Lizzie are here. I can't get in touch with my mom or Dave. I'm guessing they're probably gone."

"I'm sorry." And I was. It seemed like everyone had lost someone in this nightmare. But we couldn't pretend life was the way it had been. We had to be smart. And it had to start now. "I'm calling a meeting," I said.

Jaylee frowned. "What kind of meeting?"

"Guitar is all packed up," Zach said as he entered the living room.

"Eli called a meeting," Jaylee told him.

"Cool," Zach said.

They were all looking at me, which made me feel weird. I supposed I was about to pick a fight, and I really didn't want to, but... "We have to set some ground rules," I said.

"For what?" Jaylee said.

"For survival," I said. "Who made coffee?"

"I did," Jaylee said, grinning. "You can have some, if you want. It turned out a little strong, but really hit the spot."

"You wasted three bottles of water on coffee," I said. "That can't happen again."

"I tried to tell her," Logan said.

"You guys are not the boss of me," Jaylee snapped.

"Water is precious," I said. "We can't waste it. In fact, we need to ration it."

"But coffee is made of water," Jaylee said. "If you guys don't want any, fine. That will be my share of the water."

"Coffee is a diuretic," Zach said. "It will only dehydrate you and leave you wanting more water."

"He's right," I said. "I propose we each get one sixteen ounce bottle of water per day. No more. At least until we get to Colorado and see what our resources are. If we're going to survive, we've got to be careful. We've got to be smart."

Jaylee wasn't looking at me. Had I made her uncomfortable? I couldn't afford to care just now. "Jaylee, we're leaving in a few minutes. We're heading north to Colorado. We think maybe the water up there might be okay. Even if it's not, we think it will be safer where there are fewer people. Would you like to come with us?"

"We should try to find our families first," she said.

"Our families are dead," Logan said.

"You can't know that," she snapped.

"You were at the hospital with us. There's no way anyone survived that."

"But what if my mom never got sick? What if she's here somewhere? I can't just leave without looking."

My chest ached for Jaylee. Her not knowing what happened to her mom and siblings left her with that same shred of hope I clung to about my dad. I couldn't fault her for it. In fact, I wanted her to have it as long as possible. But I couldn't give her what she was asking for.

"This is Phoenix," I said. "Where would we look?"

"At her work, maybe."

"No one's at work," I said. "Everything is deserted, closed up, or looted."

"Well, Mom works at a bar, and with all this stress, I'm sure people are drinking," she said. "I just don't want to leave without knowing."

"You may never know for certain," I said.

"If your mother was alive, you would have heard from her by now," Logan said.

"Shut up!" Jaylee shoved Logan. He stumbled back into a lamp, which fell over with a clank of metal against the stone tile floor.

"Come on, guys, cut it out," Zach said. "This isn't helping."

"I'm sick of him!" Jaylee yelled. "I don't need to be around any doom's-dayer right now."

"The word is *doomsayer*," Logan said, "but we're not predicting impending misfortune or disaster. It has clearly already arrived."

"Shut your face, Logan!" Jaylee said. "You don't know everything."

"Logan," Lizzie said, hooking her arm around his. "Sweetie, did you forget what we talked about?"

Logan's face was flushed from his cheeks all the way to the tops of his ears. "I'm sorry, okay? I don't want to upset anyone. I just think we need to be smart."

"Now he's calling me stupid," Jaylee said.

"I'm just backing up what Eli said."

Zach grabbed Logan's other arm and dragged him and Lizzie out of the room. "Let's check the house one more time to make sure we have everything."

That left me and Jaylee alone. She fixed those brown eyes on me. "You think I'm stupid?"

"Of course not."

She sighed. "Tell me we aren't going to leave till I find my mom."

Why did I have to be the bad guy? "The problem is, we don't know where to look, and we don't have the time because it's too dangerous to stay. The four of us are going north. You're free to do what you want to do."

"I'm not staying here by myself! But I don't want to just take off without knowing the truth. Can't you understand that?"

"I do understand that," I said. "Leave your mom a note telling her where we went. Lizzie and I did that in case our dad comes home."

She chewed on her thumbnail. "I guess I could do that."

"I'm sorry this is hard, Jaylee," I said. "If things are as bad as I think they are, people are already killing for water. And we've got quite a bit of it. So we need to get someplace quiet. Someplace remote."

She wrinkled her nose. "Back to the woods?"

"I think we'll be safe there," I said. "We can look for Reinhold."

She rolled her eyes. "Great. What about Riggs?"

A chill flashed over me. I'd forgotten all about Riggs. "What about him?"

"You're just going to leave him too?"

"No," I said. While we couldn't drive all over Phoenix looking for people who were likely dead, Riggs was very likely alive. "Did you try calling him from the corded phone?"

She nodded. "He didn't answer."

"We'll drive by his house and see if he's there." I really didn't want him to come, but we couldn't just abandon the guy.

"If we find him, I can stay here with him," Jaylee said. "He can help me look for my mom."

Was she serious? I couldn't imagine Riggs agreeing to drive around Phoenix looking for Jaylee's mom. Nor was he the kind of person I'd bet on surviving an apocalypse, let alone helping others survive.

Jaylee was staring at me, and I wondered what I was supposed to say—what she wanted me to say. "You could," I finally said, slowly, like I was still thinking about it. And I was. The idea of leaving Jaylee behind made my stomach ache.

Tears welled in her eyes. "You would really leave me behind?"

Unbelievable. Girls were so frustrating. Did everything have to be some kind of test?

At the moment, I didn't care. "Yeah," I said, "if that's what you want. The rest of us are leaving in five minutes, though, so you've got that long to decide what you're going to do." I pushed past her and into the kitchen where Logan and Zach were playing with a couple walkie talkies. Three more lay on the kitchen counter.

"Look what I found," Logan said. "They were my dad's."

"Those will be great to have along," I said.

"This one's for you." Zach handed me one. "I'll keep the others in the van. I mean, there's room for all five of us to sit in the van, but I figured since we've got two vehicles, we could take turns riding with each other, you know, to give us different company."

"Good idea," I said, fighting to keep a stoic expression. This was Zach's way of making us share Logan.

Jaylee ran through the kitchen toward the front door.

"She coming?" Zach asked.

I shrugged. "She wants to look for Riggs."

"Oh, man," Logan said, grimacing.

Zach pulled a face. "I forgot about him. Again."

"Yeah, I did too, but we should at least tell him we're leaving. See if he wants to come." I *so* didn't want him to come.

"Do we have to?" Logan asked.

"Yeah," Zach said. "We have to."

"Let's get out of here," I said. "You ready, Logan?"

He nodded. "I'm ready." His voice shook a little, and I wondered if he really believed his parents were gone.

I glared at saucepan of coffee on the stove. "Someone had better put that coffee in a travel mug."

"I got one," Logan said.

There wasn't anything left to load. The only thing I saw that might be useful was a manual can opener. I already had one, but you could never have too many of those lying around if you were hoping to live off canned goods.

Zach, Logan, and I left the house. A plume of exhaust filled the pale morning as the minivan peeled out of the driveway and onto the road. Logan took off after it, sprinting to catch up.

I stopped beside Zach in the driveway, hands on my hips. "Did Jaylee just steal the van?"

"Yep," Zach said. "With your sister inside it."

Of all the . . . "Then what are we standing around for? We've got to follow them!" I sprinted to the truck and opened the driver's side door.

Jaylee drove the van to her apartment. We all got out and went inside. The air reeked here. Not in Jaylee's place, but the entire Camelback premises oozed with the fishy odor of HydroFlu. I didn't want to know how many people had died in their homes.

Jaylee's apartment was still empty. She broke down and cried. Lizzie comforted her. Zach and I went out on the balcony with Logan, hoping to give Jaylee some privacy and keep Logan from making things worse. He really had a gift for being obtuse.

Jaylee packed a bunch of stuff—five times as much as Lizzie had—then wrote her mom a note and hung it on the fridge. She wrote three more notes and placed them around the apartment, all of them telling her mom to read the note on the fridge.

As the minutes ticked by, I found it difficult to be patient and give her the time she needed. I had wanted to be on the road by now. I marveled over how well Reinhold had led the twelve of us up in the mountains. I couldn't get these people to do anything. It was like trying to corral a bunch of kittens. Every time I managed to get my eye on the last one, I looked back and found another one missing.

When we finally left, it wasn't to go north. We had to check on Riggs first.

When I said that Logan's house was massive, it was a double-wide trailer compared to the mansion that was Casa Orcut. Riggs had hosted a few youth events at his parent's place. It had eight bedrooms, a game room, and a movie theater with nine leather recliners. Every bedroom had its own walk-in closet and private bath. It was more like a bed and breakfast than a home for three people.

I parked the truck behind the van and got out. Jaylee was already pounding on the front door, Lizzie beside her. I swung my rifle over my shoulder and walked up the curling sidewalk to join them.

"His car isn't in the driveway," I said.

"It's probably in the garage," Lizzie said.

True. "No doorbell?"

"She rang that already."

Jaylee hopped into a triangle of decorative pebbles between the sidewalk and house. She picked up a large rock with one hand and pulled a key out from the hollow interior.

"You know where they hide their spare?" I asked.

She smirked at me. "Yep."

From behind me, Zach snorted. I shot him a dirty look and noticed that Logan had come with him.

"You guys lock the van?" I asked.

"Yes, Papa Eli," Zach said.

I glared at my sister. "Thanks so much for starting *that*," I said.

"Those fake rocks are the first place a thief would look," Logan said. "You can tell the rock is fake because of the color."

"Thieves are the least of Riggs's worries," I said.

Jaylee used the key to open the front door. We all followed her inside. No power in the house, but a wall of picture windows in the living room let in the hazy, bluish glow of predawn.

"Riggs?" Jaylee ran down the hallway and disappeared around a corner. The sound of her muted voice continually calling out for Riggs was like nails on a chalkboard in my mind. I kept checking my watch as we searched the house. It was almost six now. We needed to get out of here. The crazies would be waking up soon.

The garage was empty. I came back inside and told Zach. "His car isn't in the garage. We should go."

Zach slapped me on the back. "Just let her look, man. It'll only take a couple minutes."

"A couple minutes is long enough for someone to get shot, Zach. We need to get out of here."

"Now who's sounding paranoid?" Zach said. "We haven't heard any gunshots around here."

"Not yet," I said.

Where would Riggs have gone? That he might go looking for his parents seemed out of character for someone so self-absorbed. Though that wasn't fair. Even serial killers had moms, right?

Thinking of Rigley Orcut having a mom made me think of my own. Hopeless horror came like a shock. I'd lost something I could never get back. Never see again. Mom's loss was permanent and real and devastating, like a part of me had been amputated.

I shoved down the pain. I just couldn't let myself go there. Not now. Not yet.

Jaylee returned to the living room carrying a notepad, a tape dispenser, and a pencil. "I'm leaving him a note."

I didn't like the relief that rushed through me, knowing Riggs wouldn't be coming with. This disaster was turning me into a jerk. "I'll be in the truck."

I reached the driver's side door just as the sound of heavy bass met my ears. I froze. In the distance, a pair of headlights lit the treetops on Lafayette, heading west, toward the intersection. I took my rifle into my hands and inched toward the back of the truck in a crouch. The glow of the headlights lit up the intersection, brighter than the musky predawn. The steady whump whump whump of bass grew louder.

"What are you doing?" Lizzie asked.

I spun on my heels. "Get down!"

Lizzie ducked beside the minivan. I turned back to the street in time to see a black Honda Civic crawl through the intersection, fifty feet away. It continued west, likely headed into the hills and the mansions up near Echo Canyon Park.

I was glad Riggs didn't live on the corner.

I ran back into the house, dragging Lizzie with me. Zach and Logan were perusing the shelves in the sitting room. Jaylee was perched on a footstool, using a fancy high-backed chair for a table.

"There's a car out there," I said.

"So?" Jaylee said.

"We need to leave. Now."

"Because of one car?" The look Jaylee gave me—the look that said, "You're an idiot and I will never have any respect for you"—just about did me in, but I stuck to my resolve.

"Yes," I said. "And I want us to keep our headlights off and to drive cautiously, at least until we hit the freeway."

"Eli, you're scaring me," Lizzie said.

"I'm sorry. But you heard the gunshots last night. I don't want any trouble. We took too long getting ready to leave. It's almost light."

"Stop freaking out, Eli," Jaylee said. "You're worse than Logan. Besides, I'm done." She got up, ripped a piece of tape from a dispenser, and stuck her note on the front door. "I call shotgun!" She took off for the van.

"Put the spare key back, will you?" I yelled after her. "Riggs might need it."

"Good point." She slid her fingers into her front jeans pocket and threw the key at me.

I barely caught it with two hands, clapping the thing to my chest to keep from dropping it.

"Such a lovely girl," Zach said as he exited the house.

"Shut up," I said.

"If she's riding in the van, I'm riding in the truck," Logan said as he passed me.

Zach followed him, patting my cheek as he went by. "Just remember," he whispered, "Jesus loves you even if she doesn't."

I swung at him but he darted out of my reach, chuckling.

"Jerk," I said, shoving the key back into the fake rock. I paused for a moment to read the note Jaylee left on the front door.

> Riggsy,
> Since we can't find anyone, we're driving north, back to Reinhold's place.
> Come meet us, okay?

Jaylee

Riggsy? I was tempted to rip down the note and take it with me, burn it, maybe. Instead, I flipped the lock on the inside of the door and pulled it shut. I descended the porch steps and headed for the truck.

Lizzie was standing between the vehicles. "You want me to ride with you?" She glanced at the truck where Logan was climbing into the passenger's seat.

"Nah, you ride in the van with Zach and Jaylee." I honestly didn't trust Jaylee alone with Zach. She did stupid things when she got emotional, and she'd already been hanging all over Zach. Lizzie would make a good buffer.

She winced. "You sure?"

"It's not a problem. I can handle Logan."

She hugged me. "You're the bestest big brother ever. If you want a break, use the walkie. Say you need to make a restroom stop, okay? It'll be our code phrase."

"Yeah, yeah. Get in the van, will you?" I circled the front to the driver's side window. Zach had it down and was leaning out. "Imma follow you, boss."

"All right." I climbed in the truck and headed north, for Camelback Road. The walkie talkie fizzled to life as Logan messed around with it.

"Zach, do you read me? This is Logan Graham. Over."

Jaylee's voice came through the speaker. "Zach is driving. This is Jaylee."

"Just testing the walkie talkies. Over," Logan said.

"Sounds like they work," Jaylee said.

"Right," Logan said to himself, then grinned at me. "If she answered, that means they're working."

"Sure does," I said.

I stopped a few yards before the intersection on Camelback and peeked west. No sign of the Honda or any headlights, but it was light enough out now. So much for my plan of getting out of town before dawn. Maybe this was better. Headlights in the dark would have made us more visible. I turned right onto Camelback and headed into Scottsdale.

"Where are you going?" Logan asked.

"I want to get on the freeway. Loop 101 is closer."

Logan pushed the button and held the walkie talkie to his mouth. "Transport two, this is transport one. We're heading north on Camelback Road. I'll be giving you directions. Over."

"Not necessary, Logan," Jaylee's voice came back. "It's not like Zach is going to lose a red pickup truck when there are only two cars on the road."

"Plus you'll waste the batteries," I said. "We need those for emergencies."

"Didn't think about that," Logan said. He spoke back into the walkie talkie. "Transport one to transport two, let's keep the channel clear for now and save the batteries for emergencies. Over."

"You got it," Jaylee said.

"Why doesn't she say 'over'?" Logan asked. "How am I supposed to know she's done talking?"

"I don't know. I guess you'll know when she doesn't say anything else."

The road was completely deserted. Trees, bushes, and concrete walls lined both sides, hiding fancy homes from the noise of would-be traffic.

"The speed limit is 35 here, Eli," Logan said.

And I was doing 60. "I know. I just don't figure it matters right now."

I slowed to glance both ways before running a stop sign. I tensed, waiting for Logan to rebuke that latest infraction, but for once he didn't speak.

The sky was cloudy today, likely due to all the fires. The sun peeked over the horizon straight ahead, brilliant and backlighting the palm trees in a peachy orange color that made the trees look black. Gorgeous. Even amongst so much death and destruction, creation went on doing its thing. I pulled a pair of sunglasses off the visor and slid them on.

After 64th, the street had steady median crossovers with grass and trees that split the two directions of traffic. We were almost to the mall; I could see the pedestrian overpass up ahead. Loop 101 was only another eight blocks or so past it. Before I reached the overpass, though, a boy ran out into the street, right in front of me.

10

"Look out!" Logan grabbed the dashboard.

"I see him." I clutched the wheel with both hands and slammed on the brakes.

The boy reached the sidewalk on the other side of the street, but he tripped over the ledge. I parked the truck diagonally in the road, just past the intersection, tossed my sunglasses onto the dash, and got out to help. The boy was holding his knee and wincing. He looked to be about nine or ten. He had short orange hair and glasses.

I squatted beside him and grabbed his arm. "Hey, buddy. You okay?"

"Let go!" The boy squirmed, kicked at my stomach, and

when I released him, crawled away.

"Calm down, kid. I'm only trying to—"

A piercing scream drew my attention. I stood. On the other side of the road, a teen girl in a miniskirt was running this way, dragging a little girl by the hand into the street.

"Jump," she said. And when the little girl jumped, the older one lifted her by the arm so that she cleared the median in one leap. They kept running, right toward me.

The little girl was wearing a bright red hoodie and had orange hair in pigtails. The teen was barefoot. Streaks of black makeup ran down each cheek from her eyes, and her shoulder length hair was blonde and so very curly it looked like she was wearing a tumbleweed for a hat.

"Help us!" she yelled between gasps for air. Her feet slapped against the pavement, accompanied by the patter of the rubber soles of the little girl's sneakers. They were flashing with red lights as she ran.

The boy beside me had stood and was looking me over with narrowed eyes. "Are you a good guy?"

I looked down on his freckled face. "Yeah, kid. I'm a regular superhero."

"Please help!" The teen tackled me, almost knocking me down, her arms wrapped around my neck, her hair all in my face and mouth. I blew out a breath, spitting out her hair, and turned my head, trying to back away, but she held tight.

"Get off!" I said.

"Sorry!" She let go and stepped back, brushing her hair away from her face and wiping the tears off her cheeks, smearing the black make up worse. She looked to be in middle school but was dressed much older.

"He's coming!" the boy said, pointing.

Across the street, a man ran toward us. He looked to be in his late 20s, wore a plaid western shirt, tight blue jeans, and cowboy boots. He had stringy black hair and a thick moustache. He slowed to a jog, heading this way.

"You've got to help us!" The teen's eyes met mine. They were green, edged in smudges of black. "Please?"

I ran back to my truck.

"Coward!" she yelled after me. "Just leave us to the monsters, you weak, pathetic excuse for a human be—"

I grabbed my rifle off the gun rack on the back window of the cab and ran around to Logan's side of the truck.

She gasped. "You have a gun?"

I leaned over the front hood, using the vehicle for a blockade. I trained my rifle on the man, and waited. "Get behind me. Come on."

The teen grabbed the kids by the hands and moved beside the truck.

The passenger window on the truck lowered. "Eli! What are you doing?" Logan asked.

I wasn't sure. "Stay in the truck," I told him.

The man slowed to a stop just under the pedestrian bridge. Behind him, on the other side of the underpass, an old blue Ford pickup approached, driving on the wrong side of the road. It exited on our side of the underpass and stopped beside the cowboy, who climbed up into the passenger's seat. The vehicle rolled nearer.

My pulse pounded in my ears. Was I nuts? What was my plan? Would I really shoot someone? What if they drove over here? What if they rammed us?

But this wasn't a *Fast and the Furious* movie. The Ford stopped twenty yards away. The driver jumped out, raised his arms in the air, and stepped toward us. I looked through the rifle's scope. Only saw the two of them. Unlike his pal, the driver was a big guy, heavy, wearing ratty cowboy boots, faded jeans, and a Budweiser T-shirt. He had a big metal belt buckle that said Jack Daniels Old No. 7 Brand.

"I don't want any trouble!" the driver yelled. "Them's my kids running off is all."

"He's lying," the teen said. "We've never seen those guys before today."

I glanced behind me to my right. The teen had picked up the little girl, who I guessed to be a kindergartener. The boy stood beside them, clutching the teen's upper arm with both hands.

I focused back on the cowboys. "Where'd you meet them?"

"We were walking over to Coco's to see if there was anything to eat," the teen said. "They stopped and offered us a ride. I said no and they started chasing us. I don't want to go with them."

I didn't blame her for that. These were exactly the kind of people I'd been hoping to avoid. "What's your name?"

"Krista."

"Where do you live, Krista?"

"*I* live in Mesa. The kids live over on East Highland. I was babysitting them, but their mom never came home."

Babysitting. Just great. Mesa was out of my way. I couldn't start picking up strays everywhere we went. We had few supplies as it was. And here were three more mouths to feed—to water. They didn't look to be very helpful mouths, either.

But I could decide all that later. Right now we needed to lose the desperados. The big guy was inching toward us. My thumb hovered over the safety.

"Don't come any closer or I'll shoot!" I yelled.

The minivan rolled up on the other side of my truck. "Eli?" Zach called through Jaylee's open window. "What are we doing, man?"

"Being good Samaritans," I said. "Get in the van, Krista."

She squinted in Zach's direction and frowned, looked back to me. "Can't we ride with you?"

"There's not enough seatbelts." The front had a bench seat, but Zach and I had buried the jump seats in supplies.

"But I don't know those people."

"You don't know me, either."

Krista flipped her hair out of her face and looked back to Zach. "He looks really big," she whispered.

"He's a good guy," I said. When she didn't move, I glanced at her again. Tears brimmed in her eyes. "Fine. Logan, get in the van. Zach? Be ready to ride. Krista, you and the kids get in the truck. Go. Now!"

Logan got out. Krista and the kids climbed into the Tacoma.

"I'm not gonna let you take her!" the Budweiser man yelled.

"I don't see your name on her," I yelled back.

"She's mine, just the same. I don't care about the little ones. Just give me the girl!"

And he'd said they were his kids! What a creep.

Zach backed up the van and turned around.

"Things are hard enough right now," I said. "Get in your truck and drive away."

"Ain't going nowhere without the girl."

"If you don't leave, I'll have to shoot out your tire. I don't want to make trouble for you, but I will."

"Do what you got to do, punk," the man said. "Gun probably isn't even loaded."

He'd left me no choice. I couldn't leave Krista with these guys, and I couldn't have them following us, either. I took careful aim, flipped off the safety, breathed out, aimed again, and pulled the trigger. The gun recoiled against my shoulder as the shot rang out. The driver leaped away from the vehicle, swearing a blue streak. The Ford didn't move, but once my ears stopped ringing, I could hear a soft hiss coming from the tire. The truck was starting to tilt. Perfect.

I flipped on the safety but kept my rifle trained on the Ford as I edged around the front of my truck. Let them think I was going to shoot again. I got to my door, which was still hanging open, and handed my gun in to Krista, who was sitting in the middle, the kids on her other side. I climbed in, started the truck, and peeled out in a U-turn. I sailed past Zach as I headed north. My arms were trembling, so I gripped the wheel tighter, hoping Krista wouldn't notice. She was holding my rifle barrel with both hands, the butt on the floor, her knees tipped toward the kids to make room for it and me. She probably didn't know how to hold a gun.

The road became one way, took a ninety-degree curve and became Highland. I slowed to a stop at the next intersection and took the gun from Krista. "Duck," I said, checking the safety again.

She obeyed, and I twisted, hanging the rifle under my dad's in the gun rack on the back window.

"Don't touch these guns, do you hear me?" I said, looking from one face to the other.

All three nodded, eyes big.

"I want to hear you say it," I said.

"Yes, sir," the boy said. He was farthest from me, by the passenger's window.

The girl echoed her brother, but her words sounded more like, "Yes sore."

I raised my eyebrows at Krista.

"Got it," she said.

"Buckle up." While my passengers worked out how to share two seat belts, I shifted into drive, and hit the gas. I felt awkward, talking to kids like that. I sounded like my dad. But I didn't like them in here with the guns. I didn't trust them not to get curious, and kids playing with loaded rifles was the last thing any of us needed. I would switch the kids into the van the first chance I got.

"Where'd you learn to shoot guns?" Krista asked me.

"My dad taught me," I said.

"You're good at it."

"Will you teach me?" the boy asked.

See? Already the kid could think of nothing but getting his hands on my rifle. "No," I said. "Guns are dangerous. I only have them for protection."

"They worked good for that," the boy said.

I turned left on Scottsdale, glancing into my rearview mirror for any sign of a blue Ford. The road was barren but for Zach's minivan. I let out a deep breath. Needed to change the subject.

"So, what are you doing out so early dressed like that with no shoes?" I nodded at Krista's bare feet.

"I left them in the store."

"You shouldn't be outside right now. It isn't safe."

"The kids were hungry." She tugged at the hem of her skirt, trying to pull it lower. "And what is wrong with my outfit? It's cute."

"It screams, 'Attack me. I'm a defenseless female.'"

She grunted. "Don't judge me." She shifted on the seat and something sharp poked my thigh.

I glanced down to see a tag on the side of her skirt, digging into my leg. "You stole that skirt?"

She looked down to the tag, yanked it off, and tossed it on the floor. "Like it matters. No one is alive to arrest me."

"That's fair," I said.

"We were shopping at Macy's," the girl said. "Krista wanted a short skirt because her mom always says no."

"Shut up, Shy," Krista said.

I stopped at Chaparral, noted that Zach was right

behind me, and turned right. I glanced at the girl. "Your name's Shy?"

"Shy*la*. His name is Davis." She pointed at the boy.

"Nice to meet you Shyla and Davis," I said.

"You *are* a good guy," Davis said. "Did you see how he shot out Al's tire? Blam! Blam!"

"Wait. Al? I thought you didn't know that guy?"

Davis clapped a hand over his mouth.

"I never said that," Krista said.

Heat flashed through me. She'd pretty much implied it. "*Was* that your dad?"

"No!" She folded her arms across her chest and sighed. "He's not."

"He's our stepdad," Davis said.

Nuts. "I shot out that guy's tire and gave you a ride because I thought he was some kind of creeper. If he's your dad, I should take you back."

"No!" Krista and Davis said together.

"Look, you saved us, okay?" Krista added. "Trust me. Al is bad news. Don't you remember? He said he didn't even want the kids. Just me. The babysitter. He *is* a creeper."

Good point. I glanced out the window. We were passing Chaparral Lake. Almost there.

"So what's *your* name?" Krista asked me.

"Eli."

"Elijah or Elisha?"

"Elias."

"Never heard that one before. You're really skinny."

Okay, I know I'm a twig, but I don't really need strange girls pointing it out, thank you very much.

Krista didn't seem to care about manners. "You're also tall. How tall are you, anyway?" she asked.

"I'm five eleven. That's not really very tall for a guy."

Krista smiled and her teeth were perfectly white and

small, like baby teeth. "Well, I'm five foot three. But if I get my hair really poufy, I can pass for five foot six."

"Fascinating," I said.

"So where are we going?" Krista asked.

"Loop 101," I said, gliding into the turn lane that stretched under the freeway overpass.

"That's it? We're going to the freeway?"

"For now." A quick glance in my rearview showed Zach right behind me. Good. I hit my blinker and turned left onto the onramp. I tensed as the truck crested the hill and shot out onto the freeway. I hoped it would be empty.

I chastised myself for that thought. Shouldn't I be hoping there were more survivors? Truth was, I dreaded the inevitable confrontation with someone armed.

The freeway put us up high enough that we could see everything for miles. The sky was dark, like it might thunder, but it was all smoke. Phoenix was still burning, and I hadn't heard a single siren all night. Even with the smoky canopy above, the bright sunlight stung my eyes. I reached for the sunglasses on the dash and put them on. I hadn't gotten enough sleep. I didn't like the idea of getting into a wreck with the kids sharing a seatbelt. I should stop and make Krista and the kids get in the van. But now that we were finally moving, I didn't dare slow down until Phoenix was far behind us.

"We're going to the mountains," I told Krista. "We were there when all this started, so I'm hoping it's still safe. If we can find wildlife, that'll mean there is an uncontaminated water source nearby."

"What mountains?"

"Colorado."

"I have an aunt in Flagstaff," Krista said. "You think you could swing by there? See if she's . . . you know . . . home?"

No way, was my first thought as I recalled the thugs with baseball bats. But that wasn't really fair. We had to pass through Flagstaff anyway. "What part of Flagstaff?"

"University Heights. It's right when you come into town."

I glanced at her—at the thick black sharpie lines around her eyes. "Yeah, we can stop. I want to stay out of the city as much as I can, though. Too many people."

"Are you scared?"

I glanced past Krista at the kids, saw they were looking out the window at the smoke. "I'll feel better when I'm in the woods."

"You like to camp?"

This girl and her questions . . . "I just figure it's going to be crazy for a while. Whatever people are still alive in the cities, it's going to get bad." I lowered my voice, just in case the kids were listening. "People will kill for water. We're better off getting away until things calm down."

"Three extra people are going to need a lot of extra water, huh?"

I nodded. Maybe she was smarter than I'd first thought.

"Well, don't worry," she said. "We won't drink a drop. Just get us to my aunt's house, and we'll be out of your hair."

"Don't worry about it," I said, but I wasn't certain I meant it. We had quite a bit of water in the back of my truck, but for eight people, it would be gone even sooner.

The walkie talkie on the dashboard crackled. "Logan to Eli, do you read me? Over."

I reached for it and pressed the button. "This is Eli." Then for Logan's benefit I added, "Over."

The walkie fizzed a moment before Logan's voice came again. "Erin is dead."

11

There was a sound in my ears, funny and distant, like I was underwater or on an airplane. My heart was thumping like I'd been running hard. It occurred to me that maybe I'd misheard Logan—that he'd simply been worried about Erin dying.

"Who's Erin?" Krista asked.

The question made Logan's words real, and I sucked in a breath that didn't seem to have enough air. My hands started to tremble, so I gripped the wheel harder, trying to hold myself together. The knot in my stomach ached. People I cared about were dying.

The walkie talkie crackled again. "Logan to Eli, we're

stopping. Over."

I glanced in the rearview mirror. The van had pulled onto the shoulder. Someone was already out. I hit the brakes.

Krista's hands grabbed the dashboard. "What are you doing?"

I cranked the wheel and did a U-turn in the middle of the freeway. "Turning around."

"Who's Erin? Was he in the van?" she asked.

Oh, Aaron. "E-R-I-N. *She* was our friend." My voice sounded weird. Far away. Foreign. "And no, she was in a different car."

I pulled up beside the van, but it was empty. Everyone was in the sagebrush off the side of the road. Lizzie was crouched beside Jaylee, who was on her hands and knees, sobbing. Logan stood beside the girls, mouth gaping, his face totally blank but for the tears that streaked his cheeks.

I got out and joined Zach, who was standing in the back, his expression hard, the wind making ripples along the front of his Arizona State T-shirt. The air smelled like vomit. I suddenly felt very aware of my own mortality. I could feel the warm air enter my mouth and lungs. My chapped lips. How greasy my face felt after so long without a shower.

How could my mom and Erin be dead while I was still here? Why were any of us still here? Where was my dad?

Jaylee's sobbing intensified, and Lizzie answered her in a high-pitched tone laced with tears. Their voices made an unintelligible duet of panic and consolation. I didn't know how to feel about any of this. I mean, should I be crying too? What did it say about me that I wasn't crying?

I looked back to Zach. He wasn't crying either, which oddly made me feel better. "Antônia text Jaylee?" I asked.

Zach nodded.

"Where is she now?"

"In Peoria."

At the sound of our voices, Logan came toward us. "Jaylee puked," he said. "She wants us to go get Antônia."

"We're not doing that," I said, wincing at the Boss in my voice. Who'd put me in charge, anyway?

"I don't like this," Zach said. "We were all together in those mountains. If Erin and Mark got sick, shouldn't we all be sick?"

Despair struck me like a bucket of cold water dumped on my head. "If Erin is gone, does that mean Mark is too?" I asked.

"Yes," Logan said. "I mean, he has to be."

I didn't want to agree. I couldn't. "No one can reach them?" I asked.

"Jaylee's been trying," Logan said.

"Why them and not us?" Zach asked.

It didn't make any sense to me, either. "They must have done something different," I said.

"Maybe they caught the Hydro-Flu beforehand," Logan said.

"Before the comet passed?" I asked.

"Oh, right," he said.

We stood there on the side of the road for longer than I was comfortable. We were vulnerable here like this, with our entire load exposed for all to see. No one came along, though. Not one vehicle. Lizzie prayed with Jaylee. Then the girls texted Antônia, who was all alone in Peoria. Jaylee wanted us to go back and get her, but I refused. Thankfully Zach backed me up.

"We can't backtrack," he said. "It's too dangerous."

"Have her drive up here and meet us," I said. "She won't be far behind. Besides, we need to stop in Flagstaff and drop off Krista and the kids."

"Krista? That's the girl's name?" Zach asked.

"Yeah. Her aunt lives in Flagstaff."

"Good," Zach said. "Let's hope she's home. And alive."

The girls were on their feet and making their way back to the van when the sound of an engine turned my head. A gold GMC SUV was slowing down. Instinct told me to run for the truck, but there was no time. All I could do was stare and wish I hadn't left my gun in the cab.

The SUV pulled up behind my truck. The passenger's window lowered, revealing a woman. The voice that spoke, however, was male, and came from the driver's seat. "Hey, there!" A man leaned over the woman's lap. He was white and wore a cowboy hat made of straw. "What a sight! So many of you all together. That's great. I love it!"

Zach started toward the vehicle. I wanted to tell him to stay back, but if these two pulled out guns, it wouldn't matter where we were standing.

"Name's Quinn," the man said. "This here's Darby. We're heading to Mount Crested Butte."

I frowned. "The ski resort?"

"Yeah. Y'all haven't heard 'bout the Champions?"

"Champions of what?" Zach asked.

"Nah, man, those French rock stars. Loca and Liberty Champion."

"It's pronounced *Shamp-ee-ohn*," the wife Darby said with a French accent. "And it's *Liberté*, not Liberty."

"Yeah, well, they got a mansion up by the resort," Quinn said. "And it's got clean water. Safe water. Water that won't kill you to drink. Word is they've invited survivors to come up and share. Gonna build some kind of commune."

"If they have clean water, why would they share it?" I instantly felt guilty for such a comment, but the water was only going to last so long. Then things would get ugly.

"Nah, man," Quinn said. "I'm not talking 'bout jugs or anything like that. There's some creek out of the mountains goes by their house. It's clean. Hardly anyone who lives in the area has died, so they're telling people to come on up and make a life there."

For the first time in days, I felt a wisp of hope. It tingled at the base of my spine, begging to grow. I stomped it down. The idea was ridiculous. Rock stars with water? Come on.

"How can that be? Safe water?" Zach looked at me, as if I was some expert on the whole Comet Pulon water virus situation.

I shrugged. "No idea." Then to Quinn, I said, "Thanks for letting us know. Maybe we'll see you again."

"Sounds good, man. Be safe out there." Quinn waved as his wife rolled up her window. We stood there watching them as the SUV drove away.

The relief I felt was palpable.

"We have to go!" Jaylee said. "It's a sign."

"A sign of hysteria," Logan said.

"You think it's not true, Eli?" Lizzie asked.

Frankly, I didn't believe a word of it. "Look, things like this happen during a crisis. It's like a mirage out in the dessert. People panic. They're desperate. They'll believe anything if it keeps the hope of survival alive."

"Don't be such a pessimist," Lizzie said.

"I'm a realist."

"I get that it sounds kind of far-fetched," Jaylee said, "but that's why I believe it. Who would make that up? Famous musicians with water for everyone? It's too weird."

"Like the Bible," Logan said. "A common argument for the veracity of the Bible is, if you were trying to write a book to trick people into believing a lie, why would you put some of those stories in there?"

"Exactly!" Jaylee said, grinning at Logan.

Seemed like a stretch to me, but I said, "Fine. Crested

Butte is another four hours from Durango. We get to Reinhold's place, see if he's got safe water, find out if he's seen my dad. Then we'll talk about a drive up to Crested Butte." Though I really didn't like the idea of going to a place where survivors were congregating. A bunch of desperate people arriving at a place where they thought salvation awaited and didn't find it? That would make for some mass hysteria I had no desire to witness.

"Come on," I said. "Let's get back on the road."

As much as false hope annoyed me, it had lifted everyone's spirits after hearing about Erin, which I had to admit was a blessing. We made it the two and a half hours to Flagstaff without any further incidents. The temperature on my dashboard read 75. I was glad to be in cooler weather. Just thinking about the heat back in Phoenix made me thirsty.

I followed Krista's instructions to get to her aunt's place. She lived in an upscale, wooded subdivision on the south side of Flagstaff that was filled with a lot of redwood homes with suburbans in the driveways. The occasional RV.

I finally pulled into a concrete driveway in front of a redwood house with forest green trim. The yard was shaded by a forest of towering ponderosa pine and landscaped with piles of river rock boulders and ferns. An A-frame roof sat over the entrance and divided a two-car garage from the gable roof that covered the rest of the house. I liked it. I could live in a place like this.

I turned off the truck. Shyla and Davis were sleeping.

"Might as well let them rest until we're sure your aunt is here." I climbed out.

Krista got out behind me but darted past, hurrying toward the house. I grabbed my rifle and pushed the truck door shut until it clicked, hoping I wouldn't wake the kids.

"You want me to come with you?" I called after her.

She spun around and winced. "Would you?"

"Sure." I motioned to Zach in the van and followed Krista to the front door.

She knocked and we waited. When no one answered, she tried the knob and the door opened.

We entered a spotless living room that was painted and decorated in shades of beige and brown. A large river rock fireplace dominated the room. The place looked homemade, in a good way.

Krista walked into the center of the living room and stopped, like she was afraid to go any farther. From what I'd seen at Zach's house, I didn't blame her. The air didn't smell bad, though.

"Aunt Robin?" Krista fidgeted with the hem of her skirt, pulling it down. "Hello?" She turned to me, giving me a "helpless girl" look.

I tossed out an idea. "Might as well have a look around."

She led the way, and I followed her through a pink kitchen with black appliances. I doubted a man had chosen such colors. We eventually went up beige carpeted stairs to a wide and short hallway. That's when we noticed a change. We peeked into a couple of bedrooms and found clothing heaped all over. An open suitcase, empty, gave me the impression the residents of this place had packed to go elsewhere in a hurry. I said as much to Krista as we entered an office. The top drawer of the filing cabinet was still open.

"Where would they have gone?" Krista asked.

I didn't know. "What are you going to do?"

Her eyes flashed wide. "What do you mean?"

I thought my meaning had been fairly obvious. "Are you going to stay here or stick with us?"

"*Can* we stick with you?"

"Of course," I said, hoping I looked kind and sincere,

though my eyes felt like they were giving away my lie. "I mean, if you want to stay here, you can. But you're welcome to come to the mountains with us."

Krista clapped her hands over her mouth and nose and started sobbing.

"Um . . . take your time," I said, heading for the stairs. "I'll be outside."

"Wait! Take me to the hospital," she said. "My aunt could be there."

"I don't think we really want to go to any hospitals," I said.

"You have to!" she said. "Please!"

"Let's talk to Zach," I said.

"Why?"

"Because he's the closest thing we have to a doctor." I started down the stairs, eager to have some back-up where the hospital was concerned.

"What kind of doctor?" Krista asked as she plodded down the stairs behind me.

"He's a lifeguard," I said. "He's had CPR and first aid training. That's all."

"Oh."

When we came out, Zach was standing next to the van hugging Jaylee. I stopped and stared at them. Jaylee was crying again, and she'd probably hugged him, but still. I didn't like what jealousy did inside my head.

"Well?" Zach asked, still holding onto Jaylee.

"No one's here," I said. "Krista wants to go to the hospital."

"You have to take me," she said.

Zach shook his head. "Not a good idea."

"You have to!"

Logan got out of the van. "No one is alive at the hospitals," he said.

Jaylee released Zach, to my great relief. "We went to the hospital in Phoenix," she said, sniffing. "It was the most horrifying thing I've ever seen in my life."

Krista had the decency to accept that. For a moment she looked confused and very young. Then the scowl returned and she folded her arms. "Then I'm staying here."

"If that's what you want," I said.

"It is." She stomped to my truck and opened the passenger door, shoved each of the kids. "Davis, wake up. Shy. We're here! At my aunt's house. She's really nice. Wait 'til you meet her."

I glanced at Zach. I doubted the kids would ever meet Krista's aunt. It didn't feel right leaving them here. Krista might be a decent babysitter, but I didn't think she was mentally capable of keeping the three of them alive for very long.

Lizzie got out of the van and tried talking Krista into coming with us, but Krista had made up her mind. Honestly, we didn't have any right to stop her. So I climbed in the truck. Logan jumped in beside me. Zach, Jaylee, and Lizzie got back in the van. I put the truck in reverse, stretched my arm over the top of the seat, and waited for Zach to back out first. I followed, but when I stopped to put the truck into drive, I glanced at the house and saw Krista running toward us, waving her arms.

I rolled down the window.

"Wait!" she said. "Don't leave us!"

I leaned out the window and waited for her to reach the truck.

"We want to come with you," she said.

I sighed, relieved, and put the truck into park.

12

If Krista and the kids weren't staying in this house, we were going to scavenge it for supplies before leaving. We all went in and scoured the place. We found a few sleeping bags and some winter clothing that might come in handy. The pantry was stocked with a ton of canned goods. No water, unfortunately. We cleaned them out of anything nonperishable, shoving it wherever we could in the back of the van or truck. I did some rearranging to clean out the access cab of the Tacoma so that the kids could sit back there. I ended up stacking the flats of water in the middle between the two jump seats.

Once we had everything packed and repacked, I found

Krista in her aunt's walk-in closet, trying on a pair of boots that were clearly too big. "Find any clothes for you and the kids?" I asked.

She shook her head and stuck her feet into a pair of flip flops. "Nothing here fits. But there's a Target just up the road. We can stop there for clothes and shoes."

Krista, Shyla, and Davis definitely needed clothes, but Target was not on my list of stops. I didn't want to start a fight about it without backup, so I hightailed it outside, where I could confer with Zach for at least a few seconds before Krista got to the girls. Target was Lizzie's favorite store.

I strode up to Zach, who was standing with Lizzie. My sister was crying, and Zach was looking at her like he'd just told her he'd run over her dog.

"I should have told you," he said. "I'm sorry."

I didn't have time to inquire. I pulled Zach a few steps away from my sister and mumbled in one long breath, "Idon'tthinkweshouldgotoTarget."

"What?" he asked.

"Krista wants to go there to get clothes for her and the kids, but I think we should go someplace else."

Krista joined us, arms folded. "What's wrong with Target?"

"Oh, good idea, hon!" Lizzie said. "I love Target."

So much for my plan of keeping the girls out of it. "Target is a huge store on the main road," I said. "People will be drawn to it."

"So?" Krista said. "You're acting like every other person alive is evil, or something. Quinn wasn't. No one is going to bother us."

"Hey," Zach said. "Eli's in charge here. If he doesn't want to go, we're not going."

That stopped me. I was in charge?

Krista clicked her tongue and glared at me like I was Budweiser dude. Man, she ran hot and cold.

"Hey, Eli!" Logan was headed our way from the back of the house, carrying a red gas can. "It's half full!"

I left the group to join him. He handed me the can, and I set it down and twisted off the cap. A quick sniff confirmed it was gasoline. "Let's put it in the truck," I said. "It's running lower than the van."

"I'm on it." Logan snatched up the can and carried it toward the truck. On the other side of the driveway, Shyla and Davis were doing somersaults on the lawn.

I headed back over to the others, who were standing in a circle. Jaylee had gotten out of the van and joined them.

I tried to change the conversation. "Any word from Antônia?" I asked.

"Last I heard she was an hour out," Jaylee asked. "That was fifteen minutes ago."

Perhaps waiting for her would be best, though I wasn't sure she could find the place without a guide. I doubted that her phone's GPS would work.

"Why don't you ask her to meet us at the Walgreens on Wilton Road. It'll be the first one as she comes into town."

"Eli, we should at least check out Target," Lizzie said. "It will have a lot bigger selection of supplies."

"If there's anything left," Zach said.

"I'm just saying, we need to get as many medical supplies as we can. Target has a pharmacy and clothes," Lizzie said.

"There's a Walmart nearby too," Krista said, "if you think that would be better."

"You're missing the point," I said. "Smaller is better."

"No one wants to go to Walgreens, Eli," Jaylee said.

"Exactly my point," I said. "It'll be a lot safer than a huge department store."

"But I can't get clothes there," Krista said.

"They have sweats and T-shirts," I said. "Probably some socks."

Krista gave me a half-choking gasp. "I'm *not* wearing sweat pants."

"Ninety percent of the world is dead," I said. "Fashion doesn't matter anymore."

"It matters to me," she said.

I folded my arms. I wasn't going to give in. Target could very well be suicide.

"I need some clothes too," Jaylee said. "Plus with all us girls, we're going to need to stock up on tampons."

The word may as well have been magical for "burst into flame" because that's what happened inside my body when that word rolled off Jaylee's tongue. I couldn't even speak. What was I supposed to say? No, you can't have any tampons? I mean, females had managed to deal for thousands of years before modern technology had created such convenient "products." These girls might have to deal with that at some point, but I wasn't going to be the one to tell them.

"They carry feminine hygiene products at Walgreens," Logan said, approaching our circle.

Ha! "Well, there you go," I said.

"Not the kind I use," Jaylee said to Logan, then looked back to me. "Eli, I really need a certain kind. Please?"

I swallowed, exchanged a painful glance with Zach, and said, "Fine. Let's go to Tar-zhay."

Jaylee invited Krista to ride in the van, so I opened the suicide doors and showed the kids how to use the jump seats. That left Logan riding shotgun with me. I packed Dad's gun in the back, and put mine up on the dash, which wasn't ideal, but at least it was out of the kids' reach.

We drove back to I-17, which soon became South

Milton Road. I didn't realize how hungry I was until we drove by a Pizza Hut. So not fair.

All throughout Flagstaff, we passed stores with busted out windows. The words "Drink bottled only" were spray painted on the wall of a 7-11. Similar signs and messages were posted all over town. I was thankful we'd missed the insanity of looting. We didn't see anyone. Alive, that is. I saw a body on the ground in the parking lot of a Denny's and three bodies inside a car blocking an intersection. I know Logan saw one of them because he started pontificating about decomposition.

"Logan!" I said, nodding to the kids in the back. "Can it."

"That happened to a dead squirrel outside our house," Davis said from the back. "It smelled bad. Are we going to die too?"

"Not today," I said, then wondered if I should have just said no. I didn't want these kids breaking down on me. Maybe after Target, I'd make Lizzie ride with me for a while. She was good with kids. Always knew what to say.

I turned right on University Drive, scanning the Target parking lot for any sign of . . . anything, I guess. There were six cars in the lot. I pulled in the side entrance and parked in a handicapped spot in front of the store. I'd rather drive around back, but there was no way to know whether we could get in that way, so the closer I could get to the entrance, the better.

The windows and sliding glass doors all along the front had been busted. Merchandise was strewn along the sidewalk.

"Looks like the looters worked this place over pretty good," Logan said. "There's probably nothing left."

Zach stopped the van beside me, and everyone piled out.

Logan opened the back door for Davis. "Shyla's asleep," he said. "Want me to wake her up?"

"Let her sleep," I said. "I'm going to wait out here."

"Suit yourself," Logan said.

Davis stuck to Logan like a shadow. I smirked. Looked like Logan had made a new friend. I got out, grabbed my dad's gun from the back, and met Zach by the front end of the van.

"What's up?" he asked.

"One of us goes in. One of us stays with the load," I said. "It's got to be you and me. Which job you want?"

He shrugged. "Doesn't matter."

"Go in, then. You know more about what to look for as far as medicine goes. Radio me that it's clear inside. And if you have any trouble."

"You too," Zach said.

"Shyla's sleeping, so she's with me."

"Got it."

"Take my dad's gun. It's loaded. Safety's on. You got four rounds."

"Don't really want it," Zach said, but he accepted the weapon.

"What were you and my sister talking about back at Krista's aunt's place?" I asked.

"Oh." Zach stood looking in through the open door. "I told her about my family. About what we did. She was ticked off that I didn't tell her before. Said she would have come help."

"She would have," I said. "Why'd you tell her?"

"I don't know. She asked the right questions, and I didn't know how to lie about it. Or why I should, so . . ." He shrugged.

Yeah. Lizzie had a way of pulling the truth from people. "Sorry, man," I said.

He shrugged. "Guess I'll go in."

I watched Zach walk inside the store, then climbed back into the truck and started it. I didn't like having my back to the lot, so I turned the truck around and backed into the same spot I'd been parked in previously, the van now on my left. I grabbed my gun off the dashboard, then sat there on high alert, imagining every worst-case scenario I could think up. What I'd do if I heard my father's gun go off. What I'd do if I heard my sister scream. What I'd do if someone came driving in. I mean, I didn't even have a tarp over the back of my truck. My load screamed, "Steal me and live for six months!"

The walkie talkie hissed. "Zach to Eli, come in."

Skin pricking, I grabbed the radio and answered. "I hear you, over."

"Jaylee says Antônia is on the outskirts of Flagstaff. She'll be here soon. Also, so far all is clear in here. Over."

"Ten-four. And that's great news about Antônia," I said, relieved both that Antônia was close and that nothing was wrong inside. "I'll keep my eyes peeled for her car. Over and out."

I scanned the parking lot. Antônia would probably pull in on the south side like I did. I didn't see anything at the moment. I shook my leg, my rifle sitting awkwardly across my lap. There wasn't a lot of room in the cab to rotate the weapon. I could easily shoot out the passenger's side window, but if someone approached the driver's side, I wouldn't be able to get the gun pointed in the right direction very quickly.

Time ticked by, and I got bored. I started a mental list of all the things we still might need. I'd like to go by a hardware store of some kind. True Value, maybe, or an Ace. If I could find a shake siphon, that would be ideal. Then we could siphon gas from cars along the way without getting a mouthful of gasoline. I doubted we'd find any gas stations open. I wondered about Pete's place. If he was still there with his old fashioned pump. Seemed to me at some point when people stopped coming by he'd close up shop and—

I straightened and stared at the red Volvo station wagon out in the lot. I thought I'd seen some movement there. My eyes strained, watching the car. I chastised myself for being so paranoid. We hadn't seen anyone in a long time. I likely had nothing to worry about.

Still, I watched the Volvo, vigilant. Then I saw it. A dog trotted out from behind the back of the car. He was a brown Labrador retriever, looked a lot like Sammy had except for the darker color. I watched him stop to sniff something on the pavement, trot up to an army green Impala, and pee on the tire.

I felt relieved that it was just a dog, until I realized he might be with a human. Had to be, in fact. Most animals were dead. The only way one could still be alive was if someone was giving it bottled water.

The dog had spooked me, and I didn't like that I couldn't maneuver the rifle well from inside the cab. I decided it would be better to get out of the truck. With my back to the outside wall of Target, I'd be able to see the whole lot. I removed the keys, pocketed them, clipped the walkie talkie to my belt, and opened the door. A warm breeze flitted through the cab. I gripped the handle over the door and twisted to get out.

"Hold it right there."

A bearded man popped up from the front of Zach's van, pointing a shotgun at my head.

13

My heart lurched. I had my right fist around the barrel of my gun, my left hand on the handle above the door. I let go of the handle, hoping to get my hands into position on my rifle, but I lost my balance and slid out of the truck. My hiking boots thwapped on the pavement.

"Don't do it, boy!" Beardo yelled. "It ain't worth it. Leave the rifle in the cab and walk away."

"I can't do that," I said.

"You'd better."

I just stood there, staring, daring myself to move my rifle into position. *Come on, McShane, you gutless coward!*

I knew we shouldn't have stopped at Target. I *knew* it! I

was the worst surveillance man to ever grace the planet Earth. Where had this guy come from, anyway?

Beardo whistled, and the brown lab came running, pink tongue flapping in the breeze. Stupid dog! What did I care about a dog, anyway?

"Come away from that truck, now," Beardo said, jerking the gun toward the bed.

I took a small side step toward the road, unsure what to do. I couldn't let him take the truck. Besides, Shyla was in there!

I had the keys, at least. I could run into the store. Beardo was likely bluffing about shooting me. Maybe with Zach's help, the two of us could scare him off. Except the entrance was the opposite direction, and to get there, I'd be putting my back to this guy.

I took another teensy step toward the back of the truck, thinking that maybe if I could get behind it, I'd have a chance to lift my gun.

Two months' worth of water in the back of my truck. Two months' worth that we wouldn't have if I messed this up. Which I already had. That stupid brown lab that would be lapping up my share.

And who knew what they'd do with Shyla.

I inched another step to the left. My hands were shaking.

Lord help me, Lord help me, Lord help me, Lord help me.

"A little faster, will ya?" Beardo said. "And drop that gun."

I shook my head, and in one quick breath, I lifted my rifle, trained it on my adversary, and flipped off the safety.

"Hey, hey, hey!" Beardo yelled, fixing his shotgun on me. "Let's not do this, boy!"

"Get out of here!" I yelled back, my pulse pounding in my ears.

"You don't have the guts!"

"Neither do you!"

We faced off between the van and the truck. The brown lab came alongside me, sniffed my leg and panted, oblivious to the tension around him. I could feel him watching me, though I didn't dare look.

A dozen scenarios flashed in my mind. I could try and shoot Beardo in the arm or leg. I could run around to the other side of the truck. Run inside the store. Jump in the passenger's side and hit the locks. Drive away. Shoot the dog. Cry.

I did none of that. I just stood there, trembling and praying Beardo wouldn't shoot me, wishing I were smarter and could think of some way to get myself out of this.

The dog's head shifted suddenly, focused on something behind me.

Oh oh.

Something hard struck the back of my head, the force so strong I collapsed to my knees. My rifle was yanked out of my hands. I wanted to take it back, but my skull felt like liquid fire. Had I been shot? I hadn't heard any gunfire. I tried to yell at Shyla, to wake her up, to warn her. All that came out was a pathetic groan.

Since I seemed to have no control over my body, I decided to die—or at least pretend to. I slumped to my left side, the pavement hot under my cheek, the truck keys an uncomfortable lump under my left hip.

The dog's breath blew hot on my face. His tongue lapped my cheek, my lips.

I didn't move.

"He's out," Beardo said. "Check the truck."

Footsteps scuffed over the pavement. Only one set. I squinted open one eye, saw that Beardo hadn't moved. He was smart. I stayed put, unsure what else to do.

"No keys!" A woman's voice.

Beardo started toward me, gun trained on my head. "Get over here and check his pockets."

I need help, God. Send Zach out. Logan. Anything! I kept my eye slitted as the woman crouched over me. I wished I'd studied Karate or Jujitsu or something that could get me out of this fix. Being a mechanic wasn't much use here.

Hands patted down my right side. If they didn't find the keys, maybe they'd think Zach had taken them inside. Again I willed him to come out here and check on me.

"He's got a radio," the woman said.

"That's no good without another one," Beardo said. "Throw it where he can't reach it."

I heard the radio hit the pavement in the distance and slide to a stop. I should get up and run. The moment the woman had climbed inside the truck, I should have taken off. Too late now.

"No keys," the woman said.

"Roll him and check the other side," Beardo said.

She rolled me. The moment I felt her hands on my pants pocket, I curled into a ball, rolled back.

"Oh, no you don't," Beardo said.

Something hard bashed against my head. Things blurred together as pain spiked through my skull in a new spot. I think I said the word "no" or "stop." Hands were all over me, yet I managed to pull the keys out myself. I thought about trying to swallow them. The key fob was way too big for that. Instead, I threw them as hard as I could.

Beardo cursed, kicked me in the gut, then called his dog to fetch.

For several seconds, I couldn't breathe. Beardo's hard-toe boots had knocked my breath into the store. I wheezed, managed to roll over and scan the parking lot. Everything was a blur.

Behind me, a door slammed. The Tacoma started.

"No." I heard tires roll over pavement. Away from me.

"No!" I turned, saw the blur of a red truck in the distance as it stopped, then shot out onto the road, away from the store.

"Shyla!"

I wanted to get up and stop them. To run into the store. Get help. We had to follow them. But all I could do was lie there, watching, my head pulsing with waves of pain as the truck turned right out of the parking lot. I felt stupid and useless and pathetic. Immovable.

The truck gone, I shifted my eyes to look for the walkie talkie. I spotted it about ten yards away. I pushed onto my knees and elbows and started to crawl. My vision swam, but I made myself keep going. I toppled over once when my eyes shut. That just ticked me off. Stupid body, anyway. Shyla needed me to man up and get to that radio. I pushed myself back to my hands and knees, fought to get one foot under myself, then the other. I staggered a good ten steps or so before stumbling to my knees. I crawled the rest of the way. Pathetic. Too much time had passed. We'd never find the truck. Shyla.

I picked up the radio and rolled onto my side. The case was cracked, but it didn't look broken. Pushing the button brought forth static, so that was a good sign.

"Eli to Zach. They took Shyla! Help me!"

No answer came, so I repeated the call a few more times. I don't know how long I lay there, but eventually I heard my name.

"Eli!"

I opened my eyes. Logan's face appeared over me, looking down.

"What happened? Oh my gosh, the truck!" He took off.

I turned my head to follow him with my gaze and

winced at the throb in my temples.

"Hey." Zach, beside me, frowning into my eyes. "You okay? Where's it hurt?"

I grabbed his arm. "Shyla was in the truck. Help me up. We have to get her back."

14

Zach drove. We left Logan with the girls. He thought he was in charge, but I gave Lizzie her own walkie talkie too, just in case she needed to talk to us.

I had the passenger's window down, Dad's gun between my knees, the barrel pointed at the roof. My head was still throbbing but my alertness was starting to return.

"They've had a bit of a head start," Zach said, driving toward the exit. "How do we decide which way to go?"

"They turned right out of the parking lot," I said. "That's all I saw."

"Better than nothing," Zach said. "What happened, anyway?"

I didn't want to talk. I wanted to run through a forest and scream at the top of my lungs. Maybe burn something or smash something. My eyes scanned the streets as I told Zach about the dog and Beardo and his woman. "I'm sorry," I said. "I wanted to fight back, but I . . . I just couldn't bring myself to shoot him."

"You did the right thing," Zach said.

I replayed the scene in my head, me facing off against Beardo. I shivered.

"You dizzy? Confused about what happened? Nauseous at all?"

My head felt like it was going to implode. "Nah. It just feels like someone drove over my head."

"I'm so sorry, man. We should have listened to you."

Normally I would have loved hearing those words, but they did nothing to console me now.

"I only put one flat of water in the back of the van so you'd have some bottles to drink on the drive. That's all we got now. Everything else was in the truck."

"Don't worry about it," he said. "We'll get more."

I wish I was as confident.

Zach stopped when the road reached Route 66. "Which way, do you think?"

I looked right. I looked left. I had no idea. My gaze locked onto something straight ahead of us. As the street continued on the other side of 66, a line of liquid ran along the right side of the lane. "That line of wetness," I said. "It looks fresh."

"Could the truck be leaking water?" Zach asked.

"I hadn't noticed it before, but could be."

Zach's gaze shifted to mine. His eyebrows lifted. "Let's find out."

We crossed Route 66 and continued on. The water lasted two blocks before disappearing, but at the end of

THIRST

another city block, it picked up again, leading us onward.

"See that water bottle," Zach said. "You don't think . . ."

"I do if it's an Aquafina bottle," I said, recalling moving the three flats into the middle of the back earlier today.

Sure enough, when Zach rolled to a stop, it was an empty Aquafina bottle, lidless and still wet inside.

I sighed as my eyes tracked a new trail of water in the distance.

"You've got to admit, it's clever," Zach said.

"Yeah, it's clever. I just hate to see water going to waste."

"It's not going to waste," Zach said. "It's saving her."

"You're right," I said. Of course he was right.

We followed the water trail for another three bottles, checking each time to make sure they were our brand. Just when the water had finally run dry and Zach and I started to argue about continuing on or turning back to check side streets, I caught sight of something red about twenty yards ahead.

"What's that?" I asked, pointing.

Zach steered toward it, slowing to a stop in the middle of the road. I opened my door and leaned out. Red fabric. The hoodie was instantly familiar, and I snatched it up.

"It's hers," I said, hope welling inside me. "She's left us another clue."

"Smart girl," Zach said. "Now what?"

"Let's follow this road. See what else we find."

Zach hit the gas, but he went slowly, nearly stopping each time we came to another crossing.

About ten blocks down, we passed through an intersection. I spotted an object down the road on the right.

"Hold up," I said. "I thought I saw something on that road we just passed."

Zach stopped, put the van in reverse, and backed up.

Down the road, a shoe lay on the asphalt.

"A shoe," I said.

"I see it." Zach cranked the wheel and turned down the road, slowing as we approached the shoe.

I opened my door and grabbed it. Red lights lit up with the motion and lifted my spirits. "Hers," I said.

We continued down the road. I tried my best to look everywhere. What if I missed a clue? What if we couldn't find her?

The radio crackled. "Logan to Eli, come in. Over."

I grabbed the radio off the dashboard. "This is Eli, over."

"Antônia just arrived. No sign of infection. Over."

Zach scoffed. "As if he knows what to look for."

I pressed the talk button. "That's great news. Over and out." To Zach I said, "I hope he wasn't going to quarantine her."

"Yeah. I love Logan like a brother, but sometimes . . ."

"You want to strangle your brother?"

"Egg-xactly."

The road ended at a T. We hadn't found another clue, so we turned right and drove for a while. After about twenty blocks with no leads, we turned around and tried going the other way. When we found nothing on that end either, we backtracked to the road where we'd found the shoe. Zach drove five miles an hour, and we scoured every driveway.

"This is killing me," I said. "She's got to be here somewhere."

At the intersection, Zach turned around again and headed back to the T in the road. A sound caught my attention, and I perked up.

"Did you hear that?" I rolled down my window.

A small voice cried, "Wait!"

Movement in my side mirror. I twisted in my seat and

peered out the back window. A child with one shoe was running down the middle of the street, coming toward us. I opened the door and got out, holding Dad's gun by the barrel.

"Shyla!"

Her face lit up, and she stopped to jump up and down a few times. In that moment I felt immense relief and joy.

Until Shyla screamed and ran the other way.

"Shyla!" I started after her; movement jarred my aching head. I didn't make two steps before a man ran into the street and scooped Shyla under his arm. A familiar man. Though his back was to me, and though five seconds ago all I would have been able to say to describe him was "older with a bushy beard," I instantly recognized Beardo's green and white plaid shirt, Carhartt pants, and Romeo work boots.

"Hey!" I lifted Dad's rifle to my shoulder and locked Beardo in my sights.

But what was I going to do? He was holding Shy.

At least he wasn't holding a gun.

I could hear the van's tires rolling over the street behind me. I wondered what Zach was doing but didn't dare move.

Beardo turned toward me—Shyla kicking and screaming in his arms, the lights on her shoe flashing. He grinned, recognition crossing his face. "Thought you might come," he said.

"You stole several things that belonged to me," I yelled.

"All I want is the girl."

"How 'bout we trade? You give me that rifle. I give you the kid."

"You already have *my* gun," I said. "This one's my dad's. We built these ourselves. They're more than weapons to me."

"This ain't no time to get sentimental, boy," Beardo

said. "You want the girl or not?"

Before I could answer, the van sped by on my right, heading toward Beardo. He took off, back toward the sidewalk he'd first come from.

Zach hit the brakes so hard the tires squealed, but he was too far past to do much good. I lowered the gun and gave chase, following the man up a potholed driveway to an open garage. He went in. There were no vehicles parked inside—no sign of my truck. I could see Beardo's silhouette stepping over boxes of supplies, then he disappeared through an interior door.

I slowed, glancing down at the boxes as I passed by. I recognized some of my dad's tools, our sleeping bags and tent, Dad's worn survival book. That I picked up and tucked into the back waistband of my pants.

My pulse was a frantic throb, and my head was screaming from where Beardo had hit me, but I kept going. I had to. Though it seemed the most foolish move of my life to step inside this place, I couldn't leave Shyla here.

I crouched low before the open door. I could see a hardwood floor inside. The end of a kitchen table covered in a yellow checkered tablecloth. It seemed off to me that such a man would care about decorating. I peeked both ways. Laundry room to the left. Kitchen to the right. No sign of anyone.

The laundry room looked like a dead end, so when I stepped inside, I turned to the right, toward the kitchen, gun raised, heart beating so hard it was practically in my throat.

What was my plan? I didn't have one. I was an idiot to walk into this house. Beardo could be behind any door, gun ready to blow my head off the moment I came into view.

I crept over the hardwood floor of the kitchen and came to an archway. A quick glance showed a living room on one side and a hallway to the left. Still no sign of anyone.

I peeked out again, and movement caught my eye. Zach, outside the living room window, studying the house from the driveway.

Several thoughts ran through my head in that moment. Run over to the front door and let Zach in. Ignore him to keep him safe? If Zach was out there, who was guarding the van? Did he leave the keys inside the van or were they on him? I couldn't risk letting Beardo steal our other vehicle.

A child's scream from the end of the hall ended my indecision.

"Let go! Help!" Another scream.

"Will you stop it?" This a woman's hissing whisper.

I started down the hallway. I passed an office, a bathroom, and was approaching the next door when Beardo stepped out.

I braced myself to shoot. "I only want the girl," I said.

Beardo lifted his arm. He was holding a 9mm handgun.

"You shoot, you die," I said.

"You too."

We stood there, like two Old West cowboys in a standoff. I didn't want to do this. I didn't want to die here. I didn't want Zach to have to live with that outcome. I didn't want Shyla to forever be separated from Davis.

"Come on . . ." I said. "Just send her out, and I'll leave nice and quietly."

"Put down the gun."

"I'm not stupid," I said.

At this he snorted. "That you're in my house proves just the opposite."

Behind him, a woman emerged from the room. Beardo saw my eyes shift, but before he could glance behind him, the woman struck him with something big and orange. The resounding clunk was dull. I winced.

Beardo collapsed to his knees. He slumped against the

wall and stayed there, like he was praying.

The woman tucked a porcelain cat statue under her arm and waved inside the room with her free hand. "Come on, now. Be quick about it."

Shyla came to the doorway.

I lowered the rifle and held my breath, my gaze bouncing between Shy and Beardo's slack face.

"Take her and go," the woman said, shoving Shyla forward.

Shyla didn't move. She just stared at Beardo, slumped on his knees.

"Come on, Shy." I moved the gun to one hand and reached out with the other.

Shyla pressed back against the opposite side of the hallway, eyes fixed on Beardo. She inched toward me slowly. Too slowly. She wore only one shoe, and with her snail-like movement, the red lights weren't flashing.

I went down on one knee and reached for her. That was all it took. She ran to me, collided against my chest with enough force that I almost fell over. I hugged her with my free arm and used the other to clutch the barrel of Dad's gun like a walking stick.

Shyla started sobbing, deep, jagged breaths in between each cry.

I grabbed her around the legs and stood. "I got you." I carried her down the hall, backwards, not willing to take my eyes off my enemies. As I reached the corner, I met the woman's gaze. "Thank you."

"It wasn't right, keeping her," she said.

I nodded and hurried toward the front door. It was locked and bolted shut, and I had to set down Dad's gun to open it. I managed the feat and got outside, rifle in hand, without anyone chasing us.

I carried Shyla into the road, looking for the van.

"Zach!" I yelled.

"Here!" Zach came running out from behind Beardo's house.

"Where's the van?" I asked.

"There." He pointed across the street to a driveway kitty-cornered from Beardo's place. He ran past us, digging into his pants pocket. I ran after him. I wanted out of here, now, before Beardo woke up and came after us. I didn't want to think what he might do to the woman when he realized what's she'd done. Regret flashed over me that I hadn't asked her to come with us.

Too late now.

Zach jumped into the van and backed it out onto the street. I set Shyla down to wait for him and looked into her eyes. "You okay?"

She rubbed her sleeve along the bottom of her nose, smearing a stream of snot across her cheek, but she nodded and sniffed deeply, her breath starting to slow.

"Let's get you in the van, okay?"

When the van stopped, I buckled her into the seat behind Zach's and climbed in next to her, pulling my dad's survival book from my pocket. "To Tar-zhay, my good man," I told Zach.

"Right-o, boss," he said, hitting the gas.

We were silent for a few blocks, and I perused my dad's old book. So strange to have rescued one small thing from all Beardo had stolen.

I finally asked Shyla, "When did you wake up?"

"People were talking," she said. "I didn't know their voices."

"What were they saying?"

"They were happy they had a lot of water."

I bet they were.

"I got scared. I thought they stolded the truck. I knew

that would make you mad and you'd chase them with your gun." Her eyes flitted to the rifle in my hands.

"You were right."

She smiled, and I was so desperately thankful that she was safe.

"We only found you because you left us a trail," I said.

"Like Hansel and Gretel," she said. "Krista reads me that story sometimes. We have the book at my house. But I didn't have any crumbs."

"But you did have a lot of water."

She grinned. "A very lot."

A very lot that was gone now.

"I poured some out, but then I couldn't reach it so good. So I putted out my coat. And then I putted out my shoe." She frowned. "I sure am gonna miss my shoe."

"We have it," I said. "It's riding up front with Zach and your hoodie."

Another smile. I couldn't get enough of them.

"When did you get out of the truck?" Zach asked.

"After I putted out my shoe. The truck stopped, so I got out and runned away. The man yelled at me, but I runned faster. They tried to find me, but I was hiding in a bush. I didn't come out until I heard you say my name. Then I runned after you."

"You did really good, Shyla." I tugged her pigtail, feeling joy for the first time in the past few days.

Until I remembered what we lost in the truck. All that water. All my tools. My gun. A pang of sorrow shot through me. Lizzie still had her duffle bag of personal possessions, but my gun . . . I loved my gun. I'd built that gun myself.

It was just stuff. It didn't matter. Not like Shyla mattered. She was here now, and I was grateful. But the missing water was a problem, and it was not at all comforting.

15

When we got back to Target, Shyla clung to my arm, so I handed Dad's gun to Zach and carried her inside. The store looked like an earthquake had knocked everything off the shelves. There was so much stuff on the floor, I could barely make out where the aisles were supposed to be. The lack of lights didn't help matters.

A cheer rose up. It looked like everyone had congregated in the cart return area.

Jaylee ran up to me. "Oh my gosh, Eli, are you okay?" The concern on her face warmed my insides.

"I'm fine."

Lizzie hugged me and Shyla at the same time, then

pulled back, sliding her hand to my cheek. "You sure you're okay?"

I nodded.

Davis came running, so I put Shyla down. The boy hugged his sister. Krista hugged her too.

Antônia was standing with Jaylee. She was a short girl, not much taller than Krista, despite being twenty-two. She had moved from Nogales last year to live with her aunt so she could study programming at PVCC. Her English was pretty good, but she sometimes confused her pronouns.

She hugged Zach, then came over and hugged me. "Thanks for waiting for me to come," she said, her Spanish accent thick as always. "It was so scared being on the car by myself."

I could only imagine. "I'm glad you're here," I said, but I was anxious to get going. I raised my voice to address everyone. "Can you all bring your stuff to the parking lot so we can load it? We need to get going."

The group started to move, all except for Antônia. "I think something is wrong with my car. I worried I might not arrive to here. The battery, it hasn't been charging. Last night I was able to put into the tank some gas, but I worry something is broken."

I didn't like the sound of that. "Show me," I said.

I followed her out to the lot. She got in the Prius and started it up. I put one hand on the roof, the other on the top of the open driver's side door, and leaned down to look.

"This light here?" Antônia pointed at the dashboard warning light that was lit up. "I think is bad, that it's lighted up."

Crap. It was bad indeed. This car was well on its way to dead. Which meant we weren't leaving any time soon. "We're going to need another car," I said.

"What's wrong with it?" Zach asked me.

"The battery is toast," I said. "If we take this, it'll die on the road, and we'll be stranded. We won't be able to fix it."

"I thought a Prius could drive without the battery," Lizzie said.

"It *can*," I said, "but it'll be slow."

"So we find a new battery pack," Logan said.

"Finding a new battery is more work than we have time for," I said.

"If we see a Prius, we could just take that one," Logan said.

"That's another 'if' I don't want to deal with," I said.

"So we need a new car," Zach said.

Yes we did. "There are some dealerships on Route 66," I said.

Zach clapped his hands. "Let's do it."

It took a while, but we managed to load all the Target stuff into the two vehicles. There was, thankfully, no sign of Beardo, his woman, or his dog. We had to put some of the bags on the floor of the van because the back was already crammed full, but no one complained. When we finally took off, Zach drove the van. I sat shotgun, holding my dad's gun between my knees, pointed at the roof. Logan sat behind Zach, Davis behind me, watching Logan play on his Switch. In the back Lizzie sat with Shyla. Jaylee and Krista had gone with Antônia in the Prius.

Zach pulled out of the Target lot and went north on Milton Road. I drummed my palms on my knees, which were uncomfortably high since my feet were perched on a stack of Jaylee's feminine products. She certainly had stocked up.

"Well," I said to Zach, "we might not have any water, but at least we have eight years-worth of tampons."

Zach laughed, but Lizzie had, unfortunately, heard me.

"They're not tampons, Eli," she said. "They're maxi

pads. The tampons are back here. Jaylee doesn't like tampons."

"Gah!" Zach said. "Can we talk about something else?"

Lizzie giggled from the back. "Am I making you uncomfortable?"

"Yes," Zach and I said together.

Zach steered the van onto I-40. "Okay, so what's the plan?" he asked me.

Why did I have to be the one with a plan? I'd had a plan. No Target. But no one had listened. I'd never wanted to be in charge, anyway. Zach is the one people listen to. Zach should be in charge.

I stared out the window. "People listen to you, Zach. You need to be our leader."

"I'm not leadership material."

"You are too."

Zach snorted. "No, I'm the heavy. I'm the guy who gets behind a good cause and makes it happen. And I'm an entertainer—a performer. But I'm no idea person. I don't have a clue what to do. You've always been the smart one. If this group is going to live, it's going to be because of you."

Zach had never said anything like that to me in my entire life. I'd had no idea he thought of me as smart or a leader of any kind. "But I didn't want to go to Target."

"And you were right. And I should have backed you up. We can't let the girls play us," Zach whispered with a quick glance in the rearview mirror. "We're going to have to be smarter than that. I know they're looking to us to lead—at least Lizzie is."

I doubted any of them wanted us to lead. Girls liked being in charge. "We should take a vote. Make sure that's what they want."

"Maybe. But first we need to get you some new wheels. What are your thoughts on that?"

"A truck," I said. "Maybe a Ford Ranger—something with good gas mileage. We also need some supplies. I had almost everything in the back of the truck. The tents, the tools, the gas can . . . This sucks."

"So we get to go shopping. And everything is free. It's going to be awesome!"

Zach was being a little too perky, which bugged me because I knew he was only doing it to compensate for my bad mood.

Zach drove to Jim Robert's Used Cars just a few blocks away from the destroyed Downtown Diner. It had only been a day, but I was on guard for those thugs who'd taken a baseball bat to Riggs's Evoque. The dealership reminded me of an Altoids box, flat and low with red trim around the top and solid gold windows in the front—the kind that looked like mirrors. You could see out of them but you couldn't see in. For some reason, this place had survived the looting. Apparently no one had been too keen on free cars when there was water and food to stock up on.

The building sat in the center of a scummy slab of old pavement filled with shiny cars and trucks with colorful writing on every windshield that said things like, "Low Miles!" "Loaded!" "Big Savings!" "Gas Saver!" or "Drive Today!" Zach pulled into the lot and parked in the back of the building.

I turned in my seat and addressed everyone. "Listen up. Wait in the van. I'm going to go find us a new truck. Keep the doors locked and your voices down, okay?"

"Yes, Papa Eli," Lizzie said.

Shyla giggled.

I rolled my eyes and clipped an extra walkie talkie to my belt. "If anyone comes around, drive away," I told Zach. "We'll meet up at the Conoco on the outskirts of town." I got out of the van, my dad's rifle in hand, and called over my shoulder. "Logan, you're with me."

Logan whooped.

I walked around to the front of the dealership, Logan beside me. I scanned the lot, looking for the best truck. There was a 2008 Ford Ranger, royal blue with two fat white racing stripes running down the hood and over the cab like the stripes on a skunk. "That's pretty sweet," I told Logan.

"Check out that convertible," Logan said.

"No convertibles, man. We need a truck. Preferably one with an extended cab and a camper on back to hide our stuff."

There was one Tacoma, silver, but it had been converted to big wheels, so that would mess with the gas mileage. There was a shiny black Nissan Frontier that I would happily make my own if I wasn't looking for better camouflage. Black wasn't bad, but I preferred green or brown.

I felt better, having a mission. I still tried not to think about my stolen truck and all our gear. We passed by a yellow Dodge Dakota and a white Dodge Ram. "No and no," I said. "Too much gas." I also ixnayed a Subaru Baja and a Chevy Suburban.

"Ohhhh," I moaned when I saw the 2010 Suzuki Equator that had been painted in flat army green paint. "That's my girl right there." Plus it had an extended cab, four doors, and a hard folding bed cover on the back that would keep people from knowing what we had.

"Why that one?" Logan asked.

"So we can park in the trees and no one will see us."

"What about when it snows?"

"It's July, Logan. We'll worry about snow later, okay?"

"I like the Tacoma better," Logan said. "What if we have to drive up a rocky hill?"

"Why would we? And even if we did, the Suzuki would

make it. No on the big wheels. The black Nissan is my second choice. Let's go find us some keys."

We crossed the lot to the dealership's entrance. The mirrored windows along the front of the building also had colorful writing on them, the way old supermarkets used to advertise. Now that I was closer, I saw that several of the windows *had* been busted up, making it hard to read what some of them had said. The front glass doors had been broken too, but the window to the left was still intact. Neon orange and green writing proclaimed, "Guaranteed Financing Available."

"Free is my kind of financing," I said, carefully wedging myself through the jagged hole in one of the doors.

Logan followed, creeping along beside me like some kind of cartoon ninja. I ignored him lest I receive a lecture on what he was doing and why.

The keys would likely be kept in a safe or lock box in an office. We passed by a cluster of cubicles, peeked into a few offices, and headed for the big office at the end of the hall. The door was halfway opened, but the name Jim Robert on the nameplate seemed like a good sign.

Then I heard a noise. I held up my hand and stopped, then trained the gun on the open door. A shadow moved inside.

Oh, come on! Couldn't we catch a break? I was just about to urge Logan into one of the smaller offices to hide when the door swung in and someone ran out.

16

It was a young woman. Asian, maybe. She stopped when she saw me, her face a pale mask of shock. Her hair was black, long and straight and very tangled. She was wearing a filthy white tank top and a pair of short jeans, the kind that end midway between a girl's knee and ankle. I can never remember what Lizzie calls them. This girl was also barefoot and wore a silver toe ring.

All this I noticed in the space of a breath.

"Please don't shoot," she said, her English perfect.

I lowered the rifle. "I'm not going to—"

She ran, sprinting past Logan and me as if her life depended on it.

"Wait!" I called after her. "We're not going to hurt you." But she had already slipped out the jagged opening in the door and was running across the parking lot toward a silver Honda Civic.

"Good gas mileage," I said.

"Dude!" Logan called from inside Jim Robert's office. "She found the keys for us!"

I joined Logan in the office. He was looking into a narrow cabinet filled with rows and rows of hooks with keys on them. Jackpot.

"You think she picked the lock?" I asked.

"Of course she did," Logan said. "She's probably a ninja."

"That's racist," I said.

"No, it's cool," Logan answered.

Ninjas *were* cool. "Since when is lock-picking a ninja skill?"

"Lock-picking is stealth," Logan said. "Ninjas are stealth."

"You're a nut job. Look for the Suzuki so we can get out of here."

• • •

I found the key. Logan was too busy trying to decipher the code of how the keys were organized. I just searched for the word Suzuki.

On our way out, I found a mini fridge that likely once had been stocked with beverages to offer customers. It had already been raided, though. I also found a phone book on one of the desks in the cubicle area. I didn't like being out on the main strip. If we could find someplace to lay low, we could make some lists and find some smaller stores to gather supplies before we headed north. There weren't many cities where we were headed, so it would be nice to really think about what we needed before leaving Flagstaff for good.

Inside the cab of the Suzuki felt like sitting in a kiln. I tossed the phone book on the seat between Logan and me, peeled off my hoodie, and tossed it in the back seat. Much better. I started her up. Sounded like a good engine. Sadly, my new wheels were already running on empty.

I might have to try out my siphon hose and see how it worked, though I bet I could make it to a hardware store. I'd much rather find a shake siphon. I really didn't want a mouthful of gasoline.

I drove around back where Zach and Antônia were parked. I pulled up alongside the van facing the opposite direction so that my driver's side window paralleled his. "We nabbed a phone book from the dealership. Going to look for a hardware store."

"This says there's a hardware store just up the road," Logan said, phone book in hand.

"I kind of wanted to get off the strip," I told him. "We'll drive that way, but keep looking for something bigger and off the main road." I looked back out my window at Zach. "We're going to head out of town and check out a hardware store."

"You got it, boss," Zach said. "Sweet ride, by the way."

"Thanks." I drove around the dealership and back out to the main road. Zach pulled out after me. Antônia followed. It wasn't even a full mile until we reached what turned out to be a gas station with a combo garage and hardware store. It was smaller than I wanted.

I coasted to a stop by the building and looked to Logan. "How about an Ace or a True Value or Lowe's or something like that?" I was just about to drive around to the back of the gas station to get out of sight of the main road when I saw the silver Honda Civic parked at a pump closest to the gas station building. The words "Low Gas Mileage" were scrawled on its windshield in neon orange and white paint. The driver's door was hanging open, and a gas nozzle was sticking out of the tank. No sign of Logan's ninja lock pick girl.

Could the gas be working at that pump? Because if it was, I wanted some too. I put the truck in drive and steered around to a pump on the other side of the Honda. The display board was dark. No gas. So where'd the girl go?

The chains coiled around the door handles on the store ended that train of thought. None of the windows had been broken yet. I rolled just past the station so I could look down the side. Sure enough, there was an open door on the garage end.

The walkie talkie fizzled. "This is Lizzie. Zach wants to know what you're doing."

Logan dropped the phone book and fumbled for the walkie talkie. "This is Transport One. Hold for an answer. Over." Logan looked to me. "What are we doing?"

"Hold on a second." I put the truck in park and got out. "Lock yourself in," I said. "I'll be right back."

I shut the door and jogged toward the station. I couldn't stop thinking about what Antônia had said about being alone. It seemed the right thing to do to at least talk to the girl.

I slowed as I stepped inside the building. "Hello?"

A clunk. The brightness of outside made it hard to see. I suddenly felt stupid. I'd left Dad's gun in the truck with Logan.

I inched forward, blinking my eyes into focus. I could now see the store in shadows. The windows up front let in plenty of light.

"Uhm . . . My name's Eli. My friends and I are headed north. We think there might be safe water up there. If you're alone, you're welcome to join us."

"That's very kind."

I jolted. That was a man's voice. I looked toward the source, and sure enough, there stood a guy, mid-twenties, maybe. He was as big as Zach, thinner, but by no means skinny. He wore slacks, dress shoes, and a striped button front shirt. No tie, but he looked like the type to normally wear one.

"Hey," I said.

"Expecting someone else?"

I didn't like his tone. Then I saw her. The girl from the dealership. She was crouching behind a display of potato chips, staring at me, her eyes wide and desperate. She put her index finger to her lips. Oh-kay. I glanced away, confused. Was she scared of this guy?

"No," I said. "I just saw someone come in and thought I'd check on them and see . . ." I swallowed.

"You saw *me* come in?"

"I saw someone."

"A woman?"

"Uh . . . I'm not sure. Anyway." I turned and headed for the door out.

"Hey, wait up, kid," the guy said, hurrying toward me. "Tell me more about this place you're going."

Something about this guy weirded me out, and I continued toward the exit. "It's in Kingman," I said, which was the opposite way we were headed.

"Check this out. You ever seen one of these?" He walked past me, past the side door, toward the back of the store. Curious, I followed, trying to see what he was reaching for.

I was almost to him when he spun on me, swinging a long piece of metal at my face. It hit me so hard I collapsed.

My cheek was on fire, and my head pulsed with fear and

warnings to get up and get out. I rolled to my front, but before I could stand, a foot kicked my side, which sent me skidding across the concrete floor. Again the guy was on me before I could move, rolling me over. He was holding one of those metal rods used for steering wheels, to keep people from stealing your car. He pressed it against my throat. I turned my head, which only helped a little.

"You can't have her, do you hear me?" he said, his eyes wild, a vein pulsing at his temple. "She's mine!"

17

I assumed he was talking about the girl, who had clearly been hiding from this psycho for good reason. I had no desire to die for being a good Samaritan, though, so I reached for his face, remembering what my dad said to do if I ever found myself defenseless. Before I got up the nerve to stick my thumb in his eye socket, a loud thunk made his eyes roll up into his head. He collapsed on top of me. Above us stood the girl, holding a huge bottle of brown glass. She dropped it, and it rolled noisily across the concrete. She grabbed my attacker's arm and pulled. I set to work helping her, and together, we rolled the guy off me. She extended her hand, which I took, and she hoisted me to my feet.

"Let's go," she said.

She didn't have to tell me twice. We ran out the door. She went around to the front, then stopped.

"He took my keys," she said.

"You can come with me," I said. "There are nine of us."

She stared at me, her eyes the same shade of brown as the bottle she'd used to rescue me. "Okay," she said.

Okay.

I led her around front to where I'd parked. The locks clicked as we approached the Suzuki. Logan unlocking the rig from inside. I opened the driver's door. As the girl reached for the back door, I noticed a ring on her left hand. A massive, glittering diamond. She was married? She looked like a high schooler.

I got in, clicked the locks, and took off, my face and throat still throbbing.

"What happened to you?" Logan asked.

"I fell," I said, scanning the parking lot for Zach. There. He was rolling toward me, so we were good. I pulled out onto the main road and hit the gas.

"Hi," Logan said over the seat. "I'm Logan. This is Eli."

"Hannah," she said.

"Nice to meet you," Logan said.

The radio fizzled. "Eli, do you need assistance?" Lizzie. Still worried.

I glanced out the rearview mirror. No sign of anyone but Zach and Antônia following me.

I stopped where the road met Route 66 and rolled down my window. I reached out and waved Zach to come up alongside. "Logan, did you find me that hardware store?"

"Yeah," he said, reaching for the phone book that was up on the dash. He paged through it. "Ace Hardware is on 1763 East Butler Avenue."

I blew out a breath. So not helpful. "Is there a map?"

"A funny one."

I reached over. "Give it."

"You don't have to be so grouchy." Logan passed me the book.

"Sorry." I was suddenly very aware of two things: how much my face and neck hurt and the fact that my hands were shaking.

"Eli?" Lizzie was in the passenger's seat of the van, looking up at me.

"Picked up a hitchhiker." I pointed my thumb behind me.

Lizzie waved. "Welcome! I'm Lizzie."

"Hannah," the girl yelled out my window.

I looked at the map. "Okay, it's on the other side of the tracks. Off the main strip." I hoped that meant it might have missed the looting. I tossed the book on the seat between me and Logan, then told Lizzie, "I'm heading to Ace. Follow me."

I whipped the truck out onto Route 66. About a half-mile later, I took a right. I kept a close eye in my rearview, relieved when Zach and Antônia followed.

Now that I had a plan, I relaxed a bit, though my adrenaline was still pumping from my encounter with that guy and his wand of death.

I glanced at Hannah. She was sitting in the middle of the back seat, her hands gripping the top of the front bench. She had a fancy manicure job, the kind with the glossy white tips and that ring with the massive diamond. I wanted to ask about her husband or fiancé or whatever, but I didn't want to risk making her cry.

"Hannah," I said, "I'm sorry about the Honda."

"I don't need it," she said. "As long as I can come with you guys."

"Yeah," I said. "I, uh . . . I lied. We're actually headed to Colorado."

"I'm glad you lied. What's in Colorado?"

"We think there might be safe water there."

She crossed her arms on the seat back and rested her chin on her hands. "What makes you think that?"

"We were there when the comet passed. And we're alive, so we thought . . ." I shrugged.

"Comet?"

"Comet Pulon," Logan said. "It's been in the news and everything."

"Right." She nodded to herself. "I remember hearing something about that."

I took another right. "Are you from Flagstaff?" I asked.

She shook her head. "San Francisco."

"Long way from home."

When she didn't answer, I glanced at her. A tear had escaped and rolled down her cheek. It clung to the edge of her jawline, dangling. "I don't want to talk about it," she said.

"No problem. If you want to get back to San Fran, I'm hoping to gather some stuff at Ace that will help me get gas. We can find you another car, fill it up. Teach you how to find your own gas. Gas stations are useless without power, so you need to siphon gas from other vehicles."

"Okay, thanks," she said.

"Sure, but, uh . . . you really got to be careful. We came from Phoenix. The cities aren't safe."

"Lots of places were on fire," Logan said. "And people are killing each other for water."

"We didn't actually see anyone get killed for water," I said.

"Krista told me she did," Logan said.

Whoa. "Um . . . Well, that's one of the reasons I wanted

to get us away from the metro areas, for a while, at least. My guess is that San Fran will be pretty bad too."

Her brow wrinkled. "This water problem is nationwide?"

"Worldwide, from what I could gather."

"And a lot of people are dead?"

"Almost everyone, I think," I said.

"You just passed Ace," Logan said.

I flipped a U-Turn in the road and drove into the parking lot. To my delight, all the front windows were intact. "Looks like no one's gotten to Ace yet."

"How can that be?" Logan asked.

I didn't know. "It's kind of a long drive off the beaten path," I said. "On the opposite side of the train tracks. This is an industrial area. There are no houses. No other stores."

"You think people forgot about it?"

"Seems unlikely, yet here it is, looking like a shiny penny, head side up." I didn't even see any bottled water warnings.

I wasn't making the mistake of parking out in front of the store again. This time I drove around back to the loading dock. Two garage-style doors were closed. I got out to inspect them, pulled at one of the handles.

It slid up a couple feet.

Ha! I waved Zach to come help, and Logan came too. The three of us managed to slide one of the garage doors up enough to walk under. Inside was a small bay. Big enough for four small trucks, side-by side. Maybe two semi trucks.

I climbed back in the truck and backed inside. Zach did the same, parking right beside me. Antônia pulled her Prius in front first.

"Bat cave exit," Logan said when I got out.

"Right you are, Logan." If anything went wrong, I'd be able to shoot out of here without needing to back out or turn around. I caught sight of Hannah, standing on the outskirts of the group, arms crossed. She looked cold, even though it was far from cold, in my opinion.

"You can borrow my sweatshirt if you want," I said. "It's in the back seat somewhere."

"Thanks." She went back to the truck.

"I should have thought of that," Logan whispered. "Of giving her my shirt."

"You're only wearing a T-shirt," I said.

"So? She's gorgeous. I'd go shirtless for her. How old do you think she is?"

"No idea."

Zach and Logan helped me pull down the garage door, which made it very dark inside the loading bay. I found a flashlight in the van and flicked it on. Hannah returned wearing my sweatshirt. It was black with the Phoenix Suns logo on the front. I made quick introductions to the others.

"Eli, sweetie, what happened to your face?" Lizzie asked.

"Brandon," Hannah said.

Surprise rippled through me. "You knew him?" I asked.

"He's my . . ." She paused, glanced at her hand and the huge ring. "He was my fiancé."

Logan whistled low. I glared at him. He didn't even know what had happened in that store. What was he whistling about?

"He attacked Eli," Hannah said. "He was worried I'd leave with him."

"Apparently he was right," Logan said.

"You wanted to get away from your fiancé?" Lizzie asked.

Hannah nodded. "He's not . . . safe."

That was an understatement.

"Then I'm glad my brother was able to help you,"

Lizzie said, giving me a side hug. "He's good at helping people."

I laughed. "Actually, Hannah helped me more than I helped her."

Hannah's eyes pinned me. "We helped each other."

Everyone was staring, which made my face all hot. "Okay, let's go shopping."

"I'll wait in the car," Krista said. "I don't like shopping at hardware stores."

"No way," I said. "Everybody does their share. The stuff we get here is going to keep us alive. You need to know what that stuff is. Because if we get separated, you're going to need to be able to find your own stuff."

Krista rolled her eyes. "Yes, *Dad*."

"No, he's Papa Eli," Lizzie said, winking.

I ignored my sister and climbed up on the loading dock, feeling a bit on edge. I didn't like conflict, and there had been way too much of it today. I'd been assaulted, twice. My truck had been stolen. I'd almost lost Shyla. And now we'd added yet another mouth to feed to our group. It had been the right thing to do, but the dynamics facing us stressed me out.

I found the way inside. All that separated us from the store inside were a set of rubber swinging doors. "Zach, what say you and I go in and make sure the place is safe?"

"Sounds good," he said.

I grabbed Dad's rifle, and we went in. The familiar smell of rubber and metal made me grin. Sporting goods stores were my favorite, but this was close enough.

We stopped just to listen. Didn't hear a sound but for the low voices of our group out back. We teamed up and gave the place a quick search. It wasn't all that big of a store, so we made good time. Didn't find anyone.

"This place is pristine," Zach said.

"It's ours," I said.

We went back for the others, and I divvied us up.

"Okay, let's see . . . Lizzie, Antônia, Krista, and Jaylee, head over to the outdoor section, maybe power equipment? Something like that. See if you can find a portable generator. Something small with a lot of watts. And wheels, if you can find one with wheels. Also, get some extension cords and some outdoor lights, lightbulbs for them. And maybe a small charcoal grill and some charcoal. If there's any kind of camping dishes and flatware and cups—"

"We should probably get paper plates that we won't have to clean," Lizzie said, "since we don't have water to wash them."

"Yes, good point," I said. "Be smart. Think compact. Zach, you and Logan and Davis see if you can find a way to lock that garage door. It would be nice not to have to worry about the vehicles. After that, go to tools and get whatever you think we'll need." As people peeled into two groups, Shyla and Hannah remained. Guess I hadn't really thought that through. "Shyla and Hannah, you come with me and help me find some other stuff."

"What stuff?" Hannah asked.

"I'll know it when I see it. You should look for some socks and shoes. I don't think they sell shoes here but they might have some rubber boots."

"Let's hope they have something," Hannah said.

I clapped my hands. "Okay, let's do this. Get carts in the front and fill them up. Yell if you need help."

I led the way.

"It stinks in here," Jaylee said.

"Are you kidding?" I said. "That is the smell of opportunity."

I led the girls to the front of the store and stopped by the registers. The coolers were off, but they were full of bottled water and sodas, energy drinks, and iced coffee. There were snack racks too, endless amounts of candy bars and bags of chips, beef jerky, and gum.

"Oh, my gosh!" Jaylee, already pulling an iced coffee out of one of the coolers. "Eli? Can I drink this? Or are you going to get mad at me?"

I fought back a smile. "Drink up, Jaylee. Tonight, we feast."

Everyone cheered. I grabbed a Snickers bar and downed it in two bites. I hadn't realized just how hungry I'd been. Considering I'd gotten up at three this morning, it was little wonder.

I grabbed a handful of assorted candy bars and beef jerky and threw them into a cart. I headed for the hardware department. Shyla slid between me and the front of the cart, stepped up onto the bottom rack and wrapped her arm over the top to hold on. She had a Butterfinger in one hand.

Wheels rolled over the tile floor behind me, and I turned and saw Hannah on my heels, pushing a cart of her own. The child seat of her cart was filled with packs of peanuts and cashews. Interesting. She reached up to an impulse display of batteries and pulled down several packs. She raised her eyebrows. "Yes?"

I nodded, noticing how she'd bunched up the sleeves of my sweatshirt around her wrists. I'd never seen a girl wear my clothes before—except Lizzie. It made me feel cool.

I weaved through the aisles. We found four large gas cans and two smaller ones, a half-dozen shaker siphons and some hand pump siphons. I took everything they had and also grabbed several packages of vinyl hose. I figured these were going to be one of our most valuable commodities as long as we were still using gasoline.

"So," I said to Hannah, "are you in college?"

"I was supposed to start my second year of med school

this fall."

"Really." Med student. Bet she knew more first aid than Zach the lifeguard. "So that makes you . . ." I did the mental math. "Twenty-three? Twenty-four?"

"Twenty. I graduated high school with an associate's degree. Two more years to earn my bachelors."

Dang.

"I finished kindergarten," Shyla said.

"Well, Zach will be thrilled," I said. "He's a lifeguard and the closest thing we had to a doctor until now."

"I actually don't know that I'll stay with you guys."

"Oh. Right. I know. I just mean . . . Hey, look. Matches. We should take them all."

Hannah and I gathered the matches, and I tried not to feel like a total klutz around her. I don't know why, but everything I said, every move I made . . . it all felt awkward, like I was on a stage and the only person in the audience was Hannah. The weirdest part? It was also giving me a rush. I had this strange desire to impress her even though I knew it was impossible. I mean, she was a med student, for crying out loud. Like she'd really care about anything I had to say.

We found flashlights, more batteries, three big tents, two easy ups, nine sleeping bags—Shyla picked one with Toy Story pictures all over it—a half-dozen tarps, a bunch of fleece pullovers, rain gear, canteens, a few camping chairs, a variety of knives, a couple axes, and a small chainsaw. We went down the gardening row and I took every package of seeds they had, flowers too. We'd need pollinators for a healthy garden. I wished we could take the bags of soil, but we didn't have room.

Hannah found some garden shoes with flowers on them. She also grabbed a pair of rain boots. Heat retaining socks were the best she could find for socks. They'd be too warm for everyday use.

We wandered into the fishing area. "Do you think we could eat fish that live in contaminated water?" I asked.

"I wouldn't," Hannah said.

I pushed past the fishing poles . . . and that's where we ran into Zach and Logan at a glass counter filled with weapons. Guns, crossbows, knives. The place was loaded.

"Guns in an Ace Hardware store?" I'd never seen that before.

"If they're independently owned, they can stock what they want," Logan said.

I rubbed my forehead, not liking the gleam in Logan's eyes as he drooled over the rifles. "Okay, let's get all the shells they have for Dad's 30.06. Some of those knives. Ooh, a crossbow might be handy too. But I don't think it's a good idea for us all to have a gun. We need to do a gun training first, or something."

"Yeah, I'm with you on that," Zach said. "But we might not have another chance at weapons like this."

He was right. "Okay, grab the smallest gun safe they have and we'll fill it up, but it stays locked and I keep the key. Once we settle somewhere, I'll make sure everyone learns how to hunt their dinner."

"Eat meat?" Hannah said.

"Sure, if you want to live. Canned food is only going to last so long."

"If you can't eat fish that live in contaminated water, I wouldn't eat animals who drink it, either," Hannah said.

I hadn't thought about that. "Well, hopefully we're going to a place where the water is safe. And safe water would mean uncontaminated animals to hunt." I grinned.

"Then uncontaminated fish too."

"Oh, yeah. Maybe I should go back for a fishing pole."

Her brows wrinkled together. "It's really that bad?"

"Totally," Logan said. "This is an apocalypse."

She practiced flicking it open. "I can't believe a knife costs three hundred dollars," she said.

"Quality materials," I said. "A thirty dollar knife is practically disposable."

Zach and I locked the gun safe and carried it to the loading bay. Next we hauled out the generator the girls had chosen. I tried my new shake siphon and easily withdrew enough gas from the truck to get the generator started. Then I plugged in the extension cord and the lights the girls had found, and *voila*. We could now see in the loading bay.

Zach and I transferred the contents of the Prius into my new truck. I found a gun rack and installed it as well. I also filled the truck with goodies. Flashlights and windshield scrapers in the glove box. Some oil, a jack, and some other tools in the storage spaces under the back seat. By the time we had everything loaded, we didn't have much space left, and I still wanted to take along every edible item in this place. I supposed there was always the cab or the back row of the minivan.

No more picking up strays.

By the time we'd finished loading the vehicles, it was after eight o'clock. We were dead on our feet.

"Let's sleep here tonight," I said. "Get up early and get out of town before any of the locals wake up." Like Beardo. Those who lived here would eventually scavenge every store in town, and I didn't want to be here when any of them came sniffing around.

No one objected to my plan, so we rolled out some more sleeping bags, lit an oil lamp, and had a dinner of beef jerky, candy bars, chips, and soda courtesy of the checkout aisles. Zach got out his guitar and played some songs. He started with classics like "Sweet Home Alabama," "Free Falling," and "Don't Stop Believing," then starting taking requests from the girls, which was when it turned into a T

18

"Logan, come on." I glared at him and sent him to find some rope and twine.

Once he was gone, Zach and I packed a gun safe with weapons and ammo.

"Can I take one of these knives?" Hannah asked, pointing to the pocket knives under the glass.

"Sure," I said. Even Logan had a nifty Swiss Army knife in his pack.

She chose a lightweight folding pocket knife with an orange handle and a 4-inch blade.

I whistled. "Good choice. That'll cut twine *and* gut a fish."

Swift marathon. With the girls singing along, everyone looked so happy. It kind of annoyed me how Jaylee cozied up to Zach, gazing at him and singing like he was some kind of rock star. Zach was my best friend, but it didn't seem fair that some guys seemed to get all the best traits—looks, height, muscles, singing voice—while the rest of us were just plain ordinary.

Hannah found me and returned my sweatshirt. She now wore a royal blue one that said "Flagstaff" on the front. She'd also pulled on a pair of red and black plaid knee-high heat retainer socks that she somehow made look cute.

She'd managed to put together a first aid kit and insisted on putting some kind of cream on my face. I had no idea what I looked like, but my cheek right was swollen and tender to the touch. I didn't see any reason to resist, and while I could hardly breathe while she was touching me, it was a pleasant hormone-induced kind of asphyxia.

Lizzie requested "My Lighthouse" by Rend Collective, and the words felt like they'd been written for what we were going through. Plus, with the song being so upbeat, it actually made me feel better, encouraged me, like we might actually survive this thing.

After that Zach was in full-on church mode. He played a half dozen songs, and I was with him until he started singing "Just Be Held" by Casting Crowns and the words shook me.

Life, hitting me out of nowhere. People needing me to be strong. Holding it all together. The melody and words wound their way around my heart and squeezed. Too hard. Lizzie started singing harmony with Zach on the chorus. They sounded good. Really good. I knew Lizzie could sing, but I'd never heard her sound like that.

As they repeated the chorus, and the words said things weren't falling apart but into place, I walked away.

I just couldn't do it. I couldn't stand around singing and pretending this HydroFlu horror was meant to be. I paced the aisles. I acted like I was looking for something, but I'd already scoured this store. There was nothing else I wanted here. Nothing but answers. And, like the song said, those were far away.

The song finally ended, and this time, Zach didn't start another one. I wondered if they'd seen me leave. I hope I hadn't ruined everyone's good time.

Lizzie found me on the fishing aisle. "Thinking about taking a pole along?" she asked.

I shook my head. "Hannah thinks the fish are probably contaminated."

"That was really great how you helped her today," Lizzie said.

I scoffed. "I almost got myself killed."

"It was good, Eli. You're so thoughtful and kind and—"

"Don't start." Lizzie was always telling everyone all the nice things. I wasn't in the mood.

"What's wrong?" she asked.

I glared at her. "Are you kidding me?"

"No. I'm not."

"I can't just stand around singing those songs and act like God cares about us."

"Of course he cares," she said.

"He wouldn't have let this happen if he did."

"How do you know?"

"It's obvious."

"Eli, remember when you got mad at me for trying to tell you what was wrong with that robot car you built?"

"That's different."

"Is it?"

We stared at each other. The thing is, I grew up in the same family and church as Lizzie, so I knew her arguments.

Philosophical debates with my sister never went well for me.

A voice from behind us said, "I think it's end times."

Lizzie and I both jumped.

"Logan!" Lizzie said, hand against her heart.

"You know, from Revelation?" he said. "It has to be. It's the only thing that makes sense."

"The thing with the rapture." Lizzie and I had been over this.

"Only one interpretation believes in a rapture," Logan said. "Personally, I don't buy it."

"Kind of grim to talk end times in the middle of the night, isn't it?" Zach asked, as he, Hannah, and Jaylee joined us. Jaylee had put her hair up in an adorable ponytail.

"Aren't Christians supposed to get taken to heaven before the bad stuff happens?" Jaylee asked, wrapping her hands around Zach's upper arm. As if *my* arm wasn't good enough for hanging on.

I tried to ignore it and said, "Logan was just saying he doesn't believe in that."

"I subscribe to the amillennial view," Logan said. "I believe that since Jesus's time, Satan has been free to wreak havoc on earth. But it all culminates in a big battle where the Antichrist and his allies destroy the church. I think this fits."

"You think HydroFlu is the great battle of Armageddon?" Zach asked.

"Why not?" Logan asked. "It's not like anyone expected."

"I don't think so," Hannah said.

"It makes more sense than the rapture thing," I said. "Because while I could buy God leaving me and Logan behind, there's no way my dad and Lizzie and Zach would miss the rapture."

"Hey!" Logan said.

I grinned at him. "Just kidding, man." Though kind of

not really.

"No one can know the mind of God," Lizzie said. "Nor can we stand here and determine what God's plan is in all this. All we know for sure is that since we're still here, he's not finished with us yet."

She made it sound so easy. I glanced at our group and found Hannah watching me, which made heat creep up the back of my neck. I tried to smile, but I think it came out a little thin.

"So, I was wondering," Hannah said. "Should we pack up the rest of the snacks and candy and take it with us?"

"That's a big yes," Zach said. "I'll grab some more boxes from the back."

Zach returned with boxes. Krista and the kids were asleep, so we tried to be quiet as we gathered anything edible we could find.

"What will we do when we can't scavenge food anymore?" Jaylee asked.

"We'll hunt and grow our own food," I said.

"Unless rain water is bad too," Hannah said.

"True," I said, though I sure hoped it wouldn't be. I was counting on collecting rain water as one of the ways we'd survive. "It would be great if we could find some food production plants. There's probably none in Arizona or even Colorado, but if we could find one, that would be the perfect place to stock up on canned goods."

"Or chips," Zach said, crunching down on a Dorito.

"We can't live off chips for the rest of our lives," I said.

"Heck yes, we can," Zach said. "Chips are awesome."

"Agreed," Jaylee said, reaching into his bag and helping herself.

I didn't like how Jaylee had latched onto Zach ever since we'd gotten the news about Erin. I tried not to think about what it might mean.

"Anyway," I said, wanting to get everyone back on topic, "as we scavenge in the future, check canned goods labels for addresses. Maybe there will be a production plant close enough to drive to."

Jaylee's forehead scrunched in the cutest way. "I'm sure things will get better eventually. Once the government figures things out."

I had a feeling there was no government left. I didn't want to upset her, though. "Until they do, we need to be ready. Got it?"

"Yes, Papa Eli," Lizzie said, smirking my way.

Realization dawned on me that I had taken over. I hadn't meant to. I hadn't even wanted to. Zach was supposed to be the leader. "Look, does anyone have a problem with me making plans? I mean, I don't have to. Antônia is oldest. Then Zach, and he—"

"Dude, you da man, boss," Zach said. "I'd die without you."

"Yeah, Eli," Logan said. "You complete me."

I rolled my eyes. "All joking aside, guys."

"I don't know what to do," Antônia said. "But you, Eli, you have a way to—How do you say?—A *instinct* to survive."

"You're the smartest guy I know," Lizzie said.

"Hannah's in med school," I said.

"Yeah," Hannah said. "You probably can't name all the parts of the musculoskeletal system or tell me the Krebs cycle, so . . . If any of you get hurt, I'll do my best to help you live, but that's where my knowledge ends. I didn't even know you could buy a portable generator. For surviving this thing, I'm sticking with you, Eli."

I lowered my head and fought the urge to smile. That Hannah so quickly believed in me after only knowing me for a few hours felt really good.

"Not to be contrary," Jaylee said, "but surviving in the wild is not that difficult, really. I mean, we just camped in the woods for two weeks. We all know what to do."

"Yet when you had the chance to gather supplies at Target, you chose nothing but makeup and tampons," Lizzie said.

"And you used three bottles of water to make a pot of coffee that you totally wasted," Zach said.

"Hey!" Jaylee pouted and shoved Zach's arm, her ponytail swinging with the effort. "I didn't waste it. I drank the whole thing."

"Only because Eli told me to put it in a thermos," Logan said.

Jaylee rolled her eyes. "I'm just saying—and no offense, Eli, but—why do we have to pick a leader? Why can't we just do our own thing and help each other when we need help?"

That Jaylee was the only one speaking out against me as a leader stung.

"We're a team," Zach said. "We go our own way, we die. Everybody does their share in this group."

Jaylee had the decency to look embarrassed. "Fine." She shrugged and looked at me. "Should I call you Mr. President?"

"No," I said, flustered. "Everyone calls me Eli. And I need help, okay? I'm just making this up as I go, so . . ."

"It's settled then," Zach said. "Eli's in charge. And I'm his enforcer. *Capiche*?"

"Great," Jaylee said, deadpan. "I'm going to bed."

Eventually, we all followed suit.

I slept hard but woke to the sound of someone crying. A girl. Dawn had already started to creep in the windows at the front of the store. I could see forms around me, dead to the world except for whoever was crying. I lay there listening to the sad sound coupled with Logan's snore. A low voice caught my attention. I strained to hear, wondering if the voice was something to worry about, hoping no one was outside planning to break a window.

Then someone giggled. The low voice answered. I sat up, scanning the dark forms around me to see who was missing. It was impossible to tell.

I thought about flipping on my flashlight, but that would give me away, so I got up and inched slowly toward the voices. My socks weren't thick enough to keep from feeling the cool tile beneath my feet. As I went, my eyes adjusted to the low light. I looked back at the cluster of sleeping bags and counted seven, including mine.

Two were missing.

That realization slowed my steps. Whoever it was probably couldn't sleep. I followed the sound of the whispers to the customer service booth, which was square with chest-high counters on all four sides.

A girly moan sent a prickle up my spine. Oh man. I instantly thought I should go back to bed. I didn't need to intrude on whatever was happening here. But then I considered the options. There were only two guys who could be back there, and that voice hadn't sounded like Logan's.

I stepped up to the counter and peeked over.

Zach was sitting on the floor, his back against the inside counter, his legs lost in a sleeping bag, his hands gripping the back of the girl on his lap. A girl wearing a ponytail. They were dressed but . . . yeah. It looked like they were trying to eat each other's faces.

Betrayal filled me with hot anger. Jaylee had been hanging on Zach all day, so it was no surprise she'd do this. Zach, though. I couldn't believe he'd go behind my back.

I guess the end of the world changes things.

19

Fire shot through my veins, yet it felt like something was falling inside me. I grabbed the edge of the counter and took a long, deep breath. If I was going to be the leader, I couldn't freak out like some middle schooler because Jaylee had picked Zach. I had to be a man about this. Deal with it. Move on.

Be cool, McShane.

I was debating whether to walk away or say something scathing when Zach's hand slid down to the girl's waist, pushing aside her sleeping bag and revealing the number fourteen on the back of her shirt.

"Lizzie?" Jealousy morphed into shock. "What the

Hades?"

Lizzie yelped, slid off Zach's lap, and clapped her hand to her mouth. Zach lifted his arms, as if this was a stick-up and I was the sheriff. He clunked his head back against the counter and closed his eyes.

"Yeah," I said, scowling. "Caught you." I slapped both hands on the counter and walked away. I felt stupid for thinking that Zach would have gone after Jaylee, for suspecting him of something so low, but . . . my sister?

Dude. That wasn't much better.

"Eli," Zach called after me.

I didn't want to hear it. I walked back to the cluster of sleeping bags and almost ran smack into Logan.

"Jaylee and Antônia are in the back trying to get the garage door open," he said. "They took the keys from Zach's bag and are going to steal the van."

"What? How do you know this?"

"I heard them talking."

I ran to my sleeping bag, grabbed a flashlight, then started toward the back of the store. "Why didn't you stop them?"

"They don't have a key for the padlock Zach put on the door," Logan said, holding up two tiny keys. "When I saw what they were doing, I thought I'd better get you. Where were you, anyway? Looking for more supplies?"

"Just . . . looking."

When I reached the swinging doors to the back, I turned off my flashlight and pushed through. Across the room, a beam of light wavered on the right side of the garage door.

"Bring the light here!" Jaylee's voice. "I think I found a way to open it."

I flicked on my flashlight and shone it toward the sound of Jaylee's voice. "What's going on, Jaylee?" I asked.

A growl, then, "I need something in the van."

"I can help you with that," I said, crossing the room.

"No, you can't."

"Oh, that's right. Because you took the keys from Zach's bag." I reached her, and while my flashlight was pointing at the floor, its light was bright enough to illuminate Jaylee, who had her arms crossed like some kind of night club bouncer.

"Antônia and I want to go to Crested Butte," she said.

"Jaylee says there is safe water by that place," Antônia said.

This again.

"You can," I said. "After we talk to Reinhold."

"We can't waste time on him," Jaylee said.

"Reinhold's place is on the way to Crested Butte," I said.

"It is?" This from Antônia.

"Yes. It's, like, five hours to Wilderness Way and another four hours north to Crested Butte."

"Oh," Antônia said, frowning at Jaylee. "Then we should wait."

"What if they start turning people away?" Jaylee asked.

"Why would they do that?"

"Because too many show up and there isn't enough supplies to go around?" Jaylee said.

"We're only talking about a few hours," I said. "We get to Reinhold's place, and if he has safe water, great. We'll stay with him, and you two can continue on to Crested Butte if you want. And if he doesn't have safe water, then we'll all want to go check out Crested Butte."

"Not Reinhold," Jaylee said. "He won't want to go there."

"What makes you say that?" I asked.

"You know how he is," Jaylee said. "I'm sure he'd

rather be on his own."

She was probably right, but it didn't change our immediate circumstances. "A few hours isn't going to make that much of a difference," I said. "But if you really want to leave us, I'm not going to stop you."

"Really?" Jaylee said.

"Really," I said. "But you don't get to steal Zach's van. You want to leave, you can take the Prius or we'll drive you over to the car dealership and help you get another car."

"I want another car," Antônia said.

"And we want some of the supplies," Jaylee added.

I gritted my teeth. I didn't have time to deal with this, but I couldn't really tell them no either. I wasn't a dictator. "All right," I said. "Let's go back in and hash out a plan. As soon as everyone gets up, we'll figure out what to do."

The girls just stood there, staring at me.

"The keys?" I said.

Jaylee tipped her head back and groaned, like I was forcing her to stay at the dinner table until she ate all her Brussel sprouts. "Fine." She held them out, and they dangled on the tip of her index finger.

I took them casually, as if I really didn't care if I had them or not, but I was so relieved. "Thanks," I said, stepping back out of the way. "Ladies first."

Jaylee narrowed her eyes at me, but she went and Antônia followed, shooting me a sheepish smile. Frustration rippled through me as we crossed the loading bay and I chewed on the ways I could try and convince Jaylee and Antônia to stay with us. I was going to need Zach and Lizzie's help, that was for—

A rattle shook the garage door from the outside. The four of us froze. I shut off my flashlight, but Antônia turned hers on the door. I pushed her hand down and shook my head.

A scrape, metal against metal. Another bang.

Someone was trying to get in.

What should I do? Dad's gun was in the store by my sleeping bag. It wasn't even loaded. I had keys to the van. We could get inside it. Drive out if the garage door lifted.

Someone would have to be out of the vehicles to lift it.

Outside, a car door slammed. An engine roared to life. The vehicle rolled away.

Relief shot through me, but I knew this wasn't over. "We've got to get everyone up. Now." I sprinted inside the store, all the way to the front where we'd set up camp. I slid on my knees to my bag and picked up Dad's rifle. I reached into my hiking boot and pulled out the shells I'd ejected last night, loaded it quickly. Logan and the girls arrived and woke Krista and the kids. I shoved my feet into my boots and stood just as the glass on the front door splintered.

I aimed the rifle at the door.

"What's wrong?" Hannah asked from my left.

"Someone's coming," I said. "I want us gone before he gets inside. Someone grab my pack."

Hannah crouched and looped my bag over her shoulder. Another break in the glass, and this time, the curled end of a crowbar broke through.

"I don't know where Zach and Lizzie are!" Logan said.

"Customer service," I said, inching backwards when Krista and the kids ran past me.

"Leave the sleeping bags," I hissed at Jaylee, who was trying to roll hers. "We have plenty loaded."

She still picked it up and ran with it. Whatever. At least she'd gone.

The intruder yanked the crowbar back and with it pulled away a swath of fragmented glass. I scanned our camp area. It looked like we'd gotten everyone and everything we needed. I walked slowly back into the darkness, hoping that when this person got inside, he or she wouldn't be able to see me. I glanced over my shoulder, saw Zach coming my way, hopping on one foot as he pulled on a second shoe.

I lowered the gun for a moment and passed him the van keys. "Load up and get that garage door opened," I said. "I'm right behind you."

Hannah gasped. "Oh no."

I followed her gaze to the front door. The intruder had made it inside. It was a man. Something about him was familiar, but I couldn't quite grasp what in the darkness.

Until he spoke.

"Hannah!" The sound was a raw and desperate scream, like he was here to enact revenge upon the person responsible for all the terrible things that had happened in his life.

Brandon. Hannah's ex.

I twitched, recalling the feel of that metal rod on my throat. "Go," I whispered.

She slipped out of sight. I continued to back down the light bulb aisle.

"Hannah?" Brandon yelled. "I know you're in here. Where are you, baby? This isn't funny anymore. I need you to come over here so we can talk."

Dang. This guy was certifiable. I reached the end of the aisle, flipped on the gun's safety, then turned and ran, wincing when my steps ended up being louder than I'd expected.

"Hey!"

He gave chase; I could hear his footsteps slapping the tile behind me. I'd had a good head start, though, and I knew where I was going. I pushed through the swinging doors.

Yes! Not only was the garage door already opened,

Zach had driven the van out and Hannah had started the truck. The passenger's door was open and waiting for me. I hopped in and pulled it shut just as the doors to the loading bay flapped open.

"Hannah! Stop!"

Hannah hit the gas. Brandon ran toward us and leaped off the dock. He whacked the passenger window with the crowbar. With one strike, the glass shattered.

20

I turned away as glass rained over me. The truck tore out of the loading bay and turned sharply after Zach, circling to the front of the store.

The radio on the dash fizzled. "Zach to Eli, come in, over."

I put Dad's rifle on the dashboard and felt in the darkness until I located the radio. I picked it up, my hand shaking. "Eli here."

"Where to?" he asked.

"North out of the lot."

The van rolled onto the street, going a lot slower than I'd like. I glanced over my shoulder, curious who was in the truck with us. Logan, Davis, and Shyla. I was actually relieved that Jaylee wasn't here to harass me about getting her a car to go to Crested Butte.

The radio crackled. "Can you take the lead?" Zach asked. "Over." Up ahead, the van pulled to the side of the road.

"Go around them," I said, and as we passed by, the glow from the van's dashboard lights lit up Lizzie's face. I pressed the radio button. "Lizzie wanted to drive?"

"I couldn't find my contacts fast enough," Zach said. "Left them at Ace. I got some extras from Target, but I think they're in the back of your truck."

That was no good. "You okay to wait? I don't want to stop just yet."

"I'm right as rain. Liz has got this."

I pushed away my annoyance at Zach calling my sister "Liz," wondering when all *that* had happened. "We'll pull over later."

"Sounds good. Over and out."

"Take a right up ahead," I told Hannah. "We'll follow 66 for a while. Go as fast as you want. Lizzie will keep up."

"Got it."

I tossed the radio back onto the dashboard and opened the glove box, pulling out the snow brush I'd stashed there last night. I did what I could to shake the glass off me, then twisted around and started sweeping it off my seat. I brushed everything to the floor for now. While I was still backwards, I looked past Shyla and Davis's heads, out the back window. To my relief, I only saw one set of headlights behind us.

"Who was that man?" Davis asked.

I shifted my gaze to Davis's wide brown eyes. Shyla was staring at me too.

Hannah answered before I could. "He's a bad man."

"What does he want?" Shyla asked.

"Me," Hannah said. "He wants me."

I turned around and fell into my seat, put the snow brush away.

"What's he want you for?" Davis asked.

"Well, he wants to marry me," Hannah said. "But I don't want to marry him."

"That's a good idea," Shyla said, "because he's not very nice."

"You're absolutely right," Hannah said.

"If you don't want to marry him, why wear the rock?" Logan asked.

A totally rude question, but I'd been dying to ask the same thing.

"It's my great grandmother's ring," she said. "My father gave it to Brandon to propose. When we broke up, I kept it."

That made sense. It also made me feel the tiniest bit lighter inside, knowing that we weren't dealing with some psycho lovers' quarrel. This thing went one way.

"Think he's going to follow us?" Logan asked.

"I'm sure he'll try," Hannah said.

"But he has no idea where we're going," I said.

"Then how did he find us?" Hannah asked. "How did he know to come to the hardware store?"

It was a very good question, and one I didn't have an answer for. "He couldn't have known," I said. "He was out cold when we left him at the gas station. Wasn't he?"

"I thought so."

"Even if he had managed to follow us, why wait until now to bust in?"

No one had an answer, which only bothered me more.

"Don't you need to put the gun on the rack?" Hannah asked, eyeing the weapon warily.

"Not with the kids back there," I said. "That safety is on, but I can eject the rounds if it makes you feel better."

"Thanks," she said, so I grabbed the rifle and removed the shells, pocketing them.

The dashboard clock read ten after five. I wondered if Jaylee and Antônia were pressuring Zach to take them to get their own car. We couldn't really afford to mess around with Brandon in the picture. I had no doubt he'd try and follow us. I just hoped he didn't think to look around Ace first. We'd left plenty of guns behind, and I didn't like the idea of Brandon packing heat.

I noticed where we were. "Merge left up ahead onto Highway 89," I said.

Hannah did, and our little convoy left Flagstaff and Route 66 behind us forever. It felt weird, riding with this strange girl in front. She was still wearing my sweatshirt, which looked really good on her. The wind whipping in my window was going to keep it pretty cold in here for a while. I turned on the heaters.

As air started blowing from the vents, the quiet seemed to grow. I felt like I should talk to Hannah. Make conversation. "What kind of doctor were you studying to be?"

"General practitioner. I wanted to work abroad."

"Really? Where?"

"I went on a few internships to Guatemala with Doctors Without Borders. I was only an office assistant, but I learned so much. Stuff I never would have been able to see or do in the US. It's so poor there. Children are malnourished and abused. There's a lot of street gangs. A lot of rape. It's horrifying. I was considering changing my major to OBGYN so I could go back and help."

Wow. She was quite the humanitarian. Our youth group took a yearly trip to Mexicali to run vacation bible school.

I'd gone three years running, but it seemed kind of small compared to all that. I mean, we just played with the kids.

"Are your parents lost too?" Shyla asked.

"Lost?" Hannah asked.

"Our mom didn't come home. Krista says she's lost forever."

The sorrow in Shyla's voice made my throat tight. I couldn't help but think of how I'd never see my own mom again. A sharp pain in my chest threatened to pull me under, but I pushed it away. I could grieve later. Right now I needed to stay strong. Get everyone through this thing.

"Yes, my parents are lost too," Hannah said.

"How do you know?" Shyla asked.

"There was a phone in the car dealership. I called my house and nobody answered. I called my dad's office. I called their neighbors. I called the club. I called my friends. No one answered anywhere."

"Lost?" Shyla asked.

"I think so," Hannah said.

I looked back at Logan, hunched down behind my seat, playing his video game. "Hey, Logan. Why don't you let the kids have a turn with the Switch?" They needed to get their minds on something else for a while.

Logan sighed. "Yeah, okay."

It was starting to get light. I was glad. I didn't want to miss Dad's van when the time came to look for it.

"What about you, Eli?" Hannah said.

"What about what?"

"Did you have any college plans?"

"Oh. Yeah, I don't know. My dad owns his own auto shop, and I've always liked working on cars. Owning your own business gives you a lot of freedom, so I figured I'd do that. I'm not against college or anything, but I never saw reason to put myself into debt for a degree I didn't need."

"So you were going to work with your dad?"

"For a while, yeah."

"Did you ever dream of doing anything else?"

I considered the question. "I thought it might be fun to be an outdoor guide. Hiking, backpacking, river rafting, hunting. What you'll see up in Colorado, the place we're going. *That* would've been my dream job."

Would've been.

"I'm going to design video games," Logan said, his voice loud in my ear. "I'm a decent artist. I excel at problem solving and love algorithms and programming. I want to go to MIT or Berkley for software engineering technology. Maybe Oregon Institute of Technology. I've been working on designing my own game."

Logan's verbiage gave me pause. As if his college plans were still a go, as if we were all going to wake up tomorrow and find the world was back to normal.

Logan in denial. That was new.

"Have you ever played Zombies Kings, Hannah?" he asked.

"Nope."

"You can play if you want. It's fun. I can drive."

"Maybe later," she said. "Let the kids play for now."

"I want to be a singer," Shyla said. "I want to be beautiful like Taylor Swift and play a banjo and wear a pretty dress and make music videos."

"You don't look anything like Taylor Swift," Logan said.

"Hey, now," Hannah said, glaring at Logan.

I glanced at Shyla in the rearview. She was frowning at her lap. "Which totally doesn't matter, Shy, because you're already gorgeous," I said.

She didn't look up, but her lips twisted into a smile.

Crisis averted.

"I was thinking about this pandemic, Eli," Logan said, as if he hadn't just insulted a little girl. "Maybe the water problem wasn't caused by the comet so much as the comet affected certain aquifers. Maybe it only affected metropolitan communities. Because think about it. Groundwater is depleted from aquifers by over-pumping or drought. Florida has a serious problem with aquifer depletion because they overuse their freshwater supply, then salt water seeps in and contaminates everything. And Florida is where this all started in the US. Once people were infected, it spread across the country quickly."

Sometimes Logan made my head hurt. "What about the comet, then?"

"Conspiracy. The government refusing to deal with the water problems, blames the comet."

"Logan, that makes no sense what-so—"

"How do you play Zombie Kings, Logan?" Hannah asked. "If you tell me now, then later when Eli is driving again, I'll be ready to take my turn."

"Sure! It's a really great game."

Hannah suddenly became one of my favorite people on the planet for distracting Logan from his conspiracy theories. The downside was we all had to listen to a non-stop lecture on every minutiae of the Zombie Kings game. At least Davis and Shyla were having fun.

I fiddled with the radio. There were a few stations still broadcasting, but I didn't hear any announcers. I wondered if there was still power in some cities.

We passed a sign that listed Durango at 240 miles away. Another half hour or so past that to Wilderness Way Adventures. We'd be there before lunchtime. But would Reinhold be?

● ● ●

Two and a half hours later we'd long left Highway 89 for U.S. 160 and were halfway to Durango. The sun was up now. Logan and the kids had fallen asleep in the back, but I was too wired to sleep. While I could have done the whole five hours without stopping, I'd learned on the way up that that wasn't the case for others in our group. When Zach radioed that the girls needed a potty break, they vetoed my suggestion to pee in the bushes. I told them we'd stop in Kayenta at the rest stop across from the hotel. It wasn't too much farther.

I tossed the walkie talkie back up on the dashboard and looked out the window. The land was getting a little hilly but was still barren and covered in sagebrush and chaparral. It would be another hour before we hit Colorado. We'd see Dad's van before then.

Or not.

"You don't want to stop?" Hannah asked me.

"No, stopping is fine. I don't think we're being followed." I'd been watching out my rearview mirror like a hawk, and hadn't seen any sign of anyone.

One good thing about stopping was that I could get the keys and drive again. Holding the wheel made me feel in control of the situation, which was ridiculous. I mean, was anyone truly in control of anything? "Thanks for driving," I said, as if thanking Hannah would somehow cancel out my selfish thoughts.

"No problem," she said.

Exactly how far was it to Kayenta? I needed to get out of the truck. I needed to do something. Maybe when we stopped I could tape a trash bag over the passenger side window. It was letting in a lot of cold air, which in a couple more hours would be hot air.

I examined the vents, checked out the glove compartment, fiddled with the buttons on the dash, threw a couple of handfuls of broken glass out the window. My gaze eventually flitted to Hannah, who was staring at the road, intense, like there were deer lining the shoulder or something. Her manicured nails gripped the steering wheel at ten and two. She'd taken off my sweatshirt and was in her white tank top again. I noticed her arms. She was in good shape. Strong for a girl.

"You an athlete?" I asked.

She turned her head to look at me, then focused on the road again. "I played tennis."

A rich person sport. Should've guessed. She'd put her hair up in a bun on the back of her head. This called attention to her long neck and shoulders. My eyes latched onto black in between her shoulder blades. There was a tattoo there. At first I thought that was all I was seeing, but then I notice a massive bruise, all dark and purple. This brought my attention to a yellowish discoloration on the right side of her neck. Her hair had been hiding it before.

I somehow knew this was Brandon's work.

"What are you staring at?" she asked.

Heat climbed up the back of my neck and burned my ears. I looked out the window at the landscape, thought quickly. "You have a tattoo."

Her silence pulled my gaze back, and I chanced a quick peek at her expression. But there was no anger or embarrassment on her face.

"It was my one act of rebellion against my father," she said.

"You didn't get along with your dad?"

She shrugged. "He was always too busy for me. Never too busy to criticize, though. He wanted me to do what he wanted me to do, which I didn't think was fair. He hated my high school boyfriend. Shen was a troublemaker. I liked that about him." She smiled, and there was a glint in her eyes.

She was enjoying the memory. "He had a motorcycle, and he'd come to the house or to the country club and pick me up, revving the engine as loudly as he could." She smiled. "Daddy hated that bike."

Country club, wow. "So what's the tattoo?" I asked.

"Chinese symbol for independence."

Nice. "So you got a tattoo to tell your dad that you didn't need him telling you what to do?"

"Yeah . . . I guess it was pretty juvenile. I laugh about it now, and I'm thankful I didn't get something even worse, like Shen's name."

"Things with Shen didn't work out?"

"Uh, no." She laughed. "He was a little too wild for me. It was a phase. Girls go through a lot of phases. They just don't realize it until they're older."

I wondered if my sister was going through a Zach phase. Lizzie had never been the rebellious type. She'd never even dated anyone before. At least I didn't think she had. I wondered how long this thing with Zach had been going on. Would she care what I thought about it? Would he?

One thing was certain: Zach and I needed to have a talk.

Up ahead, the van pulled off at the rest stop across from the Holiday Inn. We'd reached Kayenta. A beige and green house with a stickman on the left door and a stickwoman on the right marked the bathrooms. Regular parking spots ran adjacent to the sidewalk. Long spots for trucks filled the middle of the lot. There were three other cars. A Chevy Vega hatchback, a Datsun, and an old Honda Accord.

"We here?" Logan asked, his voice sleepy.

"Kayenta," I said. "Bathroom break. Make it quick."

Lizzie pulled the van into a space in front of the bathrooms, and the doors all opened at once. Lizzie, Krista,

Antônia, and Jaylee sprinted for the bathrooms.

Hannah pulled in beside the van, and before she had rolled to a complete stop, Logan jumped out and headed for the stickman door. Davis and Shyla were quick to follow.

Zach got out of the van and came over, pausing at the door Logan and the kids had left wide open. He tilted his head up and squinted at me. "Can I get in the back? I need to find those contact lenses."

"I'll need to unlock it," I said.

Hannah turned off the truck and handed me the keys.

"Thanks." I got out and unlocked the back, then helped Zach find the Target bags with his extra contact lenses. When he found some, he carried them back to the van and used the mirror on the sun visor to help him get them in.

I stood sentry, guarding the vehicles. I wanted to try and cover the window, but not until I had someone to guard my back. Kayenta was a small town, but any town increased the chances of us meeting survivors.

Shyla and Davis were running toward the truck, giggling. It relieved me how quickly they had returned. The back door on the opposite side of the truck opened, and they climbed inside.

I gazed across the street at the Holiday Inn. It might be nice to move into a hotel. We could house a lot of people. It probably had over a hundred rooms. And there'd be a kitchen on the ground floor.

Logan was headed my way from the bathrooms, Davis beside him. I frowned, glanced at the truck. I could have sworn I saw two kids climb inside. I lunged up to the truck and opened the back door. Sure enough, two kids. Shyla was one of them, but a little stranger was sitting on the seat beside her.

21

The kid was shirtless, had long black hair, and looked to be about six years old. She was barefoot, wearing only a pair of dingy blue jeans that were frayed at the hem. I scanned the rest stop, but saw no one else.

"Hey, Shy," I said. "Who's your friend?"

"She's named Cree."

"Hi, Cree," I said. "Where's your Mom?"

The kid didn't look at me but said, "Shimá sleep."

Great. "Where does she live?" I had no desire to see any more dead people, but I wasn't loading up this kid without making sure she was truly alone.

The girl turned on her knees and pointed out the back

window at the Holiday Inn.

I sighed, frustrated. I did *not* want to linger here, but I couldn't leave this kid behind if she was truly alone.

When the kid didn't answer, I tried again. "Can you take me to her?"

"*Aoo'.*" Cree slipped out of the truck. Her bare feet slapped the pavement as she ran toward the street. I reached into the cab and pulled Dad's rifle off the dash just as Hannah, Lizzie, and Zach approached.

"What's up?" Zach asked.

"Stray kid," I said as I loaded the shells from my pocket and triple-checked the safety." I'm going to go check it out." I opened the glovebox and grabbed the flashlight I'd stored there last night.

"I'm coming with you," Hannah said.

That surprised me. "Fine." I tossed Zach the keys, and he snatched them out of the air. Proof he could see again. "Guard the truck," I told him.

"You think this is a good idea?" he asked.

"Not really, but what am I supposed to do? Leave her here alone?"

"Why can't we just take her with us?" Lizzie asked.

"I'm not kidnapping any more kids." I shot Shyla a look and took off after Cree.

Hannah kept pace beside me. "You kidnapped Shyla and Davis?" she asked

"Not exactly. Well . . . technically."

I told her the story as we followed Cree across the street and toward the drop-off zone of the hotel. The main building was beige with dark green trim, squat-looking, like a Flintstone's house. The next building over was a two-story strip of hotel rooms with entrances on the outside. Classy joint.

Cree was waiting in front of a set of double glass doors.

She opened one side and held it for us. I ducked past her and into the lobby. The walls were beige brick, covered with Navajo paintings and artifacts. It was darkish inside. No power, but the wall of windows on the entry side gave enough light to see by.

"Wow," Hannah said. "This is . . . nice."

"You stay in a lot of hotels?" I asked.

"I've only ever stayed in the penthouse suites. My dad is really picky. Was. I wish I knew."

"I hear you." I was still holding out hope that we'd run across my dad alive and well before we reached the Colorado border.

Cree ran ahead, and we followed over a dark brown stone floor, around some gaudy furniture that was missing its cushions, past a little dining area, and down a dark hallway. I slowed, already sick with the faint smell of what was ahead. The girl became a black shadow before us until I clicked on my flashlight. She eventually pushed inside a double door that swung both ways. A kitchen.

The smell about knocked me flat. I gagged, clapped my free hand over my nose, and turned back to the door. Hades, it was awful! And I couldn't see squat.

Cree's voice flitted out from the darkness. "You help Shimá?"

I pulled my T-shirt up over my nose and mouth and shone the flashlight Cree's way. I moved cautiously, panning the light over every inch of floor before I took a step. From the intensity of the pungent odor, I was expecting to find a dozen dead people, but Cree led us to a lone body, lying on two couch cushions—likely the ones missing from the lobby. The woman had dark brown skin, but her body appeared black and blue in places, almost a sickly green. Flies swarmed and crawled over her skin. Cree plopped cross-legged onto the floor beside the cushions and slipped her hand into the dead woman's.

I had no words. I closed my eyes and began to pray. I didn't know what else to do. How long had the poor kid been sitting around with her dead mom? How many other kids had been abandoned like this?

"She hasn't been gone long," Hannah whispered. "Maybe two days."

I opened my eyes and looked at Hannah. "How can you tell?"

"The flies. It's pretty warm in the building, but she's barely begun to decompose. Her body is still in fairly good shape."

"We can't bury her," I said.

"No. It would be difficult to move her at this stage and not have . . . difficulty."

That made me smile. "Difficult not to have difficulty?"

"Well . . . she might not . . . hold together. If we wrapped her first, maybe . . ."

I thought of what we did for Zach's family. "Let's find a blanket or sheet and cover her, then try and talk the girl into coming with us."

We found a laundry room full of all the sheets and blankets we could ever want. I grabbed a nice thick blanket with flowers on it and carried it back to the kitchen. Cree was waiting outside the kitchen doors, her big brown eyes watching us.

I took a deep breath and went back inside. I set down the rifle and covered the body with the blanket. Cree stared up at me and took hold of my hand. A jolt of heat passed over me as irrational fears filled my head. It was a waterborne disease. I couldn't catch it from human touch. As if to prove it to myself, I squeezed Cree's hand. I wanted to sing, like Zach had done for his family, but "Joyful, Joyful" didn't seem the right song, and no others came to mind just then.

If I wasn't going to sing, I guessed I'd better pray. "Hey, God. Uh, we pray for the soul of this woman and ask for your mercy. We thank you for her life and the love she gave to Cree, and we pray that we can love Cree as much as her mother did. Amen."

"Amen," Hannah said.

My stomach heaved. I needed to get some air. I grabbed my gun and waved Cree toward the door, but the girl ran back to her mother. She pulled at the blanket.

"No no." I scooped her up with my arm that was holding the flashlight and headed toward the door.

"*Nda!*" She screeched, arched her back, kicked and clawed, her little fingernails long and sharp.

Her reaction shocked me, and I almost dropped her. Did she somehow know she wasn't coming back? Maybe she didn't like being touched.

"Hannah, can you take the gun?"

She relieved me of the weapon, holding it out in front with two hands like she wanted it as far away from her as possible.

I was able to go faster now, and I figured it was best to do this quickly, like ripping off a Band-Aid. "It's okay," I said. "It's gonna be okay." But what did I know? Too many people were dead. And what were we going to do when we ran out of water? Was I wrong to take Cree away from her mother only to have her die with me up in the mountains?

I didn't know. And I was tired of not knowing.

Hannah held open the door for us, and I swept past into clean air and light. I took a long breath through my nose, trying to cleanse my sinuses and calm my nerves. Cree was still wailing.

Hannah and I crossed the street. Zach climbed out of the van and came running, Logan and Jaylee at his heels.

"What happened?" he asked.

"The mom didn't make it," Hannah said, and I was thankful she'd answered. I didn't trust myself to hold it together if I had to speak.

Jaylee tried to take Cree from me. "Hey, there." But Cree screamed louder, twisted in my arms, clutched my neck and wrapped little legs around my waist.

"Shhh. I got you." I tried to bounce her. She was a bit too big to be carried like a baby, but I figured it was worth a shot. At least she wasn't clawing my face and screaming anymore.

"I'll dig out some food," Hannah said. "She's probably starving."

"Good idea." I handed her the keys and followed her to the back of the truck.

"Where do I look?" she asked.

"The cooler," I said, which was where I'd put all the candy bars. Cree needed something more nutritional than junk food, but the canned goods were too far in and weren't the easiest things to eat while on the road.

"And where should I put this?" she asked, holding up my dad's gun.

"Give it to Zach," I said.

It was then that I noticed a few people missing from our party. "Where is Lizzie? And Antônia and Krista? The kids?"

"Shyla's in the truck," Logan said. "Everyone else went to check out that bookstore." He nodded to the establishment next door.

"You were taking so long," Zach said, "I figured it would be okay."

Frustration squeezed my chest, but I supposed I had no right to get mad at people for breaking the rules. I'd started it.

"We're going to take her with us?" Jaylee asked.

"Yes, Cree is coming with us," I said.

"She doesn't look so good. What if she's sick?"

"None of us look so good," I said.

"You're the doctor," Jaylee said to Hannah. "Is the kid infected?"

Hannah removed an assortment of snacks and set them on the bumper, then closed the cooler and slid it back into place. "She looks healthy enough to me."

"Were you camping too when the comet passed by?" Logan asked.

"No," Hannah said. "I wasn't camping."

"Then where were you?" Jaylee propped her hands on her hips, as if Hannah's answers were suddenly not good enough.

"Hey, now," I said, annoyed that Jaylee and Logan were giving Hannah the third degree, but to my surprise, she answered.

"I was kidnapped."

She may as well have said she was on another planet. Jaylee's eyes few wide. "By that guy?"

"Yes, though I didn't realize it was him at first. My dad is Lou Cheng. He owns MonkeyC. It's an—"

"—domain registration and web hosting company," Logan said. "It's worth billions."

"That's right," Hannah said. "Some guys grabbed me when I went out for coffee a week or so ago, put me in a van." She opened a Slim Jim and handed it to Cree, who merely stared. "I woke up in a basement, tied to a chair. I didn't know where I was until a few days ago when I escaped. Found one of my captors dead upstairs but didn't understand what had happened until I got to town and saw the CDC health alert signs."

I realized I was staring at Hannah and glanced away.

Hades. She'd been abducted? "That's terrifying," I said.

"You walked all the way to Flagstaff?" Jaylee asked.

Hannah held the jerky up to Cree's lips, and the girl took a bite. "I stole an ATV from a farm, but it ran out of gas. That's when Brandon showed up. He said he'd been looking for me. That he'd come to pay my ransom. He acted so relieved to see me, I didn't really think it through. I figured Dad had sent him. My dad doesn't understand what kind of man Brandon is. So I got in the car. But some of the things he said on the drive didn't add up, so when he stopped in Flagstaff, trying to find some gas, I ran off. Decided to find my own car. I was at the dealership when Eli came in."

Cree took the jerky from Hannah and sat back in my arms, inspecting it.

"And Brandon wasn't far behind," Logan said.

"Wait, you saw her at the dealership?" Jaylee asked me.

I nodded. "She took the Honda."

Talking about Brandon reminded me how long we'd lingered here. We really needed to get going. I glanced across the street. Still no sign of the girls. "Zach, can you go tell the girls we're leaving?" We'd been here far too long already.

"I'm on it." He took off. I noticed too late that he still had Dad's rifle.

"Here you go!" Shyla sang from the back cab, tossing me a pink wad of fabric. "For Cree."

I took it and held it up. "Look, Cree. A shirt! Thank you, Shyla. That was very nice." I tried to pull it over Cree's head, but she wrinkled her nose and ducked aside.

"No pink," she said.

"You don't like pink?"

"No pink."

Leave it to a kid with nothing to be picky over color.

"You got something other than pink, Shy?"

"Um . . . yes. I got a black one too." Shyla ducked down and quickly reappeared with a wad of black fabric. I traded her for the pink, then pulled the black T-shirt over Cree's head. She put her arms through the holes on her own. The front had a silver foil guitar on it.

Cree was filthy and smelled faintly of the pungent sweet sickness. How would any of us ever bathe again? Then I remembered we'd stocked up on baby wipes at Target.

"Cree," I pointed to the restrooms, "you need to go to the bathroom?" I hadn't thought to give her anything to drink. The poor thing was probably dehydrated.

Cree's gaze followed my pointing finger, and she smiled.

"I'll take her," Hannah said, looking at us over the front of the truck.

"Thanks," I said. "Be quick. Cree, go with Hannah, okay?"

Cree frowned but took Hannah's hand and obediently went along. I liked that obedience. I hoped it stuck around. It made things a lot easier than the screaming and the clawing.

"I'm going to go once more too," Jaylee said, following them.

"I can't believe Hannah's dad is Lou Cheng," Logan said. "And that Brandon guy was holding her for ransom."

"Yeah," I said. "Pretty twisted."

"What was it like in the hotel?" Logan asked.

"Just the mom. Didn't see anyone else." I dug into the back of the truck, looking for some baby wipes and something for the kid to drink. Behind the snack cooler I found another cooler of drinks. Behind that should be the box with the wipes.

Before I knew it, I'd crawled into the back of the truck

and was digging through tubs, looking for the wipes. I found some cracker packs with the rubbery cheese you spread over them. Cree might like those. Shyla and Davis were likely hungry too. I dumped some of the cracker packs and a few more lengths of beef jerky into the snack cooler and pushed it out to Logan, who had half-crawled in after me. I finally found the wipes and started to wiggle my way back down to the tailgate. I had barely put one foot on the ground when a strange voice spoke.

"Need a hand?"

"Hello," Logan said. "Thanks, but I think we're okay."

Somehow between my heart failure and cramped position, I managed to vault myself backwards the rest of the way out of the truck. I whipped around to see a gangly man with greasy blond hair slicked back over his head and a week's worth of scraggly beard on his face. He was wearing a wife beater tank top and a pair of dirty jeans with saggy, worn-to-threads knees.

And Zach had my dad's rifle.

22

"Sorry, man," the guy said. "Looked like you were stuck. You sure got a lot of stuff packed in there. You guys headed up to Mount Crested Butte?"

I slammed the tailgate closed, locked the cover, and pocketed the key. "Uh, Colorado Springs," I said. I didn't like anyone looking at our supplies or knowing our business.

"Hey!" From across the street, Zach sprinted our way, eyes locked on the stranger, rifle clutched in one hand like he was carrying a suitcase. Behind him, Lizzie, Antônia, Krista, and Davis were crossing the road. Zach slowed as he neared us, his footsteps plodding heavily over the old concrete road until he stopped beside me.

"Hey," he said again, adjusting the rifle in a way that signaled he was ready to use it if he needed to. "I'm Zach."

"Artie," the guy said, eyeing the rifle warily. "Stopped to let my old lady pee."

There were two of them? I glanced toward the restrooms. Jaylee was headed back. No sign of his old lady or Hannah and Cree. I eyed his white Dodge Dakota, a late 90s model. The back was piled high with gear.

"Pretty wild stuff happening, huh?" Artie said. "Everyone dying like that. Why you going to the Springs?"

"We know someone there," Zach said, as if we were actually going to Colorado Springs.

"I hear you," Artie said. "Gotta check on everyone. See who's left. Yeah, this is some messed up living we're doing right now. Almost feel guilty to be alive. We're headed up to Mount Crested Butte. Heard there's clean water up that way. Figure it's not true but might as well check it out, you know? It's not like we have anything better to do."

"We'd like to go there too," Jaylee said. "I mean, Antônia and me."

"And me," Krista added.

"After we check on my grandma," I said.

"That's what we agreed on, remember?" Zach said.

"How could I forget?" Jaylee said with way too much attitude.

"Wish I could offer you girls a ride," Artie said, "but my rig is packed to the gills."

"Oh, that's very kind for you," Antônia said, "but we must stay with our friends. Is only a few more days." She shot Jaylee a bit of a glare.

"That's the spirit," Artie said. "Y'all got to stick together. This ain't no time to be going your own way."

"That's good advice, sir," Logan said.

"Well, hey," Artie said, "I'm gonna use the can. It was

nice meeting you all. You guys don't find what you're looking for in the Springs, come on up."

"We will," Jaylee said.

Artie swaggered off to the stickman's room and went inside. Just as the door closed, Hannah and Cree came out of the ladies.

"And we're leaving," I said, taking the rifle from Zach. "We got everyone?" I did a quick scan of the faces around me. It seemed we actually did have everyone.

Shocking.

I clapped my hands together. "Load up!"

The group scattered.

"Hey," Lizzie hugged my arm. "He was nice. Not everyone is going to hit you and steal your truck."

"Yeah." I knew Lizzie was right, but I'd feel better when we were all safely locked inside the vehicles and moving away from Artie and his old lady at seventy-miles-per-hour.

"Eli," Hannah said. "Can I talk to you real quick?"

"You see a woman in the bathroom?"

"No. The door opened and closed a few times when Cree and I were in a stall. We were kind of busy."

"Right," I said, feeling suddenly stupid for interrogating her about being in the bathroom. "What's up?"

"Cree is a boy," she whispered.

I spun around and spotted Cree climbing into the back of my truck. "What makes you say that?"

"Anatomy 101." She raised her eyebrows.

"Oh." I could feel myself turning red. "No wonder he didn't want to wear a pink shirt with a heart on it." I could barely see Cree's profile through his curtain of black hair. "That's a lot of hair for a boy."

"It's tradition for Navajo people to wear their hair long."

"Right." I felt bad that Shyla and I had mistaken Cree for a girl. I wondered if he'd picked up on that.

"Logan!" Jaylee's scream pulled my attention to the van where she was standing at the sliding door, hands on her hips.

I headed that way to see what was up. Logan was sitting in the van, buckled into Jaylee's old seat.

"I was here first," he said.

"No you weren't," Jaylee said.

"You said we'd switch seats later. It's later."

"Logan, get out of my seat," Jaylee said.

"It's not your seat, okay? And I want to talk to Zach for a while."

"Fine! Then I'm riding shotgun with Eli." She ripped her purse out from the floor at Logan's feet and stomped to the truck.

"People!" I said. "Pick a seat and let's go!" It was shocking that Brandon hadn't caught up by now. The dude could have passed us three times as long as we'd been here.

"Later!" This from Artie. He waved and climbed into his truck. Sure enough, a middle-aged woman with brown hair got in the passenger's side door.

I lifted my hand in a wave and got in the truck. Great, now people were passing us. That's how slow we were.

Logan's presence in the van changed a lot more than where Jaylee sat. With her came Antônia and Krista. Shyla and Cree stuck with me, so everyone else rode in the van with Zach, Hannah included. Antônia, Shyla, and Krista sat in back. Cree squished in the front between me and Jaylee.

The day was barren and bright. It felt good to be on the road again, even better riding with Jaylee. It soon got boring, though. Jaylee, Antônia, and Krista realized they'd all gone to the same Loca and Liberté Champion concert last year in Phoenix, so they started trying to name every song they'd played. In order. Cree fell asleep. I missed having Hannah to talk to.

We were about an hour and a half from Wilderness Way Adventures, about forty miles from Pete's gas station and fifty or so from where my dad had left the van. If it was there, we'd put gas in it and drive it north. If it wasn't there, we'd continue on. Reinhold didn't live at the campground, but I hoped to find his home address in the office. It had to be written down somewhere, right? I'd find it. Then we'd drive to his place.

But what if Reinhold was dead?

"The girl smells bad," Jaylee said.

"Cree is a boy," I said, "and I imagine we all smell bad."

She scoffed. "Not me. I smell good."

She actually did. I could smell her from here. Something citrusy.

"After we visit Mr. Reinhold, we will go to the place where Loca Champion lives, yes?" Antônia asked.

"Totally," Jaylee said.

"Why do you want to go there so badly?" I asked.

"Because they have water," Jaylee said. "And because Loca is hot."

Gross. "Loca Champion is as old as my dad," I said.

"So? Your dad's hot too," Jaylee said.

Eww. Just what I needed. The girl I liked telling me my dad was hot.

"What's his dad look like?" Krista asked.

"Mr. McShane is a few inches shorter than Eli," Jaylee said, "and he's muscular—but not too muscular, you know? He's not Hispanic like Eli's mom, but he's really tan, so he almost looks it. Ooh, plus he's a mechanic, so he's always got smudges of black on him—oil or whatever. And he's got this deep, sexy voice, and thick black hair, except the hair just over his ears is salt-and-pepper, which is so cute."

I wrinkled my nose. This conversation was killing me. "Old man hair is cute?"

"Your dad is *not* old," Jaylee said.

"He's *forty two*." Sounded old to me.

"Loca is forty-three," Jaylee said.

"I heard Loca and Daniella were getting a divorce," Krista said.

"I think it's a done deal," Jaylee said. "Maybe he'll be looking for a younger woman!"

"Can we talk about something else?" I asked.

"I'm just saying we should go up there and see if what that Artie guy said was true," Jaylee said. "Can you imagine living in the same house as Loca Champion?" She squealed, which made Krista squeal too.

I adjusted the rearview mirror so I could see Shyla, but she had her head against the window and her eyes closed. So not fair.

Once the girls stopped talking about how hot Loca Champion and my dad were, they moved on to such exciting topics as how hot Riggs was, how hot Zach was, how hot Josh was, and how hot the guy on the channel 5 news was.

Nice, huh? Everyone was hot but me. Oh, and Logan, of course. Antônia gave Cristobal the consolation prize of being cute.

"Are Zach and Lizzie going out, Eli?" Jaylee asked.

The question knotted my stomach. Why'd she have to bring *that* up? I'd managed not to think of Zach and my sister's make-out session for several hours. "How should I know?"

"Don't freak out. I'm just asking. They seem really flirty, that's all."

I pressed my lips into a line until it hurt.

"Oh my gosh. You know something, don't you?" Jaylee

reached over Cree and slapped my arm. "Spill it, Eli!"

I kept my eyes on the road. "I don't know what you're talking about."

"I read faces better than anyone. Tell me!"

I thought about it. "You know? There's hardly anyone left alive. Why 'go out' anymore? My guess is we'll all just pair off at some point." It made sense, and, really, who did I trust more in the world than Zach? I chewed on that thought a moment, then said, "I can't think of a better guy to marry my sister."

"Marry!" Jaylee burst into laughter. "I highly doubt Zach is going to give up his Olympic dreams to marry your sister and live in the woods."

Really? We were back to this again? "There is no more Olympics, Jaylee," I said. "The world as we knew it is dead. Things are different now. And Zach isn't going anywhere." Not to mention that the water in swimming pools was likely just as contaminated as the rest of the water.

I squinted. In the distance, something was sitting in the middle of the road. Something yellow.

"The world is not dead," Antônia said. "Everything will—how do you say?—*bounce back* to be normal soon."

"And you didn't answer the question, Eli," Jaylee said. "So, spill it! What's going on with Lizzie and . . . Is that a bus?"

A school bus. We were about to cross the bridge that went over the Chinle Wash, but a bus was parked across the bridge near the end, blocking the way. I stopped the truck before I reached the bridge.

"Hand me the radio," I said to Jaylee.

She passed it over.

"Eli to Zach, we've got a bus blocking the end of this bridge. I don't like it. Over."

There was barely any static before Lizzie answered.

"What do you want to do?"

It didn't make sense. Artie had come this way. There were no other turn offs he could have taken. Which meant the bus had arrived just moments ago or it had let him pass by.

But why? And where had it come from?

I glanced over the guard rails on both sides of the bridge, surveying the muddy water. I didn't see a thing, though I couldn't get a good look directly under the bridge without walking out and looking over the guard rail. I wondered if Artie's Dodge was down there—if this was some sicko's idea of Billy Goats Gruff.

"Why do you stop?" Antônia asked.

"Because if this is some kind of trap, I'd rather not be stuck in the middle of the bridge."

"Smart," Jaylee said.

"But what if somebody is needing help?" Antônia said.

What if?

I rubbed my face, tired of this adventure. Tired of adulting. Of having everyone always looking to me. I wished my dad was here to tell me what to do.

Before I could decide, Logan was out of the van and knocking on my window. I rolled it down. "What's up?"

"I got this," he said, showing me the radio in his hand. "It's my turn to help."

"Logan, stop!"

But he was already jogging away, his hiking boots scuffing over the worn concrete.

I banged my hands on the steering wheel. Idiot. I rolled my window the rest of the way down and got out of the truck, grabbing my rifle off the dashboard. In less than a minute I had loaded the gun, propped it on the sill of my open door, and was watching Logan through the scope. The safety was on. I kept my thumb on it to make sure.

From the road, the bridge just looked like a lighter strip of highway with guard rails on the sides, but it was actually pretty long. Logan finally made it across, though. He first squatted down and looked underneath the bus, then went around the front.

I winced and said a prayer that he'd survive this.

Movement on the bus caught my attention. I was about to reach for the radio, to warn Logan, then I realized it was him. He'd climbed aboard and was walking down the aisle, checking all the seats.

I relaxed some but kept my eyes peeled outside the bus, inside it, hoping no one would jump out with a crowbar and try and take off Logan's head.

"Logan to Eli, come in. Over."

"Eli here, over."

"The bus is empty. No keys in the ignition. If we put it in neutral, we could probably push it. Over."

No keys? That was even weirder. I walked over to the van and passed Logan's report to Zach. "What do you think?"

"I don't know, man. We're so close, you know? We've got to get past this bridge."

I nodded. "All right. You go first. Drive all the way down there. I'll stay back, keep the rifle out in case I see anyone coming in from the sides. Think you can get the bus into neutral?"

"No problem."

"Keep Lizzie behind the wheel with the kids in the van, buckled in and out of the way. Everyone else is out helping. It looks like the back tires will hit the guard rail, so you're going to have to turn the wheel before you start pushing."

"You got it, boss."

"That's a heavy bus. It's going to be rough with only six."

"No worries," Zach said. "I got this."

I radioed Logan the plan, then Lizzie and Zach switched places, and everyone but me piled into the van. Lizzie started it up and drove toward Logan and the bus.

I waited, watching through the scope on Dad's rifle. They arrived with no interruption. The pushers got out, joined Logan, and everyone set to work. I alternated between watching them through the scope and looking at the big picture with just my eyes. The moment the bus began to move, I knew it was time I drove down there to help.

I tossed the rifle into the cab, but before I could climb in, a hand grabbed the back of my neck and slammed my face into the door frame.

23

Pain engulfed my jaw and chin, and blood filled my mouth. I tried to turn, but the hands were on me again, this time dragging me down to my back on the hot concrete. Someone straddled me, trapping my arms against my sides. I could barely make out Brandon's shadowed face looming above, backlit by the sunny sky.

He'd sprung a trap for us. I couldn't believe it.

He grabbed my neck with one hand and squeezed. "Where is Hannah, you little punk?"

Blood from my mouth trickled down the back of my throat and I started coughing.

Brandon let go and gripped my shirt in his fist. "Tell me

where she is or help me God, I'll kill you."

"If I'm dead, then you'd never find her," I said, my voice an airy rasp.

That ticked him off, and he clubbed my ear.

I tried to pull my arms up, but he had them pinned tight.

"She's not here!" I yelled. "We helped her find a car. She's driving back to San Fran to check on her dad."

He sat back, thinking this over, and I realized, that while he had my arms pinned, my legs were free. Pushing down with my hands, I kicked my right leg up as high as I could and managed to hook my knee around his head. I pulled my leg back down, and Brandon flew back and to my right. His head slammed into the footboard of my truck. I hoped that might have knocked him out, but by the time I had gotten to my feet, Brandon was on his as well, and pointing a handgun at me.

I lifted my arms, not wanting to give him any wrong ideas. It was a nice gun too. A Glock 23. Any gun in Brandon's hands was bad news, but a Glock 23 had quite a bit of power, depending on what he'd loaded it with.

Brandon glanced into my truck, slammed the door, then waved the gun at me. "Open the back door."

I obeyed. Again he waved me back with the gun, then peeked inside.

"She's not in there," I said.

"Shut up!" he screamed and slammed the back door. "The radio." He opened the front door again, head swiveling between me and the interior of the cab. He spotted the radio on the seat where I'd left it and managed to reach it with his left hand. He set it on the ground and kicked it toward me. "Call them."

Confused, I picked up the radio. "And say what?"

"Ask to speak to Hannah."

"I told you, she's not with us any—"

"Do it!" Both hands on the gun now, the barrel pointed at my face.

"Okay," I said, pressing the call button. "Eli to Hannah. Come in, Hannah."

I glanced down the road, pleased to see that the bus was almost out of the way. It looked like the back tires had hit the guardrail, though, as I'd predicted.

The radio squawked. "This is Lizzie, sweetie. What you need?"

I took a deep breath, and this time when I spoke, I didn't press the button first. "I need to talk to Hannah."

I kept my eyes on Brandon, waiting to see what he'd do. When no answer came, he waved the Glock at me. "Again! Try again."

But before I could, Lizzie came back. "I didn't get that, Eli. Over."

Brandon's eyes narrowed. "How about you make sure and press the button this time?"

I obeyed, but I spoke quickly, slurring my words. "I-need-a-talk-tah-Hannah."

Unfortunately, Lizzie knew me well enough to translate. "She's helping push the bus."

A smile stretched Brandon's lips, though the mania in his eyes only made him look crazy. Again he jerked the gun at me. "Move," he said. "Walk toward your friends. Get going."

I started walking, wondering what Brandon was going to do once we reached the other side of the bridge. It was father than it looked across. I started counting my steps, just to keep my mind off of the panic building inside me. I reached twenty, then thirty, forty. By fifty, we were halfway across.

"Don't do anything stupid," Brandon said. "I know you

think you're in charge. I've heard you all, talking on the radios. Everyone defers to you. Don't be a hero."

He'd been listening to us! That must have been how he found us at Ace. "How'd you know we had radios?"

"I met a guy who said he'd seen a bunch of kids. Said you talked on radios and I could probably find you if I got myself a CB. That took a while, and when I finally heard you, it was a good hour before one of you mentioned where you were. Didn't take me long to find the Ace Hardware. Except I was in Kingman."

I couldn't help it, I laughed.

"Yeah, real funny. Keep moving."

On the banks below, the bushes and trees were such bright shades of green against the brown mud and water, and with the deep blue, cloudless sky above, it was almost pretty.

"Stop!" Brandon said when we were close enough to hear Zach barking orders at his crew. Then he bellowed. "Hannah!"

All eyes turned our way, and shame washed over me. All my bragging about being careful, and I had gotten myself caught.

"I want Hannah out here, or this little punk dies!" Brandon yelled. "You think I won't do it? You think I care if this kid lives?"

He pointed the gun my way and fired.

The crack of the bullet rang out, and it bit into the concrete, spraying chunks up over my legs and arm. My heart about stopped, but other than a few cuts on my arm from the chips of concrete, I was okay.

The girls were screaming, but my eyes were on the little trail of smoke coming up from the baseball-sized divot in the road a yard from where I was standing.

"That's enough, Brandon!"

Hannah was storming toward us with a gait that reminded me of an angry football coach.

"You are pathetic, do you know that?" she said. "Harassing a bunch of kids who are just trying to survive this mess?"

"We belong together, Hannah," he said, gun still trained on me. "You and me. You know it's true."

"You're sick. I know you kidnapped me so my dad would promote you to partner. He would have done it long ago if he thought you were good enough. But you're not. You give up too easily and resort to tricks. Dad saw it with the Henderson merger. You're impatient. When the stress comes, you panic. You're not management material. You never were."

"Shut up!" Brandon turned the gun on Hannah, his face a mask of fury. "The only thing I care about is that we're together."

He was close to the back bumper of the van. Hannah had stopped up by the front. I was now behind them both.

"What about what I want?" Hannah asked. "You think I want to be with someone who'd point a gun at me?"

"I'm only doing it because of them!"

With his wild gesture, the gun flew my way again. I ducked a little, unsure where this standoff was headed.

"They're not your enemy, Brandon," Hannah said. "Please put it down."

"You'll come with me?"

"I'm not going to discuss it until you put down the gun."

He lowered it, and it looked like he flipped on the safety. Then he stuck it in the back of his pants, which was a stupid place to put a gun. He'd clearly watched too many action movies.

Hannah inched forward, angling herself toward the

guardrail and me. Brandon didn't find this strange and followed her lead. She met my gaze over his shoulder, and I read something there. She wanted me to help, but I had no idea what her plan was. I took a huge step toward them both. Now that Brandon was within a few paces of Hannah, he wasn't paying any attention to me. When Hannah held out both hands to him, I understood.

She wanted me to go for the gun.

I swallowed and the moment she gripped his hands in hers, I lunged up behind him. I grabbed the Glock and flung it like a discuss, out into the Chinle Wash. It hit the mud with a satisfying plop. The next thing I knew, Brandon was on me like a fly on vomit

I managed to dodge his swinging fist, but he grabbed the waistband of my jeans and flung me at the guardrail.

I stumbled, heard screaming. Zach. Several girls. I dropped to my knees, skidding on the concrete until the guardrail stopped me from going over. I sighed, relieved, until I saw Brandon charging toward me again. I braced my left heel against the guard rail, then stood to meet him. We collided, and I pushed against him with all my strength. For a moment, things felt pretty even. Behind Brandon, Zach was sprinting toward us. There wasn't time, though. I wasn't as strong as Brandon, not by far, and I felt myself losing leverage. I dropped into a crouch, pivoted on the balls of my feet, and twisted around his legs.

I was free, but Brandon lost his balance and tumbled over the guardrail.

I lunged back and caught his leg, which slowed him long enough that he was able to grab the rail with one hand. I let go of his leg and reached for his other hand.

"Come on!" I yelled. "I'll pull you up."

Hannah rushed up on my right, Zach on my left. While Zach helped me reach for Brandon's free hand, Hannah started prying off Brandon's fingers on the hand he was using to hold on.

"What are you doing?" I yelled.

Brandon slipped. I caught his hand just in time, but he was heavier than me and I started to go over.

Zach grabbed me around the waist. "I got you, man."

"Hannah," I said. "Help us."

"No," she said. "Let him go, Eli. Drop him."

"I can't!" I couldn't.

She shook her head. "You don't know him like I do. He'll never stop hunting us. He'll never stop hurting me." She was crying. Begging. "Drop him. Please!"

"Don't listen to her!" Brandon yelled. "Pull me up!"

I didn't know what to do. My gut told me Hannah was right. I'd seen the bruises on her. But I couldn't just let someone fall. It was a good thirty feet to the creek. If he survived the fall, he likely drown in the mud.

The blade of a knife entered my vision. The pocket knife Hannah had picked out at Ace Hardware. Her hand was shaking. "Don't make me do it, Eli."

Confused, I met her gaze. "Hannah, come on."

"Drop him," she whispered, tears winding down her cheeks. "Please?"

I gasped for a breath, stuck with indecision. I wanted to help her, but I couldn't let go.

Until Hannah stabbed her knife through my hand.

I yelled, a pitiful, high-pitched sound.

And I dropped Brandon.

24

In my mind's eye, Brandon fell in slow motion, arms and legs pinwheeling out around his shocked face. He hit the water on his back, and the splash was so big that droplets misted my face. Before his body could resurface, Zach pulled me to the road, and I fell onto my backside, cradling my bleeding hand against my chest, pressing on the wound with my other hand.

It wasn't that bad. Not bad at all. Just a little prick. It would heal. No worries.

Hannah was standing over me, knife in hand, her face pale and awash with tears. "I'm sorry," she breathed and dropped the knife.

It clattered to the pavement, right in front of me. My eyes locked in on the orange grip, the bloodied blade.

Hands massaged my shoulders. "Eli? Buddy? How about we get up and walk it off, yeah?" Zach, concerned about me.

"I'm fine." I sniffed and forced a cool demeanor, but I didn't know what to do with this. She stabbed me. She killed him. "We need to hit the road," I said, desperate to focus on something else. "How's the bus?"

"Totally out of the way now." Zach hoisted me to my feet and led me away, toward the truck. He called over his shoulder, "Let's load up! Lizzie?"

What happened next was a bit of a blur. I heard my sister yell at Zach, something about not putting on hip waders and going into the wash to fetch Brandon's body. I also remember the long walk back to my truck with Lizzie at my side. Apparently, while I was in distress, Zach rose up and took charge, dividing our group between the vehicles, keeping Hannah from me.

I was grateful.

A part of me understood. Brandon had been insane. Truly mad. I didn't doubt he would have kept coming for her. Would have hurt her again. He certainly liked to hurt me.

But life was sacred. It was worth protecting. That was what my parents had taught me, anyhow. And Hannah . . . she'd been studying to be a doctor. She'd been training to save people's lives. First do no harm, and all that. But she'd made sure that Brandon had fallen. She'd betrayed her calling.

"Eli?"

I snapped out of my daze. Lizzie was driving, me sitting shotgun beside her. "Yeah?"

"Zach wants to stop and check on Pete."

Up ahead, the van pulled off the road at a familiar gas station. The signs out front were gone.

"I'll wait in here," I said.

Lizzie nodded, and she, Davis, Shyla, and Cree piled out. The three least likely to make themselves a nuisance were riding with me.

Zach made a pretty good leader.

I watched the group mill about. Most of them approached the port-a-potty, but no one stayed inside for long. They also went into the store, coming out of there almost as fast. Hannah wasn't with them. I guess she was waiting in the car too.

About five minutes later, Zach came up to my side of the truck and opened my door. "Logan did a nice job patching the window," he said. "Hasn't come loose at all."

I eyed the Visqueen and saw that he was right. I hadn't noticed until now.

"So, the porta-potty is still there," Zach said, "but it's practically overflowing and smelled about as nasty as anything I've ever encountered. No one wants to go near it. No sign of Pete's fancy old-school gas pump, and the store has been cleaned out. My best guess is Pete decided to hole up somewhere and wait this out."

"Sounds like," I said.

"Hannah wants to look at your hand," he said.

"It's fine." I was still clutching the piece of gauze to it that Lizzie had given me before we'd left the bridge.

"She's going on and on about your extensor tendons."

"I don't even know what that means."

"Yeah, me either. How about you let me take a look, then?"

I sighed, annoyed, but I peeled back the gauze, wincing at the sticky sound it made.

It was a gruesome sight. My middle two fingers were

curled, the other three sticking out straight like I was Spiderman trying to shoot some web. She'd stabbed hard enough that the blade had gone all the way through my hand, leaving a wide gash on the top and a pinprick of blood in the middle of my palm where the tip had emerged on the other side. The cut itself was deep red and still oozing a bit. The skin around the cut was purple and bruised, the grayish color running up to the knuckles of my middle and ring fingers.

"Aww, I love you too, man."

I frowned at Zach. "Huh?"

He put his hand next to mine and flashed me the sign for "I love you."

"Ha ha," I said.

"So, Hannah says we should splint your fingers. Says if we don't they might not grow back the right way."

I looked at my hand, conflicted. I certainly didn't want my fingers like this forever.

"Can *you* do it?" I asked.

Zach grinned and pulled out two tongue depressors and some medical tape. "Your wish is my command."

"She gave you that stuff?"

"I'm really not trying to take sides here. I just want to help you."

"Fine.'

"I'd like to wash out that cut again too," Zach said. "We don't want that puppy getting infected."

"Later," I said, not wanting to waste any more drinking water. Zach had poured half a bottle on it back at the bridge.

So Zach set to work, splinting my fingers as per Hannah's instructions. I didn't want to be thankful about it, but I was relieved she'd known to do this.

"Anything else?" Zach asked when he was done.

"I just want to know if Dad's van is out there." I'd been

waiting all day, and we were so close.

"You got it, man. I'll round them up."

Another five minutes and we were on the road again. I kept watch for Dad's van.

"It's gone," I said once we'd past Four Corners.

"You sure?" Lizzie sounded afraid to hope.

"We were in Arizona when we came upon it," I said.

"So, that's good, right?" she asked.

"Yeah," I said, daring to hope. "That's very good."

Another forty miles and we entered Cortez. The town was abandoned. I couldn't believe that Antônia could look out the window here and truly believe everything would *bounce back*.

Shyla saw a clothing store with long country skirts in the window and begged us to stop. Another time, Lizzie told her. Next she wanted to know if this area would become our new home. Lizzie doubted it. Why? Because the deserted city was proof that the water was bad here too.

And if the water was bad, Reinhold was probably dead, like Zach's family and Erin and Cree's mother and my mother.

I didn't think I could handle seeing Reinhold that way.

The turn off to Wilderness Way Adventures was another forty-five minutes to the east of Cortez. Lizzie followed Zach, so I didn't have to worry about directing her. He turned right onto County Road 124 and headed north into the La Plata Canyon. Two-and-a-half miles in we hit the National Forest boundary and the paved road turned to gravel. The van was kicking up so much dust, I could hardly see it in front of us. Another two-and-a-half miles and we started passing the campgrounds, Snowslide, Kroeger, and a KOA. Wilderness Way Adventures was six miles in on the right. Lizzie finally turned into the gravel drive. It felt strange coming back after just being here two days ago.

No cars in the lot. That didn't surprise me. Reinhold would've gone home to check on his family. Lizzie parked the truck, and I got out. I reached for Dad's rifle, then realized I couldn't hold it one handed. I told Zach to bring it, then grabbed the flashlight and jogged up to the front door. It felt good to have a mission again. To not just sit there like a victim.

Zach joined me on the porch. "Locked?"

I tried the door and nodded, but I quickly found the spare hanging on the nail on the aspen out front and let us in. The fishy smell still lingered, but it was fainter than it had been before. Or maybe everything would smell faint to me after Cree's mom.

My flashlight made a big difference in the hallway and in Reinhold's office. We searched his desk first. Found a checkbook with a PO Box, a customer rolodex, and a Christmas card from Reinhold's mom. Zach started opening drawers. I found a stack of opened mail on a shelf under the window. Halfway through I came across a letter to Reinhold at a different address: 23700 County Road X, Lewis, CO.

"I think I got it," I said.

Zach looked over my shoulder. "What I wouldn't give for an Internet connection right now."

"No guff, Chet."

We spent the next ten minutes looking for maps. I found a US Atlas, but Lewis was nothing but a pinprick ten minutes north of Cortez on Highway 491. Reinhold was a guide. He had to have a better map in this place. Then I remembered the giant hiking map on the wall in the lobby. Duh, McShane.

We found Jaylee and Antônia standing there, looking at it. "Crested Butte is very far away still," Antônia said. "We have to go first to Montrose and then—"

"We're not going to Crested Butte today," I said. "At

least not until we see about Reinhold." I found Lewis on the map, but even this map wasn't big enough to show side streets. I did see a shortcut, though. "Looks like we'll save time if we take Highway 184 to Lewis."

"Done," Zach said. "Let's roll."

"We'll have to drive around until we find County Road X. I can't find a city map."

"Maybe we can find one in Lewis."

"Maybe."

"You and Lizzie take the lead," Zach said.

We drove out of La Plata Canyon, headed back toward Cortez, then took Highway 184 north. It was about an hour on deserted county roads. As we neared Lewis, we passed the occasional farmhouse. I started to hope that by approaching from the backside of town, we might come across County Road X sooner, it being so far down in the alphabet, but suddenly Highway 184 ended at Highway 491. Lizzie stopped at the T. A cluster of four buildings stood on our right along with a sign that indicated we'd found the local post office. A gas station, liquor store, and a diner completed the bustling metropolis.

"Which way?" she asked.

I didn't know. "Right?"

She turned onto Highway 491 and drove slowly.

"Watch the road signs," I told her. "We're looking for County Road X." Only I didn't see any road signs to watch for. "There must be more to Lewis than this."

But there wasn't. Not even a grocery store.

Lizzie spotted County Road X about three miles north of what passed for town. It was a dirt road, wheel rutted and muddy in places.

"Really?" I said.

But we turned down it and after a quarter mile, came to another T. County Road 20. At least it was paved.

"That can't have been it," I said. "There was only that one house."

"It must continue on farther north," Lizzie said.

On that theory, we took a left onto County Road 20. A mile north we crossed over an irrigation ditch and the road went to gravel. Another mile and we T'd at County Road Z.

"Why do I feel like I'm driving through a Dr. Seuss book?" Lizzie asked.

"Little Roads C, B, and A?" I said, grinning.

Lizzie laughed. "Exactly."

On Lizzie's theory of Road X continuing farther north, I had her take a left on Road Z, which led to Road 21—paved! There we took a right and went south. Sure enough, a half mile down, we found County Road X on the left. Cheers filled the cab as Lizzie cranked the wheel and sped onto the paved road.

Like Highway 184, it was pretty barren out here. Every mile to half mile we passed a farmhouse. Lots of land and open space. No wonder Reinhold liked it.

We found 23700 County Road X just around a corner. The land was enclosed in a log fence. Inside, stood a one-story light blue farmhouse, a real teepee in the grassy front yard, Reinhold's truck, a white Ford Taurus, and a silver Honda Odyssey minivan.

Dad's minivan.

25

My heart leapt, adrenaline all but shooting me through the roof like a rocket. Since I wasn't driving, I opened the door and hopped out before Lizzie even put the truck in park.

"Eli!" she yelled after me.

I sprinted into the yard, past the teepee, and up to the house. Banged on the door.

Please, please, please, please . . .

The door opened, and there stood my dad, Suns cap and all.

"Oh, thank God!" he said.

Before I could move, Lizzie shot past me and tackled

Dad in a fierce hug. For a moment, I couldn't see anything as tears flooded my eyes. I wiped them away with my good hand just as Dad pulled me into their embrace. My knees felt weak and if Dad hadn't hugged me, I might have gone down.

"I knew you'd come here," Dad said, mussing my hair. "Andy didn't think so, but I knew my son's mind."

"What happened to you?" I asked. "We saw the van on the way home but . . ."

"Ran out of gas. And let me tell you, gas wasn't easy to come by that day. Where's your mother?"

The next twenty minutes or so was an awkward mess for pretty much everyone as we told Dad about Mom, Zach told Dad about his family, we told them all about Erin, and Reinhold told us about his wife and other two kids. It was just him and Kimama now. Pretty depressing all around seeing as Logan, Jaylee, Antônia, Krista, Shyla, Davis, and Hannah still didn't know anything concrete about their families.

Would they ever? Had I done a horrible thing, hauling everyone up here? How would they ever know? Would they always wonder? Would they want to go back?

Reinhold shared his theory on Erin and Mark getting sick. "They were off in the woods together, messing around, so they missed purifying their water the night we waited for the comet. They asked me the next morning, and I got after them about it. Then I gave them the purification pellets, and off they went to fill their canteens."

"By then it was too late," I said.

Reinhold nodded. "The rest of us had what we needed to get back alive. They didn't."

It was a depressing thought, and I again wondered what had happened to Mark, Cristobal, and Josh.

Reinhold asked us to move the vehicles around back

just in case anyone drove by and saw our load. I doubted anyone would ever find this place. Zach and Logan moved the rigs, and eventually, everyone made it inside.

Dirty dishes were piled high in the kitchen sink and lined the counters too. Piles of folded laundry sat in stacks on the living room floor. The clutter gave me the impression that Reinhold and Kimama were unaccustomed to keeping house.

Kimama greeted me with a cheery, "The shadow of the owl is still circling," which made me think about Brandon at the bottom of the Chinle Wash.

"It's nice to see you too, Kimama," I said. "Sorry about your mom and sisters."

"You didn't take them from me," she said. "It's the way of the world."

I honestly didn't think I could handle such maturity at the moment.

"Mr. McShane," Antônia said, "have you heard there are people going to the Crested Butte mountains?"

Dad exchanged a look with Reinhold. "Two groups I met along the way mentioned it. And a couple news channels put out reports just before the electricity died."

"You think it's true?" I asked.

"Hard to say. I never trusted Hollywood rock stars."

"They're French, Mr. McShane," Jaylee said, coming up to my dad and hugging him from the side. I couldn't help but remember that she thought he was hot. Was she flirting with him right now?

"I don't care where they're from," Reinhold said. "Famous people are all the same. Too much freedom, too much money, too many people watching their every move. All that adds up to too much crazy. That's why half of them die young."

I didn't think that was fair. The press tended to only

show gossip and scandals where famous people were concerned. I'm sure most of them were just regular folks doing the best they could in life.

"The water here bad?" I asked.

"Yep," Reinhold said. "I've tried some different purifications. So far, nothing. We've got supplies to last a month or two, though with you all, it's likely only going to last half that."

"We've brought some supplies of our own," I said.

"I saw that. It's good. It's real good. But still, it's nowhere near where I'd like us to be."

In that moment I realized I'd done what I had to. My adulting was over. Reinhold and Dad would take care of things now. I could just help wherever I was needed. It was such a relief, I almost started crying again.

I think I needed a nap.

Reinhold was still talking. "Was thinking of going down to Cortez and ransacking some stores and houses. You see any people in Cortez? They got power down there?"

"No power anywhere," I said. "We didn't see anyone in Cortez, but that doesn't mean there aren't people there. The place was pretty picked over, though."

"I know most of you," Dad said, "but there are some new faces."

"Eli rescued Krista, Shyla, and Davis in Phoenix," Logan said. "Some creep was chasing them. And he saved Hannah in Flagstaff from her psycho ex, though he's dead now. We think. And he picked up Cree in Kayenta."

"Hi, I'm Hannah." She extended her hand to my dad and they shook. "Your son helped me out of a bad situation. I'd be dead if it wasn't for him."

The way she'd put that shocked me, and I wondered if she really believed it, or if she was just trying to make me believe it.

Dad smiled and released Hannah's hand. "Well, I'm glad to know you, Hannah." He also shook hands with Krista, Davis, and Shyla. Cree hid behind my leg, but Dad managed to get him to smile.

"You think one of us should go up and check out Crested Butte?" Jaylee asked.

"Probably at some point," Reinhold said. "Doubt it's true, but we can't afford to ignore that possibility. Even if we rounded up all the bottled water in Cortez and Durango, it wouldn't last more than a few years. We need a better plan if we're going to live through this thing."

"Rainwater and snowmelt?" I asked.

"Could be," Reinhold said.

"I still belief everything will go back to normal soon," Antônia said. "One day we can turn on the TV and the news will say there is now a cure."

"I don't think you understand the gravity of the situation," Reinhold said. "Ain't nothing going to snap this world back to what it was."

"I don't belief that." Antônia waved her hand like she didn't care, but tears misted her eyes.

"Let's get some grub cooked up for you all," Reinhold said. "We'll put you girls upstairs in the bedrooms and the boys can sack out on the floor in the den. Bring your stuff in and I'll see about fixing you something to eat."

"Thank you," I said, thrilled that I'd sleep soundly, for tonight at least, and that I didn't have to figure out what to feed everyone.

While the girls dragged their stuff upstairs, Dad pulled me aside and motioned to my hand. "What happened here?"

I told him the full story about Hannah and Brandon, how he'd chased us, and what Hannah had done.

Dad blew out a short breath. "I'm sorry, son."

"I tried, Dad. I really did. I thought I could lead them.

They said they wanted me to lead them. But it was just too hard."

"What do you mean?"

"If they all would have just listened to me, we would have been here yesterday. We never would have gone to Target. We wouldn't have lost your truck and my gun and all our stuff and Shy. We would have avoided so much trouble. But they hardly listened. I just don't have what it takes, I guess. I tried, Dad. It was so frustrating."

Dad seemed to be fighting a smile. "Wait a minute. You think being a leader is about getting people to listen to you?"

His question got stuck in my brain. "It's not?"

"Oh, son. Leadership isn't about control. It isn't about bossing people around and having them jump to obey. It's about working hard and being an example in words and deeds. It's about empowering others to be the best they can be. It's about knowing your people well, their strengths and weaknesses and motivations and the lies they believe about themselves. It's speaking truth and encouragement to your people. It's coaching them. It's getting out of the way and encouraging them to be creative and contribute ideas. It's wisdom and patience and empathy and trust and kindness and whole lot of grace."

This revelation opened a door inside me. "Yeah?"

Dad laughed. "Yeah. And you did that, didn't you?"

I thought about it. "I guess. Mostly."

"Mostly." He put his arm around me and pulled me close, mussed my hair with his free hand. "I'm proud of you. How you took care of everyone like you did. How you took in the lost—rescued others from predators. You kept all those wild kiddos alive. Frankly, it's a miracle."

I was stunned. I hadn't seen it that way at all. To me, the whole trip had felt like a disaster. So many things had gone wrong. "If we'd had to drive one more day to get here,

Jaylee and Antônia would have stolen one of the rigs and headed to Crested Butte."

Dad laughed and shook his head. "Women." His eyes misted over, and I knew he was thinking about Mom.

"I miss her," I said.

He hugged me and squeezed tight. "Me too, son."

• • •

Kimama, Reinhold, and Lizzie cooked up a dinner of fajitas using canned chicken, black beans, salsa, and corn tortillas. It tasted so good I moaned with every bite I took. I wondered how much longer bread products would last before things started to mold. Flour might keep a while longer if we could freeze it. We could freeze a lot as long as we could keep up a supply of gasoline to run the generators. Long term, though, could we figure out how to grow our own wheat and make flour? Seemed like a lot of work, especially without the Internet to show us how.

Reinhold lit some oil lamps for us in the den, and Zach pulled out his guitar and played music. Cree and Shyla fell asleep, so Reinhold and my dad took Cree, Davis, Kimama, and Shyla upstairs to put them to bed. I knew they did it so the rest of us could stay up and be kids, and I was grateful. After a few more songs, Zach put away the guitar, and we mulled over our new world and what the future might hold. Somehow our discussion circled back to the end times debate and Logan pushing his conspiracy theories. I wished my dad was down here to offer his perspective.

Jaylee put an end to Logan's intrigue. "This is boring. Let's play a game."

Lizzie groaned. "Not Truth or Dare. That's all you ever play."

Jaylee scowled at her. "Fine. We'll play something else.

This is called . . . *Your Last.*"

"I don't know that game," Krista said.

"That's because I just made it up." Jaylee grinned, and I marveled at how pretty she was, which for some reason caused me to glance at Hannah, which annoyed me, so I looked at the rug.

"If Eli's right," Jaylee said, "and the world as we knew it is over, there are a lot of things we'll never do again. So, I'll ask first. Lizzie, name your last . . . shower."

"Last Thursday," Lizzie said, wrinkling her nose. "My hair is so greasy. I feel disgusting."

"Me too," Antônia said.

"Now you ask someone else, Lizzie," Jaylee said. "And you can't ask the person who just asked you."

"Okay." My sister's gaze fell on me. "Eli, your last pizza?"

My stomach growled just thinking of it. "Mom made one the night before I left for the camping trip."

"Oh, man." Zach moaned. "I'm going to miss your mom's homemade pizza. Her crust was so good."

I was going to miss everything about her. Except how she always nagged me for leaving my socks in little balls when I threw them in the laundry. The thought made me smile. I guess maybe I'd miss that too.

"Your turn, Eli," Jaylee said.

"Okay, Logan," I said. "Last movie."

"*How to Train a Dragon.* I was babysitting my cousin."

Zach threw a pillow at Logan. "Sure you were."

"Don't judge," I said. "Those movies rock."

"Thank you, Eli." Logan reached his fist toward me and we knocked knuckles.

"Logan," Jaylee said, "you're up."

"Hannah, the last video game you played before Zombie Kings."

Hannah wrinkled her nose. "Uh . . . does 2048 on my phone count? I don't really play video games."

Logan hung his head. "That's so sad."

"Hannah, you go," Jaylee said.

"Eli, the last book you read."

Was this her way of forcing me to talk to her? "*To Kill a Mockingbird* for my English class," I said, then asked Zach about his last pool swim.

The questioning continued. It circled back to me when Logan asked when I'd eaten my last hot dog.

"Uh . . . junior high school?" I abhorred hot dogs. I normally tried not to eat anything that was processed. Ironic that all that processed food would now be keeping me alive.

This time, I wanted to ask Jaylee something. And the way we were all gathered, with Reinhold, Dad, and the kids in bed, it made me feel gutsy, like I should ask something personal. The thought made my heart race. I chickened out, of course. "Last ice cream, Jaylee."

She pouted. "Don't remind me! I can't believe there'll be no more ice cream. I had a Ben and Jerry's ice cream bar in Flagstaff on the way up to camp. It was cookie dough."

"I got one there too," I said, smiling as if this somehow made us a special pair, though mine had been Cherry Garcia.

"Zach." Jaylee's lips curved, her eyes narrowed. "Your last . . . kiss."

Zach's eyes widened and shifted to Lizzie. If he'd been trying to look sly, he'd failed miserably.

Jaylee and Antônia crooned, "Ooooooh!" the both of them grinning wide.

Zach leaned over and kissed the top of Logan's head. "There. Just kissed Logan."

This sent everyone into a fit of laughter but did nothing to help Zach and Lizzie keep their secret. It didn't really bother me anymore. Not like it first had. I mean, if Zach was willing to kiss Logan in order to keep Lizzie from being embarrassed, he was a good guy, which I already knew.

I was just going to have to get used to him kissing my sister.

"Your turn, Zach," Jaylee said.

Zach looked around the room and his gaze landed on me. His eyes narrowed, and the mischievous glint in them made me nervous. "Eli's last crush."

26

Zach may as well have punched me in the gut. I couldn't believe I'd just thought he was worthy of my sister.

"*Zach*," Lizzie warned.

"Okay, yeah. My bad," Zach said. "I'll ask him something else."

"Oh, no you don't," Jaylee said. "He has to answer. Go ahead, Eli. Who did you like?"

I stared at her, speechless, wishing I would just spit out a name. Any name. It was suddenly warm in the house, and I wished I could escape outside where the night was sure to be cooler.

Jaylee smirked, her eyes bright. "Is it someone here?"

What I wouldn't give for ten seconds with Bilbo's magic ring. I'd slip it on and run for the front door.

"It is, isn't it?" Jaylee squealed, likely delighted at the thought of discovering some juicy gossip.

"Hey, Jaylee," Zach said. "I was just messing with him. It's no one you know."

Yes. Thank you. I relaxed a bit. Next question, please.

"Then why is he afraid to say?" She pushed to her hands and knees and crawled toward me, slowly.

I couldn't look away. I wanted to, but Jaylee Jennings was the prettiest girl I've ever known, and the way she was staring at me . . . I wondered if she had some kind of supernatural ability to immobilize people with her eyes.

She reached me and sat back on her ankles. "Is it Krista?" she whispered. "Krista's cute."

Eww. I glanced at Krista, who was looking at the floor in front of her. "No."

"Antônia?"

I shook my head.

"You saved Hannah's life. That's pretty romantic."

I could feel everyone staring, but my gaze was locked on Jaylee. Her left eye. Her right eye. Her eyebrows. Her nose. The freckles across the tops of her cheeks. The curve of her lips.

What had she said?

Her eyes widened a little, showing all the whites around her brown irises. "Is it *me*?"

If I'd thought I'd been hot before, I wasn't prepared for the way my cheeks started to burn. I looked away, caught Zach's gaze. He turned his head before I could glare at him.

Jaylee gasped. "Awww!"

I closed my eyes, cursing my biology. I should have just made up some random name. No one would have known any differently if I'd said Megan or Ally or Kaitlyn.

The thing was, I knew Jaylee too well. She would act all cute about this, but then she'd patronize me. Until she got bored. And I didn't want that. Did I?

I heard movement and opened my eyes. Everyone was standing. Hannah and Lizzie were creeping up the stairs, Krista and Antônia behind them while Zach ushered Logan into the kitchen.

Oh, no. Don't leave! I shot Zach a pleading look. He motioned at Jaylee, mouthed something. Made a kissy face.

Yeah right. I wasn't like Zach. I didn't have a clue what I was doing. I couldn't even speak.

"I guess you won the game," Jaylee whispered, twirling a lock of her hair around her finger.

"I guess." Oh, look. I said something. And it was coherent. Yay me.

"So . . ." She poked out her bottom lip. "You got a little crush on me, then?"

This time the heat that flashed over me was fueled by anger. I glared at her. "Why do you have to do that? Just forget about it, okay?" I made to stand up, but Jaylee grabbed my arm.

"Wait." She ran her fingers down to my good hand and laced them between mine.

She was holding my hand.

"Oh, my gosh, you're shaking."

Yeah, I was a regular mess. I tried to stop, but I truly had no control of it.

Jaylee looked at me, and I realized her eyes weren't just brown, they were brown and gold and amber with little flecks of green.

"You've always been my friend, Eli. So you know I usually like older guys."

Here we go. I could feel the smack down coming.

"But it's not like there are a lot of single guys around

here right now. And you're cute and sweet and smart and really brave. I'm game to give it a try, if you want to."

Give it a try? What did *that* mean? I didn't want her pity. I didn't want to be her last resort.

But then she kissed me. And I felt so awkward and embarrassed and clueless and thrilled. I also thought I might have been having a heart attack.

Before I could decide what to do, it was over.

Jaylee leaned back, her eyes slowly opening. "Now *that* was fun."

• • •

I crawled into my sleeping bag that night, a happy, happy man.

"You ticked at me?" Zach asked from the darkness.

I grinned, my lips still buzzing from Jaylee's kisses. "Nah, man. We're cool."

"Yeah?"

"Yeah."

"Good. I'm glad it worked out."

"Me too."

"So, I've been wanting to talk to you about me and Lizzy."

No, I didn't want to talk about this. "It's fine," I said.

"Yeah, well, I shouldn't have kept it from you. *We* shouldn't have."

We. I gritted my teeth. "My sister is pretty great," I said.

"The greatest," Zach said.

"Which means you'll treat her better than Bekah?" Bekah was Zach's previous girlfriend, and their breakup had gotten War-of-the-Roses out of control.

"Of course," Zach said. "Bekah was crazy."

Silence stretched between us.

"Bekah is probably dead," he added.

A dark thought. "Most everyone is." Brandon was.

As if he'd read my mind, he asked, "How's your hand?"

"Better." Though I still couldn't lift my two middle fingers.

"That was pretty messed up," Zach said.

"It's weird," I said. "From the moment I met her to the moment she stabbed me, I really liked her. She'd almost made me forget about Jaylee."

"No way. You serious?"

"I just mean, she's pretty amazing."

"She still is."

"She killed him."

"I know it looked that way. That's what happened. But, well . . . maybe try to cut her some slack. I'm sure you saw the bruises."

"I saw."

"I just think there's more to the story than we know. Like she was acting in some kind of premeditated self-defense."

"He was pretty defenseless, hanging there."

"You're right. He was."

The silence stretched between us, heavy somehow.

Zach broke it. "Do you think that if we'd pulled Brandon up on the road he suddenly would have been our new best pal?"

I thought about it. "No."

"He still would have wanted to take Hannah. We still would have tried to stop him. And he still would have tried to hurt us to get what he wanted."

"What's your point?"

"My point is, leave the judging to God."

I sighed. It was good advice. The only problem? I wasn't sure I trusted God with the job of judge. I didn't exactly like how things were going right now, so the control freak in me was taking over, though I had to admit, it was very hard work, and I don't think I was doing all that good of a job, either.

Zach sighed, a happy tone in his breath. "I can't believe it. We did it, man. We actually made it."

"Yeah, we did." And it was enough. For tonight.

Tomorrow, however, everything would start new. There would be new goals. New challenges. New strangers we'd run into out there. New dangers. New betrayals. New deaths.

It was almost too much to think about, so I pushed it away, closed my eyes, and focused instead of how things had gone tonight with Jaylee. I kissed her again in my mind. That made me smile, but my thoughts quickly betrayed me. All too soon my mind filled with images of the dead: the man on the highway, the people at the Urgent Care, Zach's family, Cree's mother, Brandon. I thought of my mom.

Again I forced myself to think of happier things. Jaylee. My dad. Lizzie, Zach, and Logan. Cree. Reinhold and Kimama. All the stuff we'd collected at Ace. There were real blessings all around me. I just had to remind myself because they were continually being overshadowed by so much darkness and despair.

That was how I finally managed to fall asleep, by listing every blessing I had in my life right then. As the list went on and on, I felt lighter and lighter until I eventually drifted off to a deep and peaceful sleep.

THE END

Eli's story continues in *Hunger*

Thirst Playlist

"Alone Together" by Fallout Boy
"Demons" by Imagine Dragons
"Don't Stop Believing" by Journey
"Even If" by Mercy Me
"Free Falling" by Tom Petty
"I Just Need U" by Toby Mac
"Just Be Held" by Casting Crowns
"Keep Your Head Up" by Andy Grammer
"My Lighthouse" by Rend Collective
"Out of the Woods" by Taylor Swift
"Over My Head" by The Fray
"Pompeii" by Bastille
"Safe From Harm" by Massive Attack
"Shoulders" by For King and Country
"Stressed Out" by 21 Pilots
"Stronger" by Kelly Clarkson
"Sweet Home Alabama" by Lynyrd Skynyrd
"Trust in You" Lauren Daigle
"You Belong with Me" by Taylor Swift

Acknowledgements

A huge thank you to my husband for being my editor on this project. I so appreciate your gift for story. And to my daughter Kaitlyn, Jennie Webb, and Tracie Heskett for proofreading: Thank you!

To my readers, you read this book back in 2012 when I wrote the very first draft on my blog. Many of you read all about it again a few years later when I blogged about it on the Go Teen Writers blog. Well, it's finally here! Thanks for sticking with me on this one. I hope you enjoy how it turned out. Your feedback on that original draft was a huge help to how I ended up rewriting things, so I thank you all very much. This book wouldn't have happened without you.

About the Author

Jill Williamson has written over twenty books for teens and adults, including her debut novel, By Darkness Hid, which won several awards and was named a Best Science Fiction, Fantasy, and Horror novel of 2009 by VOYA magazine. She has also written a handful of books on the craft of writing fiction and teaches writing in person and online at storyworldfirst.com and goteenwriters.com, the latter of which has been named one of Writer's Digest's "101 Best Websites for Writers."

To be notified of new releases and to get a free short story, visit jillwilliamson.com/sanctum and subscribe to her email newsletter. You can also find Jill on the following social media platforms

Read About Eli's Descendants in:

THE SAFE LANDS SERIES
FIND PLEASURE IN LIFE

In a dystopian future, most of the population is infected with a plague. When a mutation sends city enforcers looking for the uninfected, Levi's village is raided. While the attack leaves many dead, Levi's fiancée is taken captive. Levi launches a war against the city in an attempt to free her before it's too late.

to learn more visit
www.jillwilliamson.com

AWARD-WINNING FANTASY FROM JILL WILLIAMSON

"Wonderfully written with a superb plot, this book is a sure-fire hit with almost any reader. An adventure tale with a touch of romance and enough intrigue to keep the pages turning practically by themselves."
–*VOYA* magazine

"This thoroughly entertaining and smart tale will appeal to fans of Donita K. Paul and J.R.R. Tolkien. Highly recommended for . . . fantasy collections."
–*Library Journal*

"Williamson crafts a complex and vividly portrayed epic fantasy reminiscent of George R.R. Martin's *A Song of Ice and Fire* series but less edgy."
–*Library Journal*

"[*King's Folly*] is an intense drama of biblical proportions... Wilek, Mielle, and Trevn in particular are intriguing, and the ending leaves readers wondering what adventures await this group of young people searching for truth."
–*RT Book Reviews*

TO LEARN MORE VISIT
WWW.JILLWILLIAMSON.COM

WRITING RESOURCES

**READY TO WRITE THAT BOOK?
NOT SURE HOW TO BEGIN?
YOU NEED THIS BOOK!**

Learning to write a novel from beginning to end is a challenge. But with this book as your guide, you'll see that when you're in possession of the right tools, you're capable of finishing what you start. You'll be empowered and encouraged—as if you had a writing coach (or three!) sitting alongside you.

REVISED & UPDATED EDITION!

You know your first draft has problems, but what's the best way to fix them? How do you know where to start editing? Or for many writers the bigger question becomes, "How do I know when I'm done?"

Teaching yourself how to edit a first draft can feel overwhelming, but using this guide, you'll feel as encouraged, empowered, and capable as if you had a writing coach sitting alongside you.

TO LEARN MORE VISIT
WWW.JILLWILLIAMSON.COM

MORE WRITING RESOURCES FROM JILL WILLIAMSON

You don't need to be an expert in grammar and punctuation to write great novels, but you do need to learn the basics.

This handy reference book includes all the need-to-know punctuation rules for fiction writers, and it's presented in a clear, user-friendly format with many examples for the visual learner—including some from popular novels.

Punctuation 101 will save you time and energy, which you can spend writing your novel.

BUILDING A STORYWORLD? WONDERING WHERE TO START? THIS BOOK CAN HELP YOU.

Whether you're starting from scratch or looking to add depth to a world you've already created, *Storyworld First* will get you thinking.

Includes tips on the following worldbuilding subjects: astronomy, magic, government, map-making, history, religion, technology, languages, culture, and how it all works together.

TO LEARN MORE VISIT
WWW.JILLWILLIAMSON.COM

Come hang out with us!

GO TEEN WRITERS

honesty, encouragement, and community for writers

www.GoTeenWriters.com

Made in the USA
Las Vegas, NV
18 August 2025